the pearls *of* *the* stone man

the pearls *of* *the* stone man

edward mooney, jr.

Published by Sourcebooks Landmark, an imprint of Sourcebooks, Inc.
P.O. Box 4410, Naperville, Illinois 60567-4410
(630) 961-3900
Fax: (630) 961-2168
www.sourcebooks.com

Originally published in Belgium, Wisconsin, in 2002 by Champion Press.

Library of Congress Cataloging-in-Publication Data

Mooney, Edward.
The pearls of the stone man / Edward Mooney, Jr.
p. cm.
1. Fathers and sons—Fiction. 2. Spouses—Fiction. 3. Domestic fiction. I. Title.
PS3613.O5517P43 2009
813'.6—dc22

2009036696

Printed and bound in the United States of America.
CHG 10 9 8 7 6 5 4 3 2 1

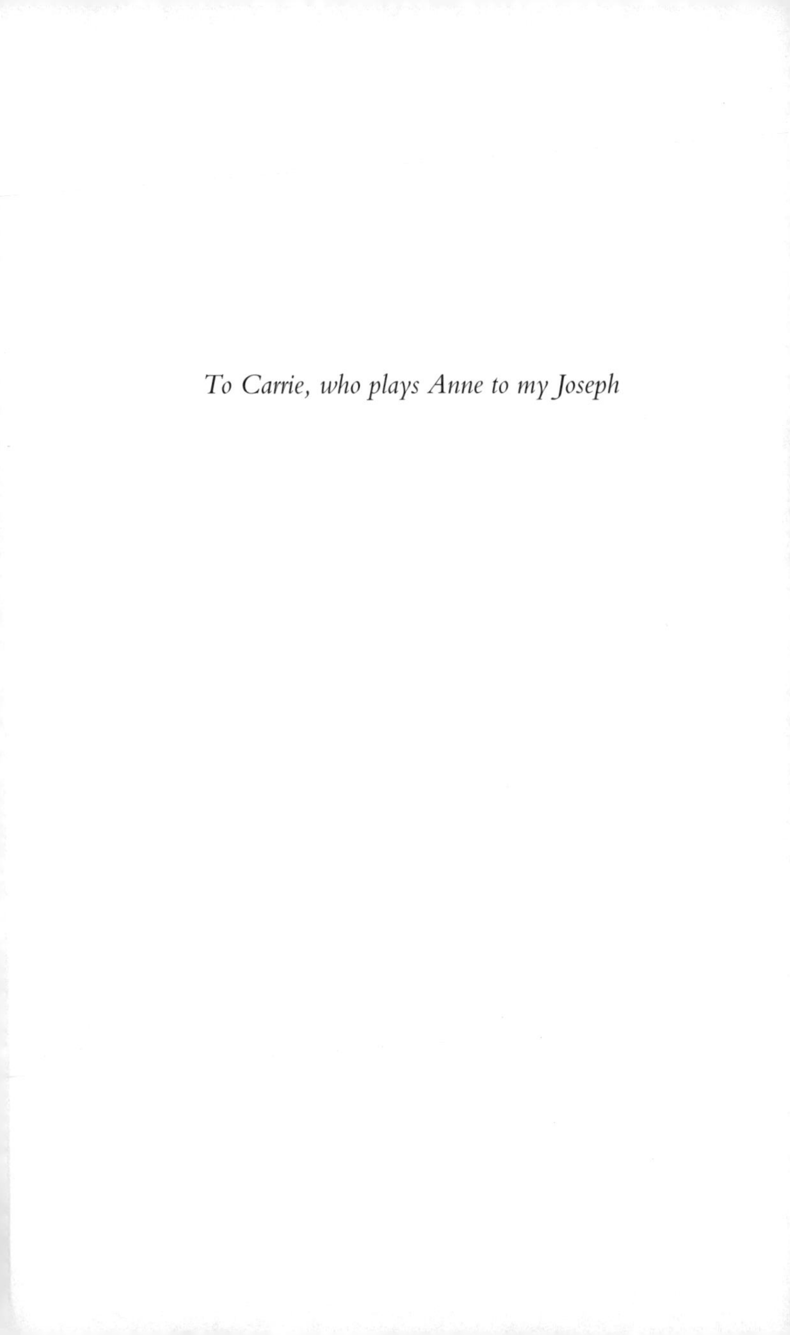

To Carrie, who plays Anne to my Joseph

Acknowledgments

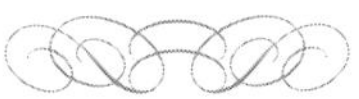

I recognize my wife, my diamond. Thank you, Caroline Houtz Mooney for love.

I recognize my children, my emeralds. Thank you, Jennifer, Elizabeth, Sarah, Patrick, and Laura, for caring.

I recognize my students, my rubies. Thank you, Cougars, Falcons, Mustangs, Bulldogs, and Rebels, for encouragement.

I recognize my teachers, my sapphires. Thank you, Lowell Schroeder, Jim Edie, and Joe Beaton, for wisdom.

I recognize my parents, my aquamarines. Thank you, Edward and Iole Mooney, for life itself.

I recognize my grandchildren, my pearls, even those yet unborn. Thank you for remembering this Stone Man.

Prologue

SATURDAYS IN SPRING BROUGHT A FLOOD OF humanity to Pine Mountain. Some travelers were returning to repair and reopen long-shuttered weekend cabins, and some came to witness the final gasps of snow on the slopes of that noble rock. Still others came to find their past. Perhaps, they thought, in the mysteries of long ago would the answers to today's questions be found.

It was on such a Saturday that a minivan with a small family rounded the many curves of a mountain highway called Mil Potrero. They came looking for a house from their past.

"Tim, I think we should stop for some drinks before we go up the hill," a pretty young woman advised the man driving. She wore her hair up, in braids.

"With the kids asleep, wouldn't it be better to just drive by, turn around and head back? We could get something to drink in Lake of the Woods, at the mini-mart," the driver responded. He was a handsome man, in a rugged way. It was obvious, from looking at his hands, that he earned his wages with some physical labor.

"But I'd like to stop and look..."

"Again? Look for what? Of all the times we've been up here you've never known what you're looking for!" Tim frowned.

"It meant something, Tim. He didn't just say it." Shannon looked out of the side window. She was angry. "I know it meant something."

"Look, I'll make a deal with you," Tim gestured with his right hand.

"Keep both hands on the wheel up here. You know how much I hate this road!" Shannon tensed further, her body molded into her seat.

"Come on hon, I've driven this road a thousand times. Hey...there're guardrails now!" Tim snickered as he teased.

"What's the deal?" Shannon said, momentarily over her fear of the curved road.

"I'll stop this time, but it's the last time. I just don't see the point. If you don't find whatever it is you think is there this time, then we'll do it my way from now on. Deal?"

Shannon looked back out the window at the passing trees. She knew she had been pursuing this strange passion for too long. Tim had been patient. Still, the idea of actually giving up left butterflies in her stomach.

"Shannon? Well? Is it a deal?" Tim whispered the words as one of the children stirred in the back seat.

"You know I don't even know what I'm looking for," Shannon matched his whispered tone. "But I know he meant it—it's too important to walk away from."

"How long, Shannon? We've been coming up here for more than a decade. It's bugged me, too. But I think it's time to write this off as just one of those mysteries we can never solve. Let's just treasure the fond memories and let it go..." Tim trailed off. He bit his lower lip.

"I'll tell you what. If no one is there, then we'll turn around and never try this again," Shannon offered. Her stomach sank as she said the words, but she knew Tim was right. Sooner or later they would have to put this behind them. Maybe some answers weren't meant to be found.

"Okay, it's a deal then?" Tim extended his right hand.

"Both hands on the steering wheel!" Shannon urged.

"I'll take that to mean it's a deal."

Shannon nodded.

"That'll be $5.27, sir." The clerk announced. She pulled out a grocery bag and started putting the cold drinks in.

"Shoot," Tim rummaged through his pockets.

"What's wrong?" Shannon asked. Two children stood behind her.

"All I have is a twenty and a five. Do you have any change?"

"I think so," Shannon opened her purse and pulled out her wallet.

"Here it is. I knew I had a buck in that pocket somewhere."

"I can't believe how much money I've collected from the couch because of your habit of crumbling dollar bills into your pockets, Tim!" Shannon shook her head. "I wonder how much we have lost that I haven't found."

"Hey, why should you complain? You've done just fine!" Tim pointed at her new blouse and purse.

"You're right. I make quite a bit of money scavenging your droppings!" Shannon smiled. It was their usual banter.

"Mom…can we eat? I wanna sandwich!" a preteen boy demanded.

"Your father wants to get sandwiches after we look at a house, Joey."

"Are we going to look at that house again?" A girl, a bit younger than the boy, whined.

"That's right, Annie. Mom's gotta do this again!" Tim leaned over and glared at Shannon. He picked up the bag of drinks and headed for the door.

"Tim! Why do you do this? You cared as much about the Stone Man as I did!" Shannon was losing her patience.

"Excuse me, ma'am…did you say 'Stone Man'?" The words came from an older woman in line behind Shannon.

"Yes. Why?" Shannon turned to face her. Tim stopped and slowly turned to look at the older woman.

"I knew someone once, a long time ago, who we used to call the 'Stone Man.'"

Shannon looked behind the woman. The tiny aisle was choked with people trying to check out. It was Saturday afternoon. The visitors needed groceries here on Pine Mountain.

"My husband and I did, too," Shannon replied eagerly. "Can we move over here? I don't want to hold up the line." Tim walked back toward his wife.

"Do I know you?" Tim asked. He had a confused look on his face.

"I don't know. You look familiar." The woman returned the same puzzled gaze.

"I used to live here. Both Shannon and I did," Tim said while gesturing toward his wife. "We used to help Grandpa Marino with his place."

"Oh! You're his grandchildren, then!" The older lady brightened.

"No…oh, no. We just called him that. We kind of adopted him," Shannon corrected the woman.

"Oh…I see. Which ones were you?"

"Which ones?" Tim asked.

"He was 'adopted' by a few kids over the years."

"We were the last ones, probably."

The woman thought a moment, her eyes turned upward as if looking back in time. "Was that about eleven years ago?"

"Yeah…about that," Tim answered.

"I remember you, then! You were in the car…in the post office!" Tim's eyebrows rose.

"The post office! You're that woman that had a thing for Grandpa!" Tim was surprised.

"Well, I did find him attractive!" The woman smiled fondly while offering her hand. "My name is Mary."

"Wait a minute…'a thing'? What is a 'thing'?" Shannon's inquiry was interrupted by an older man who nearly pushed her over while tugging at his teenage son.

"Come on…stop whining! You're never grateful for anything. That's the last time I give you the choice of dinners." The man strengthened his hold on the boy's arm. "I'm in a rush and all you can do is whine."

"Hasn't changed, has it, Shan?" Tim watched the father and son leave the store.

"No." Shannon's voice was barely audible as she found herself caught in her own memories.

"No, it hasn't. Sad. I can't tell you how many kids grow up like that," Mary agreed.

"So…what's a 'thing'?" Shannon shook herself from her private thoughts and returned to her original question.

"Well, I had a crush on him for years. Only I'm not sure he noticed." Mary looked down.

"He did…he did." Tim smiled.

"Slow down, Tim! There's somebody there!" Shannon blurted.

"Wow! How many times have we come up here and not found anything but weeds and shuttered windows?" Tim pulled to the side of the road, about fifty feet from the driveway of the house.

"It looks like they're cleaning things up."

"There's a 'for sale' sign," Tim pointed to a sign behind a tree, by a stone wall.

"Oh, Tim! They can't!" Shannon covered her mouth with her hand.

"It's their house…"

"We have to stop and talk to them!" Shannon turned toward her husband. She stared into his eyes. He kept looking away but eventually met her stare.

"Since there is someone here this time, we'll stop." Shannon rubbed her husband's arm and smiled.

Shannon walked slowly up the aspen-lined driveway. She stopped to touch one of the trees, the one nearest to the walkway.

"Hello?" Shannon called out tentatively. A man carrying a trash can stopped by the side of the house and turned around.

"You'll have to make an appointment with the realtor to see the house," he called out. He turned and continued on his way.

"No, wait…I'm not looking to buy!"

The man stopped again. He put the trash can down and started removing his gloves.

"So, what are you selling, then?" The man responded gruffly and pointed to a photo album that Shannon held in her hand.

"Oh this?" Shannon looked down at her hand. "These are just some mementos. I don't mean to intrude, but I'm looking for something; it's very important. Please," Shannon pleaded. "It's so important now that the owner is selling the place. You never know what new owners do to a place. When we bought our…"

"Shannon! Please!" Tim interrupted his wife.

"Look, I'm really busy. I've got to get back to San Diego tonight. I don't have much time. Can you make this quick?" The man glanced at his watch.

"San Diego?" Shannon whispered.

"Yeah…you from there?"

"No, Tustin. Can I ask you…no, it's not possible," Shannon waved her hand in dismissal.

"I really need to get going, so if there is something…"

"Paul?" Shannon blurted out. She was trembling.

"What?" The man looked at her squarely. "How do you know my name?" The man's tone changed.

"Paul Marino. Your wife is Meredith." Shannon was feeling more confident.

"Yeah. Who are you?" Paul's voice sounded fearful.

"I should have recognized you right away. You look so much like your father!"

"You knew my father?" Paul softened.

"Oh, yes. And your mother. I was there..." Shannon's voice trailed off.

"You're not that girl down the street...Sharon?"

"Shannon," she said affirmatively.

"Oh my God, I remember you!" Paul turned toward the house with a cupped hand.

"Hey, Merrie! You've got to come out here!"

"I remember your sister, too. Sarah." Shannon started to open her photo album.

"Yeah, Sarah..." The man's voice was barely a whisper as he looked to the ground

"What is it?" Shannon's smile turned down.

"She passed away last year. Alcohol." Paul shook his head. Shannon didn't know what to say. She looked at Tim, who just lowered his head.

"Do you want to come in?" Paul nodded toward the open front door.

"That would be nice, thank you." Shannon reached for Tim's hand.

"It's not much to look at," Paul said while shuffling toward the house. "Dusty. I've decided to sell the place. My sister used to come up from Bakersfield occasionally—but, well, now..."

"I understand." Shannon nodded as she and Tim walked into the house.

❧

"This hasn't changed a bit!" Shannon smiled as she took a place on the couch.

"So, what is it you're looking for?" Paul inquired.

"I'm not sure, really. I don't know how to explain it." Shannon looked at the dusty nightstand next to the couch. A stack of pink envelopes was somewhat hidden behind the lamp.

"Sorry about the mess. My sister never really cleaned the place. She just shuffled the junk from one spot to another, I think!" Paul was obviously embarrassed.

"No, the letters! They're here!" Shannon rose quickly and gingerly took hold of the pink envelopes.

"Letters?"

"You don't know? Oh, I have to tell you!"

"You were looking for letters?" Paul asked, still unsure what Shannon's excitement was about.

"No."

"Well, what in the world are you looking for?" Paul sat back in the easy chair.

"I know he meant something." Shannon's words came quick as she lost herself in thought. "What your father said, I mean." Her limber hands lovingly caressed the envelopes.

"My father said something about what?"

"He said, 'Remember the stone…'"

"'Remember the stone…'" Paul repeated the words slowly.

"Yes, I know it's strange but he was so insistent

when he mumbled those words to me. I know he was trying to tell me something."

"Shannon, please don't take this the wrong way," Paul leaned forward, "but that's ridiculous. An old man says 'Remember the stone,' and it's supposed to mean something?"

"I know he did mean something, Paul. His words have haunted me all these years. It's practically driven Tim crazy. I keep dragging the family up here trying to figure out what he meant."

"Lady," Paul said affectionately, "you have accepted quite the mission! There must be ten thousand stones on this property. That's a lot of stones to remember."

"Probably more like fifteen thousand," Tim smiled and rubbed Shannon's arm.

"But there's something more, let me explain."

"Okay," Paul said, getting comfortable in his chair. "But I really do need to get going in a bit, so try and make this quick."

"It was eleven years ago, right here…" and Shannon began to strip away the varnish of time.

Part One

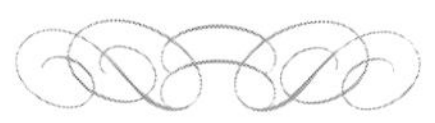

Sunset on Pine Mountain

Chapter 1

A GLINT OF SUNLIGHT FROM THE SNOW RESTING on the slopes of Pine Mountain caught the eye of the old man that fateful afternoon. Slowly he straightened himself as he turned to gaze at the broad shoulders of the peak that dominated the valley. The ache in his lower back compelled him to rely on the support of his trusty hoe.

"Well, Old One, you call out to me again!" he said as he reached into his rear pocket for his handkerchief. The sun was strong for the time of year. Rarely did the temperature reach the eighties in April—after all, they were at five thousand feet of elevation. The old man needed relief from his sweat. He removed his battered gardening hat and wiped his bald pate.

His eyes absorbed the mountain's beauty. The mountain was beautiful, he thought. "So craggy. So white with snow, and so crisply outlined against a deep blue sky." He discovered that he was whispering his thoughts, as he was sometimes inclined to do.

"Did you call?" a woman's voice called out. It belonged to the wife of the old man. He usually thought of himself as "the old man," but he never thought of her as "the old woman." He still saw her as the schoolgirl he had met over sixty years ago. She could never be "the old woman" to him. It was only the accursed mirror that reminded him of his age. And the aching back. And the many prescriptions he needed. He certainly didn't want to accept that age had caught up to him, but it had.

"No, love. I was just talking to Old Craggle-Puss up there," he said while pointing a wrinkled finger toward the mountain.

"Sometimes, Joseph, I wonder about you," the woman said with a well-worn voice. She shook her head as she returned to her petunia bed.

"Sometimes? When haven't you wondered about me?" he shot back with a chuckle heard only in a comfortable, loving relationship that spans decades, toils, children, and fears.

"When you have that look in your eye."

"What look?"

"Honestly! Fifty-three years of marriage and you still ask 'what look'? You just like to hear me talk about it," she said, with a whisper of a smile on her face.

"Talk about what?" he said with an exaggerated shrug of confusion.

"Well, they don't call them 'bedroom eyes' for nothing," Anne giggled, blushing slightly.

Joseph loved making Anne laugh and the sound of

her giggle. *After all of these years*, he thought, *she still falls for the routine.* He watched as she turned the soil over in her flower garden.

How many times has he stood watching as she worked steer manure into the ground? It must be fifty or more, he imagined. Well…there were those two years that they had lived in a cramped apartment so long ago. There was no ground available for her. She had planted flowers in a window box that he had built out of pine scraps from the housing tract down the street.

"How long have you planted flower gardens, Anne?" Joseph inquired.

"Huh? What?"

"Flower gardens. How long have you planted them?"

"Oh, I don't know. Must be around fifty years by now. Except for those years we lived in that crowded apartment, I've had one every year," she replied as she walked slowly over to her husband. He could tell that she felt like talking. He leaned his hoe against a pine tree and motioned with his right arm toward the chairs near the rear door of the house.

"I think I could use a few minutes' worth of rest," she said wearily.

"So could I."

Joseph watched her as she described what flowers she was planning to put in this year. He was a little concerned that she hadn't been looking as strong as she had in years gone by. But then, he thought, he probably didn't look that good either. Life takes its toll after seventy-eight years. Seventy-eight! He couldn't believe it. It seemed like only yesterday he was a twenty-five-year-old newlywed, fresh out of college. How could so many years have…

"…and the worms…Joseph! Are you listening?" Anne broke into his wandering thoughts.

"Huh? What? Worms?" Joseph stumbled back into the present.

"Are you taking your pills? You seem so, I don't know, so absent-minded." Anne leaned forward, concern etched in her face. "What is going on?" she asked as she gently touched his hand with her own.

"Going on? Nothing. I'm just tired, that's all. Tired."

"No. You've been struggling with something recently. What's bothering you?" Anne's voice was caring but persistent.

"Why do you think that?"

"Joseph, it's me. Fifty-three years of marriage has taught me a few things—like how to recognize when something's bothering you."

"I don't know, Anne. I don't know. I can't seem to, well, seem to stop thinking about things…" Joseph trailed off. He turned his head back toward Mount Pinos. His mouth quivered, as if fighting back tears.

"Things? What things?" Anne asked gently.

"It's hard to…" Joseph fiddled with the button on his lightweight jacket. "It's hard to…"

"Hard to talk about?" Anne finished his sentence.

"Yeah. Sometimes I feel like I'm a whimpering five-year-old. It's so damned embarrassing."

"I know it's tough, Joey, but you need to talk about it," Anne quietly whispered. She stripped away six decades of living and called him by his childhood nickname. The tears flowed freely as he turned once more toward her.

"I'm seventy-eight, Annie. Seventy-eight!"

"And I'm seventy-two. So?"

"I'm afraid," he barely whispered. Anne reached out and squeezed his arm. It was good to feel her still-strong grasp.

"We've faced so many things over the years together. We can face anything. So you're seventy-eight? You still have those wonderful sensitive feelings that made me fall in love with you. So our skin is a bit wrinkled? Inside, we're still in our twenties."

"No Anne, it's..." he was quiet as he bit his lip.

"Tell me. What can be so bad? Worse than almost losing Sarah at birth? Worse than that time you had to go out of state for work? We can face this too, Joey." Anne sat up straight as she pat his arm.

"Time is running out. I'm scared of...of..." he faded off again.

"Death?" Anne simply said what was on Joseph's mind, if not his tongue.

"Death." Joseph repeated with a mixture of anguish and relief.

"We've got lots of time, sweetheart. We've got

so much we want to do. We have reasonably good health, a comfortable pension, a decent house, grandchildren to visit with, and our love. We're doing fine," Anne said, her voice upbeat. "Besides," she continued, "you have so many projects to finish—so many dreams to pursue."

"Yeah, but that's the problem. There isn't much time." Joseph fought back tears. Anne put her hand under Joseph's chin and turned his head toward the mountains above.

"When are you going to climb that mountain?" she asked. "You've been talking about it for thirty years."

"I've just been so busy."

"No! That's not it. You keep putting it off! You're down because you're carrying so many regrets, so many unfinished pieces of business. What happened to that list of things you wanted to do? You know, the one you made seven or eight years ago?"

"I still have it. It's on my closet door." Joseph began to perk up.

"How many of those items have you done? Be honest, now!" Anne had a definite assertive tone in her voice. Joseph recognized this tone. It was the same tone of voice that pressured him to complete his graduate work, so long ago.

"Oh, I don't know. Maybe three or four." Joseph responded sheepishly.

"I don't think so, Joseph Marino. Three or four? Name two projects that you have finished!"

"There was that shed that I built..."

"Shed? You mean the one that we bought and had the boy from the hardware store put together? Try again." She was pushing; he could tell. He knew that he couldn't win this one, it was a repeat of the many "discussions" he had lost in the past.

"Okay, maybe I haven't finished many. But I've started a few."

"Hah! And they still sit there. Unfinished!"

Joseph knew what she was doing. She was prodding him, in her own indomitable way.

"Well, I can finish any one of them anytime," he said with a grand sweep of his arm.

"How about finishing one this month? Pick one!" she urged.

"You pick one. It doesn't matter which one. I could finish *any* of them!" he boasted.

"No, you wouldn't want that. I've always had a specific one in mind, and you know it."

Joseph sunk into his chair. He knew which one she was getting at. It was the one that he'd done the least amount of work on. He had good intentions, but, well, something would always come up.

"I know it," Joseph said in the sheepish voice that got so much practice this sunny afternoon.

"Finish it, Joey," Anne pleaded. He turned to look at her and was startled to see that she was crying. Her eyes were wide and round, like the ones he remembered when she pleaded with him to have a baby so many years ago.

"It means that much to you Annie?" he asked in a quiet, tender voice. She nodded as she wiped back the tears. "I'm sorry, honey. I knew it was important, but I underestimated how important. Why have you wanted it so much?" Joseph had gleaned his own insight in fifty-three years of marriage, and he knew there was something Anne had never told him about the stones.

"I've wanted an ivy-covered stone wall since I was a little girl." Anne looked up, her gaze tracing the shadows growing on the snowy walls of the sentinel mountain overhead. "And I'm afraid..."

"You're afraid?" Joseph interrupted.

"Yes. I'm afraid that I'll never see it."

"Why is it so important?" he asked. She had never really explained her obsession with a stone wall. Like he dodged the topic of aging, Anne had never confided her closely kept story. Now, as they sat there together, he truly wanted to understand.

"So very long ago, I used to wait for my father to come home from the mill," Anne's voice took on a reminiscent tone and her eyes welled slightly. "I used to hide behind the wall and pop up when he rounded the corner to come through the gate. Years later I'd hide a bottle of cold ice water for him. I'd smile, say hello, reach into the ivy, and pull out a cold drink. And when a pack of wild dogs chased me home from school, it was the strong stone wall that saved me from them. Joey, so many memories of my childhood were in that wall. It devastated me when they tore down that old wall and house to make room for that damned shopping center. Can you understand? Does it sound senseless? Part of my heart, my life, was there."

She had a grip on his arm that was vise-like. It was the same grip she had locked onto him with during childbirth.

"I understand," he said in a whisper, "and I'll do it. For you."

"For us, Joey…it is something we can do together. You do so much better when you accomplish something. You need goals. I need a wall. For us." She wiped away the tears that had spilled over onto her cheeks.

"For us. For us," he repeated.

The old man stood up and stretched his legs. They made a creaking sound and even felt creaky. He looked beyond the garden patch that they were working in and looked at the rudimentary beginnings of the stone wall along the road. He had to do it, he thought. For her.

She had given him so much in this life: companionship, children, understanding, and a good tongue lashing when he had deserved it. He wanted to give her something back—something that touched deep inside her.

The wall.

"You go back to your garden, Annie. I need to look at something by the road." Anne followed him partway down the path but stopped to watch as he began straightening the few stones piled at the bend of the road. She smiled as she returned to working the soil of her beloved garden.

Joseph took stock of the stones and realized that he was woefully short. He estimated that he was only about five percent finished, or, more realistically, ninety-five percent unfinished. He turned to look back at his wife, who had resumed her stooped-over position in the garden.

"It will be finished, Annie. I promise you," Joseph whispered the words with clenched fists. He realized that he didn't feel seventy-eight at that moment. He knew he was a man of thirty-eight. Well, maybe forty-eight.

He looked down at his wheelbarrow, which had been sitting next to the unfinished wall for a year now. It had rusted a bit over the winter, but, with a little oil and elbow grease, it would soon be fit for transporting rocks again. He grabbed onto the wooden handles and lifted, feeling renewed strength in his arms.

"Anne! Hey, Annie!" Joseph called out.

"What?" Anne turned with a quizzical look on her face.

"Forget seventy-eight! Look…forty-eight!" Joseph beamed as he struggled to push the rusty wheelbarrow up the slight slope toward the house. He was showing off. He felt like he was a teenager again. He remembered how he used to flex his muscles for Annie when they were in school and how she would giggle because a big, strong older boy paid attention to her.

"Oooff....!" Joseph hit a rock with the wheelbarrow and nearly fell.

"Hah! You haven't changed a bit!" Anne laughed.

"But..." Joseph started as he was trying to catch his balance.

"You still show off. Only now I can see through your 'muscles.' You are still trying to impress me!" Anne laughed.

Joseph regained his balance and smiled a shy, embarrassed smile. He felt a deep happiness as he looked into her eyes and heard her laugh. His smile disappeared, though, as he noticed a change in her expression.

"Joey...Joey..." Anne called out. She dropped her small shovel and clutched at her chest. She was reaching for a nearby tree.

Something is wrong, he thought. *Oh my God! She is falling!*

Joseph dropped the handles of the wheelbarrow and ran toward Anne. She was not going to reach the tree. He felt the cold, clammy sensation of panic welling up inside of his chest. He could feel his labored breathing as he stumbled up the rocky path toward her. He began to pray.

"Oh, my God! No! Jesus...*No!*" His labored breathing muffled what he wanted to be a shout.

Anne was heading toward the ground. She fell first to her knees, then slumped over on her left side. Her right arm was still holding her blouse over her heart. Her left arm was extended away from her body. Her head was back, and she appeared to be staring at the sky. It seemed like minutes stretched into hours for Joseph. He felt like Anne was falling at full speed, but he was running at half speed.

He stumbled and fell as he got within a few feet of her. Joseph didn't want to waste the time to get up, so he crawled toward her. Terror gripped his heart and mind—the terror of death.

As he reached her, he put his hand under her neck. He tried feeling for a pulse, but his panic, trembling, and shallow breathing hampered him. She was looking up into the sky, but he couldn't tell if she was alive or not.

"*Annie! Annie!* Talk to me! *Annie!* You can't die!" he sobbed. He heard a raspy gurgling coming from her mouth. She seemed to stir. Her eyes closed slowly. Her breathing was shallow and erratic. He fought the panic inside.

"Got to calm down. Got to do something. What can I do?" Incoherent thoughts raced through Joseph's head. Everything seemed hazy as he struggled for focus. Joseph took a deep breath and looked at Anne's face. It was the face he had looked upon every night for over a half a century, and the face that he had pushed wedding cake into so many Octobers ago.

"Phone," Joseph's mind cleared. "I have to get to the phone!"

Joseph tried desperately, but he couldn't lift Anne. He turned his head toward the house and back to her. He had to leave her. But what if she...? Panic gripped him, but he stuffed it back down.

He ripped his shirt out of his pants, unbuttoned it, and placed it under her head. Rising, he looked into her face one last time, turned, and ran to the house. It was a terrible fight to keep back the tears.

Joseph pushed open the door, ran to the kitchen, picked up the phone, and pushed the buttons:

9-1-1

Chapter 2

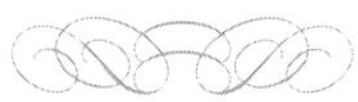

THE TELEPHONE DIDN'T LOOK VERY STERILE, Joseph thought. His eyes wandered to the clock, and he questioned if someone regularly cleaned it. Panic swelled from within.

"Mr. Marino?" A stern voice crashed into his fright.

"What?" Joseph answered as he turned toward the source of the voice. A man in a white coat came into focus. He was earnestly studying something on a clear plastic clipboard.

"I need to ask you some questions about your wife's medical history."

The man spoke crisply. There was an air of authority in the way he said the word "medical."

"Who…who are you?" Joseph said, almost whispering.

"I'm Doctor Terabian, the staff physician on duty." He continued to study the clipboard he held near his face. *Too near*, thought Joseph.

"I filled out some forms and I spoke with the nurse. Is there something else?" Joseph asked while fingering the button on his gray cardigan sweater.

"Yes. Just a few more questions." The man wrote something as he replied. There was a yawning silence.

"My wife, will she…I mean, how is she?" Joseph stammered.

"There will be time for that, sir. First, the questions," the doctor said in a monotone.

"But…"

"Mr. Marino, I have thirteen patients to attend to. I have little time for chitchat. Please. The questions."

Joseph felt a rise of anger as the man spoke. He wondered why the doctor wouldn't even look him in the eye.

"Can't you even take the time to look at me? I'm not a speakerphone, ya' know! I'm a person, not a machine that spits out information!" The emotions of that night reared their ugly heads across Joseph's face.

The doctor, startled, looked up. "This is exactly why we aren't allowing you to sit in her room, sir. We've found that most relatives of patients tend to overreact emotionally at a time like this."

"Overreact? Overreact? I'll show you overreaction, you insolent…" Joseph shouted, as he rose and rolled up the sleeve on his right arm.

"*Dad! No!*" a woman sternly chastised as she grabbed Joseph's arm.

"Sarah…he has no respect for me, for your mother, or for anything other than his damned statistics!" Joseph shook with rage and a mixture of other emotions. His knees felt weak, and his hands ached from the fierce pressure in his fists.

"Dad, please…sit down. We're under a huge strain right now."

Joseph broke his icy stare with the doctor in the white lab coat and turned to his daughter. The tears on her cheeks softened him somehow.

"You answer my question, you poor excuse for a doctor, and then I'll answer yours. That's all I ask. Do you understand?"

The young doctor swallowed hard.

"Mr…" the doctor began, with a tone that dripped with exasperation.

"Answer his question, Terabian!" an older voice ordered. Joseph glanced to his left, and saw the familiar outline of Susan Waller, the family's longtime physician, breaking the bright glare from the hall lights.

"But Doctor Waller, we have procedures that…"

"Answer the damned question. Now." Doctor Waller said in a barely audible voice. A long silence blanketed the room.

"Critical condition. But expected to survive," Terabian answered curtly. "Now, Mr…"

"Thank you, doctor!" Doctor Waller replied, with a voice heavily laced with relief, "I'll ask any questions that are necessary. Let me have the form."

"This is not proper procedure, Doctor Waller! I must protest this intrusion! Marino has been most uncooperative…"

"That's *Professor* Marino to you! The lack of respect that I have witnessed in this room has come from *you,*

Terabian. File a complaint, if you dare, but give me the clipboard." Terabian handed over the papers and left the room muttering.

"I'm sorry, Joseph. I've never understood why some people become doctors." Doctor Waller shook her head as she spoke in a calm, soothing voice.

"To hell with him, Susan! God, I'm sorry. I've probably created quite a scene around here," Joseph whispered as he saw the crowd disperse from the window outside the waiting area.

"Forget it." Susan put her hand on the old man's sleeve. She led him back to his seat, and motioned for Sarah to sit down.

"Why do they act like that?"

"That's tough to answer," Susan shook her head in disdain for the young doctor. "I'm sorry that you two had to deal with that. But more importantly right now, I've got to get some information. It's for Anne."

Joseph swallowed hard. Susan gently patted his arm in encouragement.

"She never complained. I've seen her make funny squinting expressions and noises at the strangest times."

"How long has this gone on?" Waller looked surprised.

"I don't know. One, maybe two years…"

"Two years? I've seen her in the last two years, and she never mentioned anything about this."

"She only visits you when she feels she needs to, Susan; you know that. I'd ask her about the expression, or the noise, and she'd say it was nothing, just a sore muscle from working in the yard or in the laundry room." Joseph slipped into a quiet stare. "I should have insisted that she see you. I should have questioned her more instead of just believing it was an ache or pain. If only I had..."

"Stop, Joseph. Let's not travel down Guilt Avenue." Waller put her hand up in a policeman's gesture. "That won't do you or Annie any good right now."

"Doctor Waller, what can you tell us?" Sarah asked. She was leaning over, with her arms in her lap.

"Not much, Sarah. Your mother had a heart attack. And not a mild one. I suspect that she's been having mild ones until today. But this one was, well, very damaging, to be honest."

"Is she in much pain?"

"Some, but we've heavily sedated her. She's resting, and in and out of consciousness. The next forty-eight hours are going to decide which way this goes." Waller removed her glasses and rubbed her eyes.

"When can we see her?" Joseph was almost afraid to ask.

"Just a few more questions and then we'll go in."

Joseph quietly provided Doctor Waller with a few details about Anne's recent attack. He could tell that she was searching for clues and for understanding. No one spoke for a terribly long time as Doctor Waller scribbled her notes.

"Susan?" Joseph asked with a tremble in his voice.

"Yes?" Susan continued writing.

"Will she have to…I mean, will this mean…?" The old man stumbled. When caught by fear, Joseph stumbled on his own words. This was one of those times.

"I think my father is worried about what will be next," Sarah interjected. Joseph nodded his agreement.

"Well, it's a bit early to say. There are a few options. A medical approach, a surgical treatment, or a combination of these." Waller looked up at Joseph.

"I understand."

"Joseph, I think you're just plain scared. Am I right?" The old man nodded, then lowered his eyes to stare at his shoes.

"I'd rather be in there, the one with the pain. I could deal with that better."

"We both are scared, Dad, but together, we can make it." Sarah squeezed her father's rugged hand.

"Come on guys, let's go see how she's doing." Doctor Waller rose from her seat.

Chapter 3

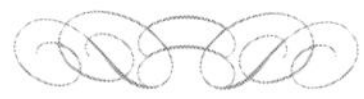

JOSEPH WAS GREETED BY LOW WHOOSHING, AIRY sounds and an occasional mechanical "beep" as he quietly pushed open the door. It seemed dark in the room. Too dark. Something moving to his left caught his attention.

"Can I help you?" the shadowy person whispered.

"I'm her husband," Joseph stammered, startled by the woman.

"It's all right, Julie. Mr. Marino is here to see his wife," Doctor Waller whispered from just behind Joseph's left ear. The nurse nodded and stepped back to allow Joseph's entry.

Joseph felt weak, almost too weak to walk. *Tired,* he thought. *It's been a long day.* He grabbed onto the bed frame when he was able to see Anne's face.

Even in the poor light he was able to see that her skin was a sickly ashen color, and she seemed not to be breathing. He felt faint.

"Dad? Are you okay?"

"Fine, just a little tired." Joseph trailed off, never taking his eyes from his wife's shadowy face.

"Joseph? Can you hear me?" Doctor Waller gently questioned.

"Uh, yes. I'm fine." Joseph continued to stare.

"She's doing fine, Joseph," Doctor Waller said reassuringly. She reached out and squeezed his forearm. The tenderness in her touch distracted him, and Joseph looked around, finding himself staring into Doctor Waller's face.

"Why don't you go ahead and sit down next to her," the doctor gently suggested. Joseph shuffled toward the left side of the bed. Just before the small chair, he stopped.

"Are you sure I won't disturb her?"

"Oh, no. She's fine. Sit right in that chair by her side."

Joseph searched and found the chair. He lowered himself gently, and reached for Anne's frail hand. Slowly his fingers laced with hers.

Odd, he thought. *She seems so cold.* He looked down at the back of her hand. He hadn't noticed how much it had changed since he had slipped that wedding ring onto her ring finger all those decades ago. She had old hands now. His gaze moved to his own, which also seemed impossibly wrinkled and covered with veins. *Is it over? Is this the beginning of the end?* Sweat began to form on his brow. He felt his heart race.

"Joseph why don't you sit back and take this?" Doctor

Waller handed him something, which he swallowed with a cup of water, without stopping to ask what the object was. A firm hand grasped his right shoulder.

"Dad, are you sure you're okay?" Sarah whispered.

"Sarah? Oh, yes…I'm fine. Just tired." His hand rose to meet hers, and he felt the anxiety drain as he was renewed by the strength of her hand, the softness and youth of her skin, and the stroking of his back by her other hand.

Joseph opened his eyes and tried to shake the dust out of his head. It was hard to focus and everything seemed foreign. The lights, the furniture, and the ceiling were all wrong. Confusion whirled around him. He remembered a strange, eerie dream. He was walking down a corridor in what seemed to be something like a hospital. Anne was sick…

"Anne!" Joseph shouted as he realized where he was and what had happened. He tried to sit up but felt dizzy; he returned to his horizontal position. A door opened.

"Mr. Marino? Did you call?" a pretty young woman inquired.

"Am I in the hospital? What's happened? How's my wife?"

"Shhh…everything's fine. Yes, you are in the hospital. Doctor Waller and your daughter decided you needed to stay here for the night. You fainted. Do you remember?"

"Everything is so cloudy. I don't remember much." Joseph ran his fingers through his thinning gray hair.

"That's understandable. Doctor Waller gave you something to relax you. You'll be better in an hour or so. You just need to wake up and have a nice breakfast." The nurse began to straighten Joseph's blankets.

"Breakfast? What time is it?" Joseph was stunned.

"About nine in the morning," she replied, pushing the button to raise the head of Joseph's bed.

"Nine? But I remember being here in the evening."

"Yes, you came in last night. You've slept quite a bit!" The nurse moved the rolling tray over to Joseph's bed.

"Anne! What about my wife?" He sat up.

"Slow down Mr. Marino," the nurse gently rested her palms on Joseph's shoulders. "Your wife is doing much better this morning. She's awake. You can walk next door and see her as soon as you have found your feet!"

"'Found my feet?'"

"When you've shaken out of the sleeping pills the doctor gave you. Give yourself an hour and you'll be all over this hospital."

"I'll have to take your word for it. Right now I feel like the whole room is bouncing around like a cork on the ocean."

"Anne?" Joseph whispered.

"Huuhhmm..." Anne mumbled.

"It's Joey. I'm here." Joseph smiled and stroked her hand.

"Jo...ey?" Anne struggled to open her eyes.

"Hey...you got it! Joey! I'm right here, honey!" Joseph was definitely pleased that she recognized his voice.

"Joey?" Anne replied, a bit stronger.

"Yeah, honey. I'm here. Can you feel my hand?"

"Uh-huh..." Anne nodded. The light glinted off of the plastic tubes coming out of Anne's nose.

"You've been pretty sick. Had me worried." Joseph smiled.

"Uh-huh..." Anne nodded again.

"Can you see me?"

Anne struggled to open her eyes. Their eyes met and the corner of her mouth turned slightly upward.

"You...have...to comb...your...hair..." Anne whispered.

"Ha! Always criticizing my grooming!" Joseph laughed, a tear of thankfulness rolling down his cheek.

"Somebody has to keep you from looking like a bum..." Anne winced as she deliberately pronounced each word.

"Shhh...not so much, Anne." Joseph was so excited to talk with her, he noticed he was rambling. "I'm always talking too much." Joseph felt a twinge of fright when he saw her expression of pain.

"Always..." Anne smiled.

"Ahh...I see you two have met," Doctor Waller

said with a smile as she entered the room. "How are both of my patients?" the doctor asked as she reviewed the chart next to Anne's bed.

"Trying to pad the bill, eh, Susan?" Joseph smiled.

"You took quite a drop, old man!" Doctor Waller shot back.

"Why don't I remember?" Joseph asked with a smile. He was fidgeting with his shirt button.

"Joey…stop…" Anne whispered. Doctor Waller looked up.

"Stop what?"

Anne lifted her arm and pointed at his fidgeting.

"Oh…sorry." Joseph mumbled.

"He always does that, when he's…nervous…"

"He has nothing to fear today. Your vitals are much better, Anne."

"What…happened?" Anne asked in a barely audible whisper.

"You had a heart attack. You're on your way out of it, though," Waller replied flatly as she returned to studying the chart. Joseph felt uneasy. There was something unsaid in her reply.

"What…about…" Anne swallowed, "…Joseph?"

"Oh, nothing. He's just a crusty old coward!" Waller grinned.

"Coward? Coward am I?" Joseph went along with the teasing.

"Fainted. Straight out! Had to check him into the hospital for observation. He was pretty wiped out from the experience yesterday." Waller smiled at Anne.

"That's...him!" Anne smiled.

"Well, Anne, I've ordered a few tests today. Not much, since you need your rest, but we'll get some solid information within the next twenty-four hours."

Joseph felt uneasy tension grip him again.

"Susan?" Joseph fought to catch up with Doctor Waller in the corridor.

"Yes..." Waller stopped and turned.

"What aren't you saying?" Joseph reached for his shirt button.

"It's early yet, Joseph. She's doing well, considering."

"Considering?"

"Considering she just had a heart attack." Susan's voice went flat again.

"Susan, we've known you for a lot of years. Please, I need to know. There's something in your tone of voice. You know me. I read things like that."

"Let's sit down in the waiting area." Waller gently touched Joseph's sleeve and guided him into a pair of seats in the corner of the nearby waiting room. "I'll be straight, Joseph. It was a pretty bad heart attack," Susan said gently.

"Bad?"

"Major damage to the heart, I believe. A colleague

of mine has reviewed the EEG tapes with me and some other test results. We're very concerned."

"What does that mean?"

"It doesn't mean anything yet. We need more test results. She's stable right now, but we need a plan and an idea of what we are dealing with before we can proceed."

"I understand. It sounds like the prudent thing to do." Joseph nodded as he twisted his button.

"You'll break that button if you keep pulling at it like that," Susan smiled as she pointed at his chest.

"Just what Anne would say. Do you know how many buttons she's sewn back on over the years? And always the second one from the top!" Joseph laughed softly as he gripped the button firmly and tears welled in his eyes.

"Joseph, I wanted to talk with you before we go in to see Anne today. This is Doctor Ball, a cardiologist. I've asked him to sit in and offer his opinion. Do you mind?"

"No, of course not. I appreciate your input, Doctor Ball." Joseph rose from the conference table and extended his hand. "This is my daughter, Sarah."

"Good to meet you, Sarah." Ball turned and reached for her hand.

"Let's get right to it," Waller said. "We have quite a number of test results back from the last three days.

We want to make sure you understand what we are seeing here." Waller opened a large chart file with the name Marino typed across the top.

Joseph's fingers reached habitually for his button.

"Yes, let's get to it," Sarah concurred. "How is my mother doing?"

"Today she's able to walk around and is showing great improvement." Waller smiled, seemingly happy at the developments.

"But, what's the prognosis?" Joseph interrupted.

Waller sighed and dropped her hands to the table. "There's major damage to the heart muscle." Waller's eyes found Joseph's as she spoke.

"Unfortunately, I must concur, Mr. Marino. Almost half of the heart has been affected," Doctor Ball added.

"But she's pulling out of it, right?" Joseph grew tense.

"Joseph, listen to me." Waller reached out for his hand. "She was lucky this time. Darned lucky. You saved her life. It's that simple. You bought her more time."

Sarah began to tremble, her composure giving way to tears as her head fell to her hands. Joseph reached over, gently stroking his daughter's back, his eyes never leaving Waller's.

"How much time?" he asked, his voice wavering.

Waller turned and looked at Doctor Ball. "That's hard to say. A month, six months. Maybe a year," Ball offered.

Joseph closed his eyes for a long moment.

"What about treatment? Surgery? Medicine?" The old man's voice pleaded as the button was turned tighter.

Snap! The button flew across the table, landing in a chair on the other side. Joseph bit his lip, fighting back tears while Sarah reached over and retrieved the button.

"I wish that this was that easy, Joseph. Unfortunately, Anne is a poor candidate for surgery. Of course, there is medical treatment, which we will use aggressively, but..." Waller turned to look at Ball, who was nodding in agreement.

"But...?" Joseph interrupted.

"But all it does is buy time," Waller faded off.

"What should we do? There must be something else." Joseph shook his head in disbelief.

"Joseph," her voice was calm and caring. "Go and live your lives. Fulfill dreams. Laugh with tears and smiles. Fill your days with spontaneity! Find joy, forgive, and give to each other. You have been given a chance to spend some more time together. Seize that gift and live." Waller fought back the tremor in her own voice.

"Our lives are like dreams in the vapor. Soon they vanish like a mist." Joseph turned away from everyone, letting the hurt, anger, and sadness of the past four days overtake him as the sobs emerged from deep within his soul.

Chapter 4

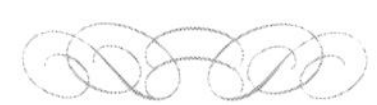

THE LEAVES ON THE WILLOW TREES WERE FULLY opened to the late spring sun the day that Joseph drove Anne home from the hospital. The sky was an oil-paint blue, peppered with clouds that seemed splattered from an errant paintbrush. Each turn of the tree-framed Mil Potrero Road seemed to bring a new, refreshing vista to Anne.

"Oh…how beautiful the leaves are, Joey! The trees were so bare when I saw them last!"

"They've come out to welcome you home." Joseph beamed, but not because of the leaves. It had been a long time since he had been called Joey. Anne sounded so full of hope and happiness. It was as if she was seeing this old, familiar road for the first time.

"Yes…yes!" She replied and turned to look at her husband. Joseph caught himself staring at her grayish-blue eyes.

"Watch out!" Anne shouted as a truck came straight at them. Joseph corrected and returned to his side of the road.

"Sorry," the old man replied, shaking his head.

"Joey…after all of that…to end up back in a hospital on the day I am released." Anne chuckled.

"Well, then we'd have side-by-side beds!" Joseph grinned with false humor. *Damn,* he thought. *Watch the road.*

The wind seemed to gently speed their way home. The gritty sound of gravel under car tires welcomed the old couple. Joseph turned the key to stop the engine. He turned toward his wife.

"We're home, love. How does it feel?" He put his arm behind her, and she reached over her shoulder to grasp it.

"Good. Scary." Anne fought back tears that had been trying to surface all day.

"Scary? What's going on, honey?"

"I don't know…" Anne's shrugged her shoulders.

Joseph waited, giving her a chance to scan the yard and the front of the house. A mockingbird landed on the bush near the car.

"Look, Annie…one of your friends has come over to say hello." The old man pointed a worn finger from behind Anne's shoulder.

"Oh, Joey…Joey…I'm so scared…" she said, her voice finally cracking.

"Of a little mockingbird? They're your favorite."

"Look at your fingers, Joseph," Anne commanded.

"You're scared of them?"

"No…look at them. Look at mine. They've

grown old while the years have passed us by!" Anne continued crying.

"Ah, Annie, we've got lots of time. You were just saying so yourself," Joseph knew that was before the heart attack. That was before time had knocked on the door with its cold reality.

"No we don't!" Anne interrupted in a gruff voice. Joseph pulled his arm back.

"But..."

"But nothing. You are almost eighty and I'm not far behind you."

"Annie." Joseph's voice grew faint. "We have today. Let's find what happiness we can." Joseph felt the slow crawl of a tear across his right cheek. Anne's hand, which looked more limp than before, gently brushed it away. Joseph wrapped his arms around his wife and pulled her tightly to him. He hated this. He hated the way time had hidden in the closet, unseen, only to emerge with its tolls and chimes echoing last moments and finality. Joseph closed his eyes and listened to his wife's sobbing and the formless wind, caressing the sides of the car.

"Sit right here," Joseph urged his wife as he pointed at the chair near the door. Under each arm were the typical bags one carries from a stay in the hospital.

"I think I'll go right into bed, Joey. It must have been the trip up the mountain. I'm so tired." Joseph decided not to argue with his wife. She slowly made her way to their bedroom. He followed, his arms stretched out behind her, as if to catch her if she fell.

"And bring my bags in, will you?" Joseph stopped in the hallway as Anne continued on to the bedroom. He stood a moment confused...should he follow her. or get her bags? Deciding not to upset her, he turned and went for the bags.

The next few days brought relief to Joseph's anxieties. After a day or two, Anne seemed to gain energy and motivation. Rest, he thought, was all she needed. On the third day Joseph was surprised in the kitchen.

"I'll handle that oatmeal pot," Anne ordered. Joseph was startled to see his wife in her robe next to him.

"You might give a guy a warning," Joseph replied with a grin as he handed over the pot holder.

"So, what are the rest of our plans for the day?" he teased.

"Well," Anne answered as she stirred some milk into the pot, "how about a game of tennis and eighteen holes of golf?" She had a smile on her face. Joseph sat down slowly, feeling a lump in his throat. How he wished it was all that normal. How he wished they could grab normalcy and cling to it once again.

"Better go slow, Annie. How about only the golf?" Joseph smiled lovingly.

"What's the matter? Can't keep up with an old

lady?" Anne plopped the oatmeal into the two bowls waiting on the table.

"Never could!" Joseph picked up his spoon to eat.

Chapter 5

It was early summer, and it had been one of those postcard days with that perfect weather that drives people outside to garden or play ball. The sky had few clouds, and the wind wound its way that evening through the narrow mountain valley that surrounded Joseph's house. The sun had little time before it fled the valley for the night. Joseph balanced a tray as he tried to open the screen door to go outside.

"Do you want some help?" Anne asked.

"Nah, when have I ever needed your help?" Joseph said with a grin. A handful of crackers fell from the platter.

"I see..." Anne bantered.

"I mean, when have I needed your help *other* than with a screen door when I am carrying a tray?" Anne rose to pull the door open.

"Maybe it's time to fix those springs, Joey..." Anne quietly prodded.

"Ah, yeah. The springs. I'll put it on the list," Joseph said with a resigned sigh—another chore that he was behind on.

"Here, let me take that before we end up having to feed those crackers to the squirrels." Anne reached for the tray.

"Well, if you insist." Joseph didn't mind that Anne wanted to take over. He had seen that she was terribly tired when they had finished their gardening that evening. He had volunteered to fix a light dinner, and she had agreed. This surprised him, for she was always the master of their kitchen. It was nagging at him. Why had she agreed now? Why did everything have to change?

"Well?" Anne was exasperated.

"Oh, the tray..."

"Joseph," Anne nudged. "I took the food; why don't you put the serving tray on the pine chair?"

"Of course, yes, the chair."

"What has gotten into you?" Anne's eyes searched Joseph's face. "I swear that recently you have not been all there."

"Where have I been?" Joseph smirked and looked around the porch at his feet.

"Stop. I mean it." Anne continued, "You seem lost in thought so very much. What is going on?"

Joseph sat down, holding his back as he did. "Oh, it aches tonight," he mumbled.

"Talk to me. This last month you've been so absentminded." The worry in her voice was evident.

"C'mon, Anne. It's been a rough month." Joseph reached for a sandwich.

"What were you thinking about before I interrupted you?"

"Let's see." Joseph bit into his special turkey, wheat bread, and cheese sandwich.

"Put the sandwich down. It can wait." Joseph stopped chewing and slowly put the food down.

"Annie...there have been so many changes recently. So much is unknown." Joseph hated to bring his own fears to the surface with so much stress already on Anne's shoulders, but her pleading eyes offered him no other choice.

"Like whether we should fertilize the aspen trees?"

"Well, that, of course, is the big one..." Joseph said with sarcasm.

"What else?

"I don't know, maybe how little things have changed."

"Like?"

"Well, I made dinner," Joseph said in an almost whisper voice.

"You're mad about that?" Anne stared at him, disbelief etched on her face.

"No, it's not the dinner." Joseph couldn't help the agitation in his voice.

"So what is it?"

"Why does everything have to change?" Joseph exploded, smashing his hand into the arm cushion on the chair. Anne's eyebrows went up and she pursed her lips. Joseph turned his face away from her and began rubbing his hand. Silence settled over the evening and the small porch. Finally, Anne spoke.

"Not everything has changed, Joey. What has changed that has bothered you? The dinner tonight? I was feeling dizzy," Anne said with a trace of guilt in her voice.

"Oh, Annie. I know." Joseph felt guilty for his complaints. The doctor had told her to rest if she felt dizzy or short of breath.

"It's okay, I think I understand."

"No…I'm sorry. I'm messing everything up. You're hurting, and all I'm doing is feeling sorry for myself." Joseph rose quickly and walked from the porch, moving quickly to the aspen tree near the driveway. The wind caressed the young leaves, and they shimmered in the fading light. Joseph cried, holding back the sobs as best he could. He felt a gentle stroking on his back, one so soft that he wondered if it was really there. Perhaps it was the wind.

"You always loved this tree," Anne whispered.

Joseph was startled, but he didn't turn around. He didn't want her to see the mix of tears and anger that crossed his face.

"I always loved aspens," Joseph said, his voice cracking.

"But this one, over all of the others, seems to be your favorite."

"I think it was because of Mr. and Mrs. Fuzzball." Joseph had to smile when he thought of the squirrels so many years ago.

"Yeah. They were quite a couple!" Anne added.

"Do you remember how they used to scamper up the driveway carrying whatever they found?" Joseph turned around slowly, wiping his eye.

"And how they would try to steal food from the kids' plates on the porch?" Their eyes met and a long silence followed. Joseph reached out and pulled Anne toward him. Joseph caressed Anne's cheek, and she clenched her arms tightly around his back.

"Hah!" Joseph exclaimed, "I remember when Paul tried to chase that big brown one all over the yard."

"Oh...I remember! She had taken his cookie!"

"How old was he then? Do you remember?" Joseph furled his brow.

"I don't exactly...wait...it was the same year that he broke his arm! I remember his arm waving stiffly, all covered in white plaster."

"That was when he was in seventh grade." Joseph smiled.

"Thirteen, then," Anne said after doing some quick arithmetic.

The couple slowly walked arm in arm back to the porch.

"Are you doing all right, Joey?" Anne asked.

"Oh, I'm fine. I'm just a bit confused and maybe overwhelmed. My feelings just seem to be bubbling out all over the place." Joseph sighed and looked down.

"This isn't easy for either of us, honey." Anne

reached over and touched Joseph's knee. "Remember what that psych Doctor Svenska said."

"You're right. Anger. Fear. Confusion. I guess we're just about right."

"I think that we are probably normal, all things considered." The couple sighed in unison.

"Well...shall we eat now?" Joseph asked with a bittersweet smile.

"You still haven't answered my question," Anne trailed off as she reached for her salad. She stirred the lettuce around as Joseph slowly picked up his plate. Anne stared at the dressing spread all over the salad.

"I think that whenever I'm reminded of your heart problems I wander away." Joseph picked up his sandwich.

"I kind of figured," Anne said before biting into a cracker. "You've always been like that. It's your way of protecting yourself, I guess."

"So, how's that dressing?" Joseph anxiously asked.

"Good! Did you make it? I wondered what it was."

"My special 'Million Islands Dressing.' That's what I decided to call it. It's Thousand Island dressing, plus a lot more!" Joseph sat up straight as he answered proudly.

"Okay...I'll bite. What did you put into it?"

"What, and give my secret away?" Joseph feigned a pout.

"Yeah, right. Like how much mustard did you add

to the bottle of what we've already got in the pantry?" Anne smiled.

I remember that smile, Joseph thought. *That was the same smile that she had when she caught me trying to sneak a piece of birthday cake many years ago. And when I tried to find my Christmas present in the closet one year…*

"It wasn't just mustard…" Joseph teased.

"Oh, yeah," Anne swallowed a bite, "and onion."

"But…"

"Worcestershire sauce," Anne continued in between bites of her salad.

"That's not all…"

"And a dash of oregano," Anne said just before she took a drink of her lemonade.

"Okay, once again you have guessed my secret recipe. What do you think?"

"Ummm…how shall I say it?" Anne looked up.

"Excellent? Unique? A wonderful touch?" Joseph pleaded.

"Well, those weren't exactly the words I had in mind."

"Well, then, what?"

"Interesting? No, too vague. I know!"

"What?" Joseph urged.

"Better on an overdone cheeseburger?" Anne smiled. He had played this game many times over the years. He concocted a dish with marginal acceptability, and she always found some "better" use for it.

The phone rang. Joseph and Anne looked at each

other wondering who would answer it. Joseph rose, then stopped to pull a bottle of real salad dressing from under a towel on the serving tray. "Here, use the real stuff." He laughed as he handed her some dressing.

Joseph walked into the house as the phone beckoned him again.

"Hello?" Joseph said with a chuckle.

"Dad?" asked the voice on the phone.

"Yep. How are you doing, Sarah?"

"I'm fine. How are you?"

Joseph had never been one for the idle chitchat that Sarah always engaged in. "Horrible. I cut off my leg with the chain saw."

Just then Anne, who had come inside to find out who was on the phone, slapped him on the arm. "Joseph! Enough!"

"Oh, that's nice…uh…you did *what*?" Sarah asked with a startle.

"Nothing…just kidding…"

"Oh. How is Mom?" Sarah continued.

"She's just fine. Do you want to talk to her?" Sarah answered affirmatively and Joseph quickly handed the phone to Anne.

Anne eased into a chair, phone in her hand. The old man wandered out the front door and sat in his old, comfortable chair. He watched as the sun started touching the mountains. He loved this time of day, this time of year. His gaze came to rest on an empty chair.

Someday, he thought, *this will be all there is to share*

these moments with me. Just then the screen door shut, and Anne approached the empty chair.

"Let me guess. Another reminder?" Anne inquired.

"Yeah, I guess so. I am having a hard time accepting all of this." Joseph spread his arms in grand gesture to the world.

"Accepting my illness?"

"Not just that."

"Death?" Anne whispered.

Joseph nodded. "C'mon. Let's finish this food before it spoils." Joseph picked up the remainder of his sandwich, eager to change the subject.

Anne obliged. "Sarah wants to come up this weekend and visit."

"That would be great. Seeing the little ones always lifts my spirit."

"They'll be here Saturday." Anne paused and then raised her eyes to meet Joey's. "I hope you'll forget it…" Anne shook her head, picked up her salad bowl, and leaned back in the chair.

"Forget what?" The seriousness on Anne's face worried him.

"Paul," Anne said quietly, without looking up. It was the "subject to be avoided."

"No more. There is nothing I will say about this." Joseph held up his hand.

"It's been five years." Anne glared at her husband.

"I didn't do this, Anne." Joseph felt himself grow angry at the mention of his name.

"You did it. He did it. What does it matter?" Anne was not backing down.

"Leave it alone, Anne. We've talked about this before; nothing has changed."

"Yes something has changed," Anne shouted.

"Tell me then, what the hell has changed?" Joseph met her anger with his own.

"I'm dying Joey..." Tremors and tears overcame Anne as she rose and rushed toward the house.

Chapter 6

Joseph removed his old weathered glove and rubbed hard at the large blister that had spread across his palm that day. He stared at the worn surface of his hand and remembered how he, as a young boy, had been fascinated by how water could gather under the skin like that. But now it just hurt.

The wind tugged at his hat as he rested that next morning, leaning on the handle of his shovel. He tried to catch his breath as he watched Anne sitting on the porch writing. She had spent many hours the last month writing, but she seldom shared any of it with Joseph. He wiped the sweat off his forehead.

He had been in the garden since before sunrise, shoveling for the foundation of the stone wall she had wanted so much. By flashlight he had begun, working feverishly, as if time were not on his side.

"I'm sorry, Anne," he whispered under his breath. "I've never finished anything for you. This pile of stones, the problems with Paul…hell, I've never finished that shed either. That changes today…"

He picked up the worn shovel and continued digging the shallow trench that would serve as the support for the wall. He winced as the butt of the tool crushed against his tender palm.

He remembered how he could have dug a trench all around the yard in this length of time. Had he really dug the foundation for the cabin all alone? Had he really come up after work and on weekends just to spend countless hours digging in the rocky soil of Pine Mountain Club? This trench seemed so endless, so difficult now. A tap on his shoulder interrupted his thoughts.

"Breakfast, Joey. Didn't you hear me?" Anne asked with exasperation in her voice.

"Already?" Joseph blurted, trying to catch his breath.

"Been ready for ten minutes!"

"Okay…let me…just…catch my…breath and clean…up." Joseph paused for a moment before rising from his shoveling position. "What are we having?"

"You don't remember? This morning?" Anne's frown grew.

"Oh…that's right. The clubhouse."

"That's right. It's Wednesday."

"Let me clean up and we'll go…" Joseph leaned the shovel against the pile of river rocks that had been sitting for years, waiting for a place in the wall.

Joseph opened the screen door of the clubhouse restaurant and gallantly swept his arm, as if royalty were entering. Anne walked slowly through the open portal.

"Welcome, your majesty!" Joseph teased under his breath.

"Good morning, Squire Joseph," Anne returned in a whisper. It had been a habit for years, this entry on Wednesday mornings. Some weeks it was knight and queen, others, judge and bailiff. But it was never just husband and wife.

Stacey, the woman who had run the small diner for eight years, sauntered slowly over to the door to join in the merriment.

"Your highness! You look grand this morning!"

"Oh...um...good morning, Stacey...we're just playing around, like we always do..." Anne was embarrassed that someone had overheard their exchange.

"I know. It's a legend around here. You've got a lot of husbands upset with you, Joe." Stacey winked. Joseph squirmed, for he never liked being called Joe.

"Is our regular table available?" Joseph asked, trying to deflect the embarrassment from Anne.

"Of course, right over there." Stacey pointed with her order pad.

Sitting on the table was a large basket of fresh, colorful fruit.

"Who did that?" Anne inquired, surprise in her voice. She turned to look at Joseph.

"Don't look at me. I have no idea." Joseph shrugged and wished he'd have thought enough to order something like it, especially considering how much Anne liked fruit. Joseph pulled Anne's chair away from the table and stood waiting as she reached for the gift card attached to the basket.

"It says a 'Secret Admirer'!" Anne exclaimed.

"A what?"

"Secret Admirer." Anne blushed slightly.

"Anything else? No clues?" Even after fifty-three years, Joseph couldn't help feeling a bit vulnerable and threatened.

"That's all," Anne said as she sat down. Joseph slid the chair under her as she did. He took two large strides and pulled out a chair on the opposite side for himself.

"Oranges, cherries, and some limes. Someone sent this who really knows you, Anne!" Joseph said as he leaned over to study the contents.

"Definitely. All my favorites!" Anne was giddy then she caught Joseph's eye. She saw his uneasiness and was just about to speak when the waitress interrupted.

"So, what's this I've heard about you being sick the last month, Mrs. Marino? You two haven't been around," Stacey said as she opened up to a new order form in her tablet.

"Heart attack. I'm just now able to get out and about. The doctor's been pretty strict with me," Anne said as she unfolded her napkin.

"Oh my gosh. Are you all right?" Stacey asked, concern flooding her voice.

"Time will tell," Anne said, inspecting her silverware.

"She's doing great, Stacey. What're the specials this morning?" Joseph interrupted, anxious to get about the business of ordering so he could focus on solving the mystery of the basket.

"Well, we have your favorite on special today. French toast, bacon, hash browns, and sourdough rye toast."

"Joey's Blue Plate Special." Joseph beamed.

Stacey scribbled quickly on her pad and was just about to turn toward the kitchen when Anne stopped her.

"Not for me, Stacey. Today I only want oatmeal, orange juice, and grapefruit."

"What? Not the usual?" Joseph asked nervously.

"I can't. Remember what the doctor told me."

Joseph tried to conceal how much this upset him. *It's just breakfast,* he thought. He remembered, although he had tried to forget, the doctor's words.

"You can always have a bite of mine," Joseph offered. But he knew the words came too late; his upset was apparent. Joseph slunk into his chair as Stacey left to place the order. "I'm sorry hon—this is all just taking me a while to get used to," he offered.

"I know, there's no need to apologize." Anne reached across and stroked her husband's hand. She cupped it within her own.

"Ow!" Joseph exclaimed.

"What in the world?" Anne turned over his hand to reveal the large blister formed in the palm.

"It's just a blister."

"A terrible one! Didn't you wear your gloves?" Anne scolded.

"Well..."

"This has happened every time you've dug a hole, for any reason. You always forget to put your gloves on. When you finally do put them on, you've got a whale of a blister!" Anne reached into her purse for the little first-aid kit she always kept.

"Not here, Annie..." Joseph pleaded.

"I'm just going to lance it and clean it with a rubbing alcohol pad." Anne's motherly nature emerged as she quickly revealed her supplies.

"Yeah, but we're having breakfast."

"We've been through this many times before. If you aren't going to take care of yourself, I'm going to do it. Here..." Anne pulled his hand into the middle of the table. "This won't hurt a bit."

"Owww..." Joseph grit his teeth as the needle slid beneath the surface of the blister.

"What a baby! It doesn't hurt," Anne said without looking up. She put pressure on the blister, forcing the clear water out and onto a small tissue she had pulled from her purse.

"I know, but it is so much more dramatic when I let out a wail!" Joseph grinned. Anne finished the procedure and handed him a tissue. He gently massaged the new cut in the blister. A ruckus to his right distracted him.

"Hey, how about some service?" A teenager shouted as he pounded his table. Two other teens sat near him and laughed.

"Yeah, where's the waitress?"

Joseph turned back toward Anne, who was staring at the young people.

"It's so sad Joey."

"It's sad that the sheriff isn't here," Joseph replied curtly.

"No, those kids. They're running wild, growing up without guidance, without love."

"You're right. No guidance. Maybe I need to give them a little 'guidance.'" He turned again as the noise got louder.

"No ketchup! Hey! No ketchup!" the boy shouted.

"I'm going to say something, Anne." Joseph shook his head.

"No…let Stacey handle it. You don't need this aggravation." Anne reached out for his hand.

"You're too soft."

"These kids have no parents around. School is out, and there's nothing to do."

"They should get a job, like I did," Joseph shot back.

"Where? This is a small town in the mountains. There aren't enough jobs to go around." Anne held her ground.

"Then they shouldn't be living here." Joseph glared at his wife.

"That's ridiculous. Their parents made that

decision, not them." Stacey arrived with their breakfast as Anne made her point forcefully.

"Yeah, well, Mrs. Marino, I wish their parents had made a different choice," Stacey said as she placed Anne's oatmeal in front of her.

"But they didn't." Anne looked down at her grapefruit.

"Don't bother, Stacey. When she gets like this she is like steel. You can't bend her or break her."

"Hey…grandma…where's the ketchup?" the teens interrupted.

"She's not your grandmother, loudmouth!" Joseph said as he turned to face them.

"Ooohhh…tough talk from a weak old man!"

"Would you like to find out how weak I really am?" Joseph pushed back his chair and started to rise.

"Joseph! No!" Anne grabbed her husband's arm. At that moment two California Highway Patrol officers entered. One was glancing at the local newspaper.

"Is there a problem here?" the older looking officer growled at the teens.

"Yeah, that old man is threatening us," the tallest teen said, flipping back his long hair.

"Sure. I believe that. Now get the hell out of here," the officer barked with a voice that sounded used to giving orders.

"Same crap again, Bill. Crackers, water, and ketchup, but no order and no cash." Stacey shook her head as she recounted the usual problem.

"We oughta round 'em all up and put 'em in detention camp. Then they'll learn some respect," the officer replied.

"No, they won't," Anne replied simply. All eyes in the restaurant were focused on her.

"What?" the officer replied.

"Detention camps will only make them more bitter. When will anyone get it? Caring and love produce caring and loving people. Harsh punishment and harassment only produce lonely, bitter, antiauthority people," Anne said firmly.

"These kids are like wild animals," Stacey added. "It's not a matter of love."

"That's only because they have been forgotten and harassed," Anne continued. "Nobody is raising the kids nowadays. Everybody is working because they've got to keep the boss happy and get that new expensive car. These kids are the real cost of the new cars, the expensive trips to Europe."

"But these kids are incorrigible! Some have parents around."

"Have you ever tried just talking to them? Not yelling at them and throwing them out of wherever they are hanging out?" Anne inquired.

"Yeah..." said the older officer.

"When?" Anne asked, her disbelief evident.

"Well...last week, at the high school. We were called in to break up a fight."

"And you were able to talk with them then?"

Joseph reached across the table and squeezed Anne's arm.

"Yeah, well, after they broke it up! Hey, lady... they're always looking for trouble. You can't turn around without finding one of them in trouble."

"How else would you suggest they get the attention of adults around here?"

"Anne! Leave it alone," Joseph said nervously. He figured they had created enough of a scene already.

"Leave it? These are kids, not hardened criminals!" Anne shot back at her husband.

"C'mon, Annie! We can't fix everyone in this world."

"Well how many can we fix? It seems that no one is trying to 'fix' anyone."

"Annie...calm down..." Joseph pleaded. He had noticed how red her face had become. He started panicking.

"I'm fine. Eat your breakfast."

"I will if you will." Joseph watched Anne stir the oatmeal mindlessly.

"I can't," Anne whispered.

"Huh? Why not?"

"The oatmeal is cold."

Chapter 7

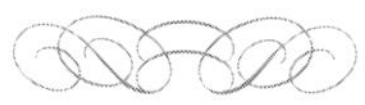

THE UNDERSIZED SHOPPING CART CREAKED AS Joseph leaned into it to turn left as he rounded the potato chip rack at the end of the aisle. He slowed as he spotted a bag of his favorite snack.

"How about some chips, Annie?" He asked tentatively. Anne continued to scan her coupon wallet. "Annie?"

"Too much cholesterol," she replied in a matter-of-fact manner. Her chin was pressed into her chest and her glasses were low on her nose.

"C'mon...I haven't..." Joseph started.

Anne turned and stared at him, over the rims of her glasses. She shook her head slowly. Joseph frowned.

"I guess you're right. You're a lot more important than the temptation of having a bag of chips around."

"I hope so!" Anne chided.

"Excuse me!" A woman wearing a very expensive looking business suit brushed past Joseph, nearly knocking him into forty bags of Ruffles potato chips.

"What's the hurry?" Joseph bit back with sarcasm.

The woman reached right over Joseph, pulling a box from a high shelf as a teenager turned the corner.

"Hey…Mom. What about some Oreos?"

"Yeah, whatever. Let's go. I've got to be in town in two hours, and it's an hour-and-a-half drive." The woman pushed her cart past her son.

"What about my…" the boy started to protest.

"That's enough! You'll have to change your plans. I can't drive you, and your father is in Bakersfield until late tonight." Her exasperation was apparent.

"Shit!" the boy replied. The woman grabbed the boy's arm and pulled him away from Joseph and Anne.

"Watch your damn language! Haven't I taught you…" The voice trailed off as they scurried down the aisle.

"What was that?" Joseph asked, to no one in particular.

"Someone too busy for their own child," Anne replied.

"How can anyone raise kids like that?"

"Things have changed, Joseph. Just like we have changed."

"But why do they live like that, Annie?"

"Well. Do you want their reasoning or the truth?"

"What d'ya mean, 'their reasoning'?"

"What they tell the older women at church." Anne pulled out a coupon.

"What do they say?"

"That they can't afford to live on one income like we did for so many years."

"Well, we couldn't afford it either! But we made a choice."

"They say that there is no choice." Anne reached for a jar of tomato sauce.

"Not that one, Anne. Garlic and oregano!" Joseph would interrupt any train of thought when it came to choosing the right tomato sauce. Anne pulled her hand back and grabbed the one on the next shelf.

"Sorry. I forget sometimes."

"The cost of growing old. Or maybe the blessing." Joseph lowered his head.

"Is that woman with the teenager getting you down?"

"I guess." Joseph was uncertain.

"We did the right thing. We invested in our children. Her priorities are her things." Anne put a box of rigatoni into the almost-full basket. "I think that we've picked up everything we need."

"Except those shortbread cookies I like," Joseph added quickly.

"They don't carry them here or anywhere on the mountain. We'd have to go into Bakersfield for them."

"Oh, yeah. Maybe next week when we go in for the doctor's appointment!"

"I swear, sometimes you're about eight years old!" Anne grinned.

"Nine?"

"Nine then! Let's go check out." Anne put her list and coupon wallet back into her purse.

"And away we go." Joseph picked up the pace with his cart.

"Joseph..." Anne said nervously as she rummaged through her purse. "I don't have the checkbook!"

"Where'd you leave it?"

"I wonder if it dropped out in the car. I had it as we left the house, when I was locking the door..."

"I'll just run out and check the car." Joseph left the cart and walked out the back door of the Pine Mountain General Store.

Joseph found the checkbook quickly. It was in between the front seats of their car, right where Anne always put her purse. He grabbed it and shut the car door. At that moment three teens walked by. One threw a cigarette butt between the cars, just missing Joseph's pants.

"Hey! Watch it with that thing," Joseph scolded.

"Sorry, bald one," said the young man with a spike of orange hair running down the middle of his shaved head.

"Don't you have any respect? 'Bald one?' Can't you be more original than that, 'bug-catcher head'?" Joseph's anger seethed.

"Don't mess with me, old man!" the orange-maned boy replied as he turned to meet the threat.

"Hey, leave him alone. Come on Isaiah..." The girl behind him tugged at his arm.

"Yeah, he's not worth it," added another from the group.

"Not worth it? I'll show you how 'worth it' I am!" Joseph shouted, as he moved toward the boy called Isaiah.

"Joseph! That's enough!" Anne commanded as she rushed out the front of the store.

The three teens turned toward the gray-haired woman.

"And you three need to find some respect." Anne vented her anger at the young ones.

"Hey, let's dump this crap, Tim," Isaiah growled as he flashed an obscene gesture toward Anne.

"Why, you lousy..." Joseph charged the boy with the orange hair. Even as he moved, he regretted his decision. Although his anger held all the ferocity of his younger years, he recognized the strength of his body could no longer match it. He grabbed the boy's gesturing arm and tried to pull it behind his back. Isaiah whirled and effortlessly shoved Joseph to the ground. The girl jumped between the two combatants.

"Stop, Isaiah—he's an old man for God's sake!"

Isaiah's breath was heavy and his eyes like fire. "Yeah. You're right. Not worth getting in trouble over." With that, Isaiah shot an angry look at the elderly couple and led his troop to some other place.

Anne ran to Joseph's side, helping him rise.

"Damned scum!" Joseph grumbled, rubbing his left arm.

"You're bleeding." Anne was scrounging through her purse trying to find her handkerchief. Joseph looked down and saw blood dripping on the ground. He ran his right hand up his upper arm and felt a terrible sting.

"Damn!"

"It looks like you fell against the edge of that dented bumper there," Anne said as she pointed. With her tender touch, she carefully pressed the handkerchief to the wound.

"Ahhh...that hurts." Joseph watched his wife tend to him. "That's not doing much good. Why do they make women's handkerchiefs so small and thin?"

"They don't make them anymore...I've nursed this one for years." Anne tugged at Joseph's waist and ripped a piece off Joseph's old work shirt. She fashioned a bandage and wrapped it around his upper arm. "We'd better get you to the doctor. That's going to need stitches."

Chapter 8

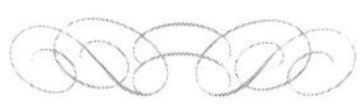

"ANNIE...CAN YOU HELP ME WITH THIS SHIRT?" Joseph asked, wincing as he tried to pull his arms through the long sleeves of his shirt. His recent wound, slow to heal, made dressing difficult.

"Hold on, let me finish zipping up my dress." Anne clenched her teeth as she fought with the zipper.

"Here, let me." Joseph reached for the back of her dress. Slyly, he slipped one hand inside the cloth and tickled Anne's side.

"Joey," laughter overtook Anne's attempt to sound stern. "I don't need *that* kind of help!" She did a turn to escape Joseph's hand.

"There...now, let me see your button." Anne turned as she finished zipping up. She tugged on his sleeve and gently fastened the button on the end of Joseph's cuff.

"Have you taken your medication tonight?" Joseph asked as she finished with his shirt.

"I'm glad you reminded me; I nearly forgot." Anne looked at the clock on the wall and moved toward her medicine cabinet.

"How are the prescriptions? Do we have to go into Bakersfield soon, or do you have enough?" Joseph straightened his tie while inspecting himself in the mirror. He had been looking forward to the semi-annual Las Vegas Night at the clubhouse for some time. He admired his choice of tie while waiting for Anne's response. For the life of him, he had never been able to get the length of the tails quite even. He fumbled with the knot trying to adjust the length.

"Anne? How is..." Joseph turned to ask again. Anne was lying on her side on the bed. She was quiet and still.

"Anne? Annie?" With two quick steps he was by her side, his heart beating strongly, his mouth dry. Slowly, he reached for her arms, his voice a whisper. "Anne? Are you...are you..."

"Humph?" Anne stirred. Joseph let out an audible gasp.

"You're all right...?" the old man asked, his confusion apparent.

"Just...feeling...tired..." Anne whispered back.

"Maybe we'd better skip tonight. We don't need to push it too much. Besides, you were working awfully hard out in the midsummer sun today." Joseph struggled to regain his composure. Within an instant he had gone from the fear of death to discussing the day's sun. He wanted to ask her what had happened, if her heart was hurting; most of all he wanted to climb inside her body and alleviate her pain.

"No, no—I want to go. I just need a little rest, love. Give me a few minutes." Anne opened her eyes and stared at the mirror on the closet door.

"Can I get anything for you?" Joseph asked helplessly.

"No. You've already helped. I'll be all right in a minute..." Anne trailed off.

"Was it..." Joseph started to form a question, but he was unable to finish.

"Was it what?" Anne asked as she rolled to her other side to face him. Joseph sat on the edge of the bed and began rubbing her neck. Anne closed her eyes as a smile grew on her face.

"I know how much you like neck rubs," said Joseph, purposely changing the subject.

"You know that I turn to putty when you do that." Anne continued smiling.

"I know."

"I had a pain. But it's better now. I just needed to lie down, that's all." Anne knowingly answered Joseph's unasked question as Joseph's hand slowed on her neck.

"Why don't we just stay home?"

"I'll be fine. I want to go. I really do. How about if we compromise and make it an early evening?"

"Anne, are you sure?" Joseph wondered how much of her desire to go to the party was for her—and how much was for him.

"I'm sure. You've been looking forward to this for months." Joseph supported his wife as she slowly rose off of the bed. He stood for minutes watching her as she finished dressing. Little things captured his sight—the curve of her calf; the peppered look of her brown-gray hair; the wrinkles on her jaw line that weren't there a half-century ago. He turned and stared into the mirror on the bedroom door. His skin also held many lines that weren't there fifty years ago. And he had lost most of his hair many decades ago. A lump grew in his throat. Where had that little boy gone? He felt an old, old feeling. It roared out of the mist of the long-ago past. It was strange. He knew the feeling so well. A faint voice, long unheard, echoed in the fog of his mind.

"Mom..." he whispered.

"What Joey?" Anne turned. "I didn't hear you."

"Oh...nothing. I was just remembering...ah... our...our senior prom." Joseph snapped from his daydream.

"Prom? What?"

"Our prom—you were dressing, and it reminded me of our high school prom."

Anne walked over to her husband and put her arms around him. She reached up to touch the corner of his eye.

"Our prom wouldn't bring tears, Joey," she said softly. "And you didn't watch me dress that night, either. I dressed in my parents' house." Anne looked deep into Joseph's eyes. He said nothing. "Why did you say 'mom' honey?"

"It was nothing," Joseph dismissed the moment. "I just get too sensitive and sentimental sometimes." He shook his head, as if to throw out the sleep cobwebs from a bad dream.

"I've been telling you the same thing for too many decades. In fact, that's one of the reasons I married you."

"I thought it was because I was a head higher, enough for a tall woman like you." Joseph forced a smile. "Look at the time! We've missed forty-five minutes already," Joseph exclaimed.

"Let's get moving, then!" Anne led the way out the door.

Joseph eased the car forward in the clubhouse lot toward the handicapped square. It felt strange to be using the handicapped spaces since Anne's heart attack. Every time he pulled into a spot he felt that the blue and white sign screamed, "Your wife is going to die." Instead of looking at the signs, he diverts his gaze with a bush or a sign on a building.

Thud!

"What was that?" Anne shouted. Joseph snapped his head forward, discovering that he had driven into the disabled sign pole. He put the transmission into reverse and slowly backed away. He turned off the engine as Anne was opening her door. Quickly, she made her way toward the dented sign.

"What happened?" she repeated. Joseph walked around his door to join her. The blood of embarrassment rushed into his neck and face.

"Sorry. I guess I was a little distracted." He leaned into the steel signpost and pushed. His injured arm sent a sharp pain up his neck.

"That's enough, honey. Nothing serious. Leave it alone."

Despite his wife's urging, he felt something deep inside. Something compelled him to fix the signpost, in spite of the pain in his arm. His proximity to the post allowed him to see that it was galvanized, made up of splotch silver and gray steel.

"I guess you're right. It'll do." Once again he longed for the strength that had long deserted his muscles. He pulled away from the cold, dark shaft.

Inside the clubhouse, they were greeted by a wave of noise. Talking. Music. Laughter. Multicolored lights were everywhere.

"Look who's here!" a man shouted from the crowd. A number of people, all dressed in evening finery, turned toward the couple.

"Yeah, Bill...we made it," Joseph growled back as he rubbed his arm.

Of all the people in the town there was only one he didn't want to see tonight. Bill Morton, the retired real estate developer. Talking to him was like talking to a used car salesman when you wanted to buy a new car. A woman moved out from the crowd.

"Anne! I've been wanting to see you! I heard that

you've been ill!" Barbara Dane called out. She took Anne by the arm and led her to one side.

Joseph stood on the clubhouse steps, nursing his aching arm.

"C'mon, Joe, get in on the poker game!" Bill slammed his oversized paw into the empty seat next to him. Joseph quietly slid into the chair.

"I'm in," Joseph said to Scott, the dealer. Outside of Vegas night, Scott was the kid who took care of the golf course.

"Deuces wild. Seven card stud. Ante up two chips to get in." Joseph handed him a ten-dollar bill. Scott slid three stacks of red, white, and blue poker chips across the green, felt-covered table. Joseph felt the familiar passion that arose when joining a good poker game. Scott flicked the cards around the table like a professional. Two cards went out 'down,' hidden to other players. Joseph pulled in a two and a seven. Scott proceeded to toss cards to the players face up, for all to see.

"Bill opens with a trey," the dealer announced. Morton winced.

"Marino pulls a fiver."

"Marty slips through with a deuce!" The sunburned man at the other end of the table grinned, and his upper plate fell into his lap. Now toothless, the table roared with laughter. Joseph couldn't help but chuckle and shake his head.

"Looks like he's brought his own deck!" Joseph teased.

"I'd say a 'flush'!" Scott blurted out. Marty sighed as he picked up the plate and returned it to his mouth.

"All right, enough. Are we gonna play cards or what?" Scott quickly resumed his dealing.

"Anyone wanna open?" Scott asked. When no one volunteered, Scott dealt another set of cards. Three deuces stared at Joey. He felt his pulse rise with excitement.

"I'll raise three!"

"Mr. Poker-face!" Bill chortled, throwing his cards into the pile.

"I'll stay," said Marty, keeping a level gaze.

"I'm definitely out." Scott shook his head and tossed his cards onto the table's center.

"Whattya got, Marino?"

"Read 'em and weep!" Joseph proudly displayed his hand.

"Damn! Wipes me out." Marty shook his head and Joseph pulled the winnings toward him.

"Joseph?" Anne stood behind him.

"Hey! Just in time honey." He smiled up at his wife. "I'm paying off the mortgage!"

"Look's like it." Anne glanced approvingly at the chips. "I've arranged a table for us to eat. It'll be ready in fifteen minutes. Is that okay?"

"More than okay, I'm starving."

Joseph's luck continued as the rounds flew by.

"Here we go. Last card up, then one down," Scott announced.

"Morton lands a lady." Bill looked down at the queen of hearts.

"Joe, the one who came to rob us all..." Scott paused to heighten the drama of the moment. A familiar shape appeared as the card landed on the green felt. "Ace of spades, the death card!"

Scott's words echoed through Joseph's mind as the color drained from his face. The death card. He picked up his cards and tossed them into the center of the table.

"I fold," he whispered.

"So, I heard that you were the big winner tonight..." Barbara, a friend of Anne's, blurted at the table.

"Yeah, twenty bucks ahead." He tried to sound excited, but he couldn't. The vision of the card haunted him as he sat sullenly, looking at his plate.

Overall, the evening was an enjoyment for them both, and the couple rode side by side in the car, an unusual silence overcoming them.

"What are you thinking about honey?" Anne looked at her husband's profile amid the night's shadows.

"I've been thinking a lot. I need your help with something."

"What?"

"Paul." Joseph was silent for a moment before turning to meet Anne's eyes. "Can you help?"

"You know that I will."

"Will you call him? You know that he'll hang up the phone if I call him." Anne nodded in the darkness.

"I want to try…it's been too long." Joseph kept his gaze fixed on the road in front of him. He was scared that choked-back tears would overflow if he met his wife's eyes.

"He's out of town right now, but will be back next week. I'll call him first thing."

Joseph could hear the smile in his wife's voice.

Chapter 9

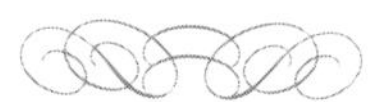

THE LATE MORNING SUN LEFT FEW SHADOWS ON the mountains above the Marino homestead. Like every morning, Joseph strolled onto the porch and addressed his old friend, Pine Mountain.

"I overslept this morning, Old Man. But when you're retired, it doesn't matter. Well, got to get some work done around here."

The wind whistled its response through the trees.

"What's that? Going to have some winds today from the valley? I guess it is getting to be that time of year. It is warming up." Joseph rubbed his injured arm as he moved toward the edge of the porch.

"Don't forget your hat, Joey," Anne called from inside the house.

"Got it on," Joseph said as he reached back through the door surreptitiously, carefully replacing the door so it did not slam.

"...and take care of that arm."

"Yes, dear."

Something caught his eye as he crossed the yard.

A few stones had fallen from the middle of the wall. Joseph slowly walked toward the breach in the wall. He was sure the dirt had been disturbed. As he drew closer, his suspicions were confirmed by the footprints in the dirt…fresh ones.

He knelt down to inspect the remains of the footprints and found more evidence left behind. Cigarette butts littered nature's floor on both sides. Joseph felt anger grip at his chest. He held one of the fallen stones inside a clenched hand.

"Damn! Go out for one night and this is what someone does to your work. Set me back two days," he said to no one except the mountain. In a world where days were dwindling like a bouquet on its last breath, two days felt like two years.

Joseph turned toward his work shed, then stopped dead in his tracks. Painted on the side of the small outbuilding was a large yellow swastika and words that Joseph had never said aloud.

"Damn!" He threw the rock as far as he could. Anne came out onto the porch.

"Joey? What's wrong?" she asked as she crossed the small area that separated them.

"Those idiots ruined my wall and painted obscene words on my shed!" Joseph could feel the heat of rage rush through his entire body.

"Who? Take it easy, honey. No use working yourself up over this." Anne turned to inspect the focus of her husband's rage.

"Working myself up? How can anyone not get worked up over *this*?" Joseph barked as he pointed toward the shed.

"That is bad," Anne said sadly. But just as quickly, she turned toward a solution. "We still have some of the paint for the shed don't we? I'll help you paint over it. Don't worry. We'll fix it."

Joseph opened the shed door and grabbed his shovel. He didn't acknowledge Anne's soothing. He plodded to the opposite end of the yard, near a dead pine tree. Anne watched, without saying a word.

"To hell with it all," Joseph yelled as he lifted the shovel high above his head. He swung his arms with all of the strength he could muster and slammed the shovel into the branches of the tree. Twigs and pieces of pinecone flew across the yard.

He hit it again. And again.

And again.

"To hell with the doctors! To hell with teenagers!" All of his rage, all of his frustration, channeled through his arms and into the handle of the shovel.

"To hell with growing old..." Joseph dropped the shovel and slumped down to a sitting position on the ground. He tried to catch his breath, and the wind blew off his hat and cooled his brow. Tears of regret, frustration, anger, and times lost crawled down his cheeks. He grabbed at his tortured left arm and let his forehead fall against the earth.

"Joey..." Anne whispered. She had walked closer but still stood a bit away. Matching tears made their way down her cheek. She hesitated, longing to run to him, but knowing these were pains that no one could nurture away.

"Why...why...why..." the old man's fingers clawed repeatedly into the soil. So many questions had to be answered but few were. Clouds had passed overhead, covering the sun and casting their shadows over the yard.

Anne slowly made her way over toward her husband. She hesitated every few feet, reaching out her hand, pulling it in, and continuing. The crying slowed to low sobs.

"Joey?" Joseph just stared at the trees and the mountains. "Can you hear me, Joey?" Anne's voice was trembling. Still, he said nothing. "It's me. It's going to be all right. You're tired, and you've been through so much recently. Don't worry about the shed."

"Shed..." the old man repeated. He glanced at his wife, his face blank.

Anne knelt next to her husband and began stroking his gray hair. He reached up and touched her elbow.

"I'm sorry."

"It's okay, love."

"Sometimes it's too much Anne." The back of his hand swiped at the wetness on his face. "Years ago, I could handle all of this—but now, it's just too much."

Shame overwhelmed him. Where was the man that could handle everything?

"I understand."

"We're supposed to be enjoying life now. We worked hard for years." Joseph turned to look at his wife's face. He stopped mid-thought when he noticed Anne's tears.

"I know..." Anne whispered.

"I'm sorry, honey." Joseph struggled to sit up, his injured arm reminding him that it would not be easy.

"Nothing to be sorry about..." Anne sighed.

"You didn't need this."

"Neither did you." Simultaneously, they reached for each other, finding strength and hope, as they always had, in each other's embrace. Joseph held her tightly, feeling her heart beat against his own. It was good to feel her skin, her shape, her breathing.

At the property's edge, there was a flicker of movement. Joseph gently pushed Anne away. He was sure he had seen a face, peeking out from beneath a tree.

"Someone is watching us," he said quietly. "Don't turn around."

"Who is it?" Anne asked, alarm in her voice.

"I don't know. I can't make much out. It looks like a girl." Just then, the person in the forest turned and ran. She wore a brightly colored vest and blue jeans. Her hair was light brown, the way Anne's used to be, and long.

"Is she still there?"

"No…but I could tell that it was a 'she.'" Anne turned to look, squinting at the distant outline of the girl.

"She's wearing one of those new vests that I've seen all teens wearing," Anne observed.

"I'll bet she knows who did this."

"But we don't know who she is," Anne reminded him.

"There was something in her expression…" Joseph's voice trailed off.

"What?"

"I could swear that she was crying."

Chapter 10

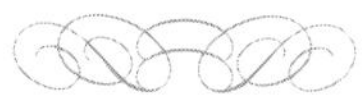

JOSEPH WIPED HIS HANDS CAREFULLY, INSPECTING for paint hiding under his fingernails. He hated dirty, long nails. Always had. He sat down on the log beside his work shed and leaned back admiring his craftsmanship.

"Yellow—" he couldn't help but chuckle as he looked at his handiwork. He had decided to paint his shed a color that would catch everyone's eye. To hell with the town planning committee and their "natural colors only" ordinance, he thought. He felt a certain youthful vigor when he pictured how the environmental officer would gasp when he saw the shed. The screen door slammed shut, with the creak of still unoiled hinges. He knew Anne's footsteps. After more than a half a century of marriage he could tell her mood from the shuffle or clop or stomp of her shoes. He tensed. The footstep sound was not a pleasant one.

"Joseph Marino! What in the world have you done?" It was more of a statement of surprise than a question.

"I told you this morning what I was going to do. I painted the shed." Joseph had a sardonic grin on his face.

"Yellow? Yellow?" Anne repeated herself as she pointed at the right side of the very visible outbuilding. The pitch of her voice rose as she spoke. "Get the brown paint out. That has got to change!" Anne demanded as she walked toward the edge of the porch.

"Ahh, c'mon, Annie. Why? You know I've always liked yellow. This might be my only chance to paint a building yellow."

"And what's next? Running around with yellow underwear outside?" Anne asked sarcastically. She stopped suddenly and grabbed her chest. She reached out for a nearby tree.

"Anne? Slow down..." Joseph jumped up and rushed to her side.

"I...can't...get...my breath..." Anne gasped.

"Shhh...sit down. Slow down, honey. Yellow is only the first coat, anyway." Joseph was talking quietly now. Nervous sweat beaded on his forehead.

"First...coat?"

"Yeah...look over there, by the shed door. Brown paint. I just did this for fun, that's all." He stroked her gray hair.

"I'll be all right..." Anne said as she stared at the yellow shed.

"Really, I painted it yellow for a reason, honey..."

"You don't have to explain," Anne interrupted.

"It's an old trick. Paint one coat the same color as the graffiti. Then cover with the desired color. That way the words and the swastika won't show through..." Joseph pleaded.

"Yeah, that makes sense. Now whenever the shed is scraped a yellow streak will show through."

"How are you feeling?" Joseph leaned over to wipe her forehead.

"Better. I just got too worked up."

"Do you want to get up...or stay seated for a bit?"

"I'd better get up. I was coming out to tell you that Sarah is on her way. She called from Lake of the Woods. She should be here in about fifteen minutes." Anne struggled to stand, with Joseph's help.

Joseph and Anne stood side by side on the porch as the minivan pulled into the drive. Two little ones waved excitedly from the back seat.

"Are you sure you don't want me to call the doctor?"

"I'll be fine, as long as I can sit down for a few minutes," Anne replied through her own wide grin, as she waved. She exchanged a short glance, and a nod, with Joseph.

"Grandma! Gramps!" the children exclaimed.

"Hey! How are the munchkins?" Joseph crouched down to catch them in his arms.

"Why do you keep calling us that?" a pony-tailed girl asked.

"Because you're small and lovable and you wear bright clothes, Laura!"

"Hey! Yellow! Neat color!" Laura pointed over her grandfather's shoulder.

"Picked it out myself, you know. Grandma didn't like it," Joseph grinned.

"And he's going to paint over it today, right now." Anne stared at her husband.

"Oh, all right, but I kind of like yellow." Joseph picked up his granddaughter. "Who's going to help me?" the old grandfather asked.

"I'll do it! Me! Me!" little Joey exclaimed.

"Oh, well…I guess we do need some paint all over the backyard!" Anne smiled as she stroked little Joey's tousled hair. "Can they have ice cream?"

"They are full of ham sandwiches, cookies, and candy. Let them run around!" Sarah replied. The children groaned with disappointment.

The family walked to the porch, where Anne found her favorite seat. Joseph scurried around to plump up the pillows for her. Anne had a difficult time getting down into the chair, so her husband gently held her as she settled down.

"She needs a little rest, Sarah. Can you see to her while I finish the shed? I'll have the little ones help me." The worry in Joseph's voice was apparent.

"I'll be fine, Joseph. Quit fussing and just get that shed finished." Anne waved him off.

"Don't worry, Dad. She'll be fine."

"Do you need anything, Anne?" Joseph asked as he shaped his hand as if he were holding an invisible bottle of medicine.

"Go..." she pointed purposely toward the shed, a grin on her face. Joseph locked his eyes with hers—unspoken words passed between them. The moment was interrupted by the two kids tugging at his hands.

"C'mon Grandpa!"

"We have to wash off the paintbrushes first, kids. Can't put brown paint on with yellow streaks in it." Joseph proudly demonstrated his knowledge of painting.

"Aren't you going to use that ter-teen?" Laura asked as her grandfather rinsed the brushes in a bucket under the faucet.

"Ter-teen?" Joseph asked.

"You know...that smelly stuff that cleans the brushes! Daddy used it last year when he painted the house."

"Ohh...turpentine! Well, uhh, I guess we should, but, um..."

"Why don't you tell her Joseph," Anne had walked over to check on the progress.

"Are you listening in?"

"Tell me what, Grandpa?" Laura asked as she inspected a stiff, yellow paint-coated brush.

"Well, I ran out of turpentine," he whispered to the kids, trying to avoid Anne's earshot.

"Tell her the truth," Anne prodded.

"You may be sick, but there's certainly nothing wrong with your hearing!" Joseph shook his head in disbelief.

"What happened to the ter-teen, Grandpa?"

"Oh, well...can't win...I left it out in the yard last week, with the top off, and I forgot and..."

"Just tell her..." Anne scolded.

"I forgot it was out there and I threw dirt all over it when I dug out some plants. There!"

"But you're supposed to put your things away after you finish using them. Mommy always says that..."

"I know...the same thing *her* mommy told her. 'Care for it or cry over it...'"

"Didn't you listen to Grandma when she would say that?" Laura asked.

"No, he didn't, Laura." Anne stared at her husband with smug satisfaction. The satisfaction disappeared quickly when she noticed that Joseph was not returning her smile.

"We better get to work, little girl. Enough talking." He sent the kids to retrieve a few items and then turned to Anne. "Messed that one up, too," he mumbled.

"It's nothing, Joseph. I was just playing." Anne's voice had softened.

"Yeah. I'll finish this in no time."

The old man grabbed a worn brush for each of the children and then picked up the large, newer roller and pan for himself. Vigorously he poured out some dark reddish-brown paint into the pan, and then pushed the roller deep into it. The children had returned and watched his demonstration.

"You get some paint on your brush, just like I'm doing with this roller...and...then...you place the brush or roller on the wood...and go to it!" He said in between the strokes of his roller. The children tentatively dipped their brushes into the paint and began to smear it wherever there was yellow. They were obviously trying to do it neatly, but their inexperience and youth showed through—just like the yellow they were painting over.

"Perfect," he encouraged.

Together, they quickly covered the shed. The grandchildren painted first and he followed, rolling over their efforts.

"We're over halfway done. How about a drink break, kids?"

"Yeah," they shouted together. "I want some soda." Joey had already dropped his brush in the dirt and was running for the porch.

"Do you have root beer?" Laura asked as she gently placed her brush on the roller pan.

"Why don't you two go in through the back door and find out?" Joseph wiped his hands as Laura and Joey ran off around the back of the house.

Joseph slowly walked toward the side of the porch and then stopped just outside of Anne and Sarah's view. Something in Anne's expression worried him.

He leaned up against the wall, behind a tree, where he could make out the side of Anne's face. She was writing in her notebook.

"Mom…you haven't been listening to me. What are you writing that has completely pulled you out of our conversation?" Sarah was exasperated.

Anne lowered her tablet.

"My journal, Sarah. I seem to be unable to write out all of the things I need to say." There was a sadness, a longing in Anne's voice.

"But why not just say them? Why the rush…" Sarah's voice tapered off as she heard her own words.

"Someday your father won't be able to hear what I have to say. For more than fifty years we have been together. I'm worried about him." She paused and looked out at the mountain. "He acts so gruff sometimes, but, underneath, he's a scared little boy mostly. He looks like an old man, but inside…"

Joseph held his breath, feeling awkward for listening and touched by what he heard. A branch from the tree caressed his face as the wind nudged past him.

"But why not just tell him what you want him to know?"

"I don't want to say…someday…well, just realize that I want something that stays…" Anne drifted off.

"I think I understand," Sarah comforted her mother.

"Grandpa! Root beer! You got my favorite!" Laura ran around the corner of the building. She stopped and looked around.

"Grandpa?" Little Joey emerged at Laura's side carrying a can of soda and an armful of cookies.

"Where is he, Laura?" Joey asked.

Joseph gently worked his way out from behind the tree. He could, he thought, just explain that he…

"He's right here, kids…behind the tree!" Anne shouted.

Joseph turned wondering if Anne would instantly know that he had overheard their conversation.

"Just picking some weeds," he explained unconvincingly.

"Sure, old man. Sure." Anne smiled at him, the love in her eyes as strong as ever.

"They're really tired out. They were asleep before I was able to finish the story." Joseph sat down at the old table in the living room, between Anne and Sarah.

"You don't look so fresh yourself, Dad," Sarah teased.

"Good Lord! You're more like your mother every day."

"She's a lot smarter than I ever was, Joseph."

"Mmmm…I'm not so sure." Joseph rubbed his two-week beard growth as he studied Anne's face.

"So, what's with the beard, Dad?"

"Ask your mother."

"Mom?"

"I've always liked him with a beard. He's doing this for me. But I think he likes it, even though he won't admit it," Anne leaned over toward her daughter and winked.

"That's not entirely true, Sarah. You know how your mother keeps me wrapped around her little finger." Joseph smiled at his wife and daughter. How he loved the time with them both—how he wished he had cherished it always, like he did now.

"How long are you staying this time, honey?" Anne asked her daughter.

"Well, Michael will be back in two days. I plan on leaving tomorrow afternoon."

"I wish you could stay longer," Anne whispered.

"I know. I like visiting up here, too. It's so different from Bakersfield. Cooler. Quieter."

"I'll say," Joseph blurted. "I've had my fill of Bakersfield."

"You always look forward to a trip into town," Anne protested.

"And after this past month, I will always look forward to the trip *out* of town."

"Speaking of tired," Sarah let out a yawn, "I'd better get to bed...good night, Mom...Dad..." Sarah stood up and turned toward the small bedroom on the first floor.

"So early?" Joseph asked.

"It's past ten and I've been up since before six this morning." Sarah came over and hugged him, and then her mother.

"That's the way you used to do it years ago. Two bear squeezes." Joseph grinned with the memory.

Anne watched her daughter walk from the room. "It seems like yesterday, Joseph. Where did the time go?"

"I don't know. We lost the time when we started running around, doing errands, fixing bikes, paying bills…"

"It went too fast…" Anne had a funny tone in her voice.

"'It?'" Joseph asked.

"'It,'" Anne responded. There was quiet.

"It's bad, isn't it…" Joseph whispered. He reached out to touch her hand. It was clammy, and she held his hand in a shaky iron grip. Anne nodded.

"Should I call the doctor?" His voice was lower than a whisper.

Anne shook her head, to Joseph's surprise.

"But…why?"

"I'll be all right. Let's wait until after the kids leave. I'll just take it easy."

"Anne…" Joseph pleaded.

"I want it this way, Joey. I'll be all right, I said. I mean it." Her voice was stern and stubborn.

"But I'm scared…" he confessed.

"Faith. Have faith. You know how much seeing those little ones means to me. I don't want to scare them. This day has brought me a great deal of happiness. And you know what the doctor will say."

Joseph nodded and rested his head against Anne's shoulder. He could feel life fading in the air. Anne stroked his sparse gray hair.

Joseph chuckled, out of context.

"What? Are you all right?" Anne wondered.

"Yellow!"

"Yellow?" Anne had a confused frown on her face.

"Yellow paint! Under my fingernails. I'm scared. Yellow paint. Scared. Yellow. Get it?"

Anne joined him and they laughed together, like they had so many times, on the couch that they had owned for over a quarter of a century.

As they lay quietly in their bed, Joseph called out to Anne.

"Annie?"

"Hmmmpphh...?"

"Are you awake?"

"I am now. What is it?" Anne whispered in a slurred voice.

"I forgot one side."

"You forgot one side of what?" Her voice was muffled by the pillow.

"The shed." Joseph was frustrated.

"Oh...good night...you woke me up for that...?" Anne mumbled before quickly fading back into her dreams.

Chapter 11

It seemed that this drive took longer than usual to get into Bakersfield. The many exits from the freeway had the same names…Copus Road…Union Avenue…White Lane…but the distances between them seemed so much greater today. Joseph scratched his beard as he pondered why a journey took so much longer when one knew there was pain at the other end.

A passing eucalyptus tree, alone in a familiar field, reminded him of another drive…another daydream… another day long ago…

"Joseph? What about my drink?" Anne pleaded.

"Uhh…Drink?" Joseph stirred from his daydreaming and pondering.

"Oh, come on. We just passed the truck stop and I already told you that I was thirsty!" Anne wasn't as patient as she usually was.

"I'll get off at the next off-ramp."

"Please!" Anne looked out the window.

"Are you all right?" Joseph shot a quick glance toward his wife.

Silence.

"Anne? Annie?"

"What?" Anne snapped.

"What's wrong? Do you want me to pull over?" Joseph asked as he turned to look back to the lane to the right, preparing to move across to the side of the freeway.

"No, I just want something to drink."

Joseph gently corrected and returned to the center of the middle lane.

"Honey, it's all right. We're just going in to make sure..."

"Make sure of what?" Anne snapped, interrupting him.

"Make sure that we're doing all the right things for you."

"Make sure I'm not about to die—isn't that what you mean?"

Joseph shook his head in frustration. "Anne...I know that this is hard to deal with...I'm doing pretty poorly about all of this..."

"You wanted to do this. Not me."

"Damn it! You can't run and hide forever in Pine Mountain and think that this will go away. Anne...I'm trying to do the best thing for you," Joseph said, controlling his anger as best as he could. He twisted around to find an open spot in the traffic flowing in the right-hand lane.

"Exit! There's an exit! We can get a drink at Burger King," Anne said tersely.

"I know, Annie. I'm moving over." Joseph flipped his turn signal to the right.

Joseph pulled the car into a disabled parking spot next to the main entrance of the restaurant. He turned off the engine and sat.

Silence filled the car but neither of them moved. Joseph looked down and ran his finger around the car company logo in the center of the steering wheel. He was searching for the right words to say. He felt angry…resentful. Ever since the heart attack he hadn't been able to read her anymore. There was always this unspoken tension—this unspoken knowledge—the unspoken fate.

"Would you rather just go through the drive-through?"

"No. I want to get out of the car for a while. It's been almost an hour."

Joseph opened his car door and was greeted by the force of incoming heat. "Oh…hot! Isn't air conditioning a wonderful thing?"

Anne didn't respond. She continued staring through the window, looking away from him.

Joseph shut his door slowly and moved around to the other side of the car. Anne had her eyes closed and instantly he felt his mind race with panic and fear. Quickly, he realized the source of the fear. He closed his eyes. How would he find her…when would he find her…when… And how did he live, how did they live, when they didn't know what life offered them one day to the next? And what happened to the damn old "happily-ever-afters?" How he longed to rewrite their story, to give them perfect health and so many more years.

Forcefully, he turned from the thoughts that haunted his every day and invaded his every dream. He shook his head. He opened his eyes and found Anne looking straight at him, through the window that separated them. She had opened the door a crack.

"I'm sorry, Joey..." Anne whispered as she reached for his arm, which was extended as an offer of help.

"C'mon, Anne. We're both tired of this stress...but we can't make it disappear. We have to get through this together," Joseph responded as he closed the door behind her.

The sound of Anne's laughter broke the tense moment. Joseph turned to see what held her attention. The handicapped parking space was adjacent to a window in the men's restroom. An unsmoked pane of glass had, obviously, just been placed in a broken section of the window. Anne had a wonderful view of the men's urinal area.

Just then an obese man in coveralls stepped up to the urinal nearest the window and began to strip off his outer garment. Joseph felt a grin grow on his face.

"Good God... we'd better get out of here, Anne!"

"Why? This is entertainment that deserves to be on live cable TV!"

"Maybe, but my heart can't stand the shock that I think I'm about to get."

"You're right! There are some things a human being cannot endure!" Anne laughed and reached for her husband's arm. They walked off together.

"I'm on a diet right now. Nothing but crackers and water for me..." Joseph offered.

"He makes you look like the height of fitness!"

"Let's go back, then...you might get hot for me..." Joseph chuckled.

"I always have been!" Anne smiled up at her husband.

"A hearty laugh...that's what we need!"

"Definitely. And that was definitely a hearty laugh!"

"Anne Marino to see Doctor Waller," Joseph told the medical receptionist, while leaning into the open window.

"Does she have an appointment?" the pretty blonde asked.

"At eleven. We're a few minutes early." Joseph felt the ugly ice of fear rising inside. It was the same fear and anxiety he felt whenever he was in a clinic or hospital. It was the fear and anxiety that started around age sixty. Mindlessly, he started tapping on the counter. Anne gently touched his hand and he stopped.

"Here are some papers for you to fill out. Have her answer the questions on both sides." The blonde handed a clipboard to Joseph.

Anne went over the questions and, dutifully, answered every one thoughtfully.

"Mrs. Marino?" a nurse announced at the door leading into the back area of the medical office. Joseph and Anne stood up and followed the crisp, neat nurse into the "inner sanctum" of Doctor Waller's office.

"Right here in Room 3," the nurse pointed the way. Anne nodded politely. She had been unusually quiet.

"I'll ask you some questions. After I leave slip into that hospital gown, okay?"

The couple was left alone after the nurse took Anne's blood pressure, temperature, and asked a few questions. Anne slowly disrobed, hanging her clothes neatly on a hook on the back of the door.

Silence filled the room. Joseph and Anne found themselves staring at the travel poster on the wall next to a door on the opposite side of the long, easily divided examination room. Anne was sitting on the examination table.

"Look...that other door takes you to Sweden!" Joseph joked.

"And you've always wanted to go there," Anne smiled nervously as she flattened the cloth gown in her lap.

"Well, at least I have a Swedish flag," Joseph smiled.

"This reminds me of another medical situation, a long time ago. Do you have an idea about what I'm talking about?"

"Ummm...a travel poster? I don't have a 'travel poster memory' from a doctor's office."

"It wasn't a travel poster..."

"Was it in a doctor's office?"

"Well, sort of. Let me give you a hint."

"OK...shoot." Joseph leaned back on the counter.

"When we went in, there were two of us. When we left, there were three of us." Anne swept her arm around from one side to another, toward the door.

"That's a tough one, had something to do with the birth of one of the kids, huh?" Joseph scratched his beard.

"So far, so good."

"Hmmm. How about another clue?" Joseph shrugged.

"Okay...here it is: 'in a bathroom...'" Anne trailed off, tilting her head toward the door.

"Let me get this straight. In a bathroom in a doc... oh, wait a minute...in the hospital...in a bathroom... I've got it!"

"Out with it, then!"

"You wore a hospital gown!"

"No...that's not quite it..." Anne shook her head and smiled. She was obviously enjoying this game of charades.

"Bathroom in the hospital. Kid being born. Another clue, please." Joseph winked.

"Lights..." Anne smiled.

"The red light switch...I remember! Between labor contractions I used it to get your mind off of the pains...'look at the strange red light switch...'"

"Bingo. How long have you known what I was thinking of?" Anne smirked.

"Oh, long enough. Actually, I remember that scene every time we are in a situation like this. One can never forget when one's first-born child enters the world." Silence filled the room. Anne looked down at the floor.

"We'll call him tomorrow, Anne. I promise. It's been too much anger for too long." Joseph looked down at the floor. Anne reached out and squeezed his arm. Joseph raised his eyes and found a warm, friendly look coming back at him.

"Well...look at the two lovebirds. Do we need a chaperone?" Doctor Waller said as she entered the room.

"You'd better get one, Susan..." Anne jokingly implored.

"That must mean you're feeling good?" Susan asked. Something in her voice told Joseph that Anne's answer was irrelevant to the matters at hand. They all knew what this was. This was the small talk. This was the "let's all try and act like there are other things on our mind besides how long Anne will live" chitchat.

"Go ahead, doctor," Joseph urged. Neither he, nor Anne, had ever been one for small talk on the face of a problem. Anne and Joseph reached out for each other's hands at the same time, as if they had done it for decades. Doctor Waller shuffled through the pages, apparently looking for something.

"We're going to have to change the medication. Go to a stronger dosage," Waller said in a soft voice. She reached out to hold Anne's hand.

"How bad is it, Susan? Please. Just tell us straight."

"As soon as you settle down a bit. No need to get all worked up, Anne..." Waller responded in a quiet voice.

"You're right."

"Do you want something to calm you down?"

Anne nodded and Doctor Waller reached into the cabinet next to the examination table. She pulled out a few sample medication packets.

"Here...take one of these. How are you doing, Joseph? You two look really worn out."

"Maybe I'd better...no...I'm driving." Joseph put his hand up and shook his head.

"Can you stay in town tonight? I'd feel better if you two weren't traveling all the way into the mountains after this." Waller raised her eyebrows and looked from Joseph to Anne.

"We've prepared for the possibility..."

"Good! Now..." Waller paused, her mouth open.

"Go ahead, Susan...you can tell us." Anne reached out and patted Waller's hand.

"You need to slow down," Waller met Anne's gaze and held it. "It's getting worse."

"I thought so," Anne looked down.

"But, Anne…you always say…"

"I know, Joseph. I know," Anne whispered.

"You've got to be honest with him, Anne. He can help."

"But I'm worried about him," Anne defended. "He's hurting, too." A tear escaped the corner of Anne's eye.

"He's a big boy now. He can take care of himself," Doctor Waller pronounced.

Waller's words stuck in Joseph's mind.

"…he can take care of himself"

"…take care of himself…"

"…himself…"

Panic gripped his mind. He concealed it and again held Anne's hand tighter.

Doctor Waller wrote out two new prescriptions and chatted for a few moments before leaving. The room was quiet, so quiet that every sound in the hall seemed amplified a hundred fold.

"Joey?" Anne broke the silence. Joseph was staring at the Sweden poster. "Are you okay?" Anne got up and stood next to him. She lowered her head onto his shoulder.

"Yeah."

"What are you thinking?"

"Wondering about Sweden…"

"What about it?"

"Nothing really," Joseph cleared his throat. "Better

get dressed, Anne. You know how unflattering those hospital gowns can be..."

Chapter 12

"Crap!" Joseph mumbled to himself as he rubbed at the bruise on his thigh. He had ruined another pair of pants on the latch of the rear door of the car. He thought he had studied the design of this vehicle before they had bought it. He always tried to see every angle of what would be useful, or what would cause problems, in a car or truck. But something always seemed to sneak past his inspection.

In their last car, there was a little bump in the leg area of the driver's front seat. He had hated driving long distances in that car. His left knee always ached whenever he got out of the car. This car contained the latch that had "bitten" three pairs of his pants. It was time for a new car. Joseph didn't care that the car was only three years old. It was time for a new one. If he didn't trade it in, his pants expenditures would keep climbing.

"Joseph are you…Oh no, not again." Anne called from the porch of Sarah's house. She had obviously seen Joseph rubbing his leg.

"Yeah...again. Time for a new car, Anne. I can't afford to buy a pair of pants every time this happens."

"Or we could be more careful when we load our suitcases in the back."

Joseph knew that she was right. Even an extra twenty dollars a month spent on new pants would still be cheaper than buying a new car. But, hey, he had his eye on a new minivan.

"You're right," Joseph said with resignation. Anne liked buying a new car every now and then, but she was far more conservative about how often that "now and then" would be.

"Come on, kids...Grandma and Grandpa are leaving! Get out here if you want to say good-bye!" Sarah shouted back into her house.

Joseph watched his daughter as she brushed off her hands on her sleeve. *The same way Anne always does*, he thought. He was startled, as if he hadn't noticed before, how much Sarah looked like Anne. Thirty-five years ago Anne did the same things. Spending two days at his daughter's house had revealed their similarities like looking into a mirror.

"All loaded up, Joe?" Michael, Sarah's husband, asked.

"Yeah. Got a problem with that stupid rear latch, though. Messed up quite a few pairs of pants...I oughta write to General Motors about it." Joseph always tried to use "guy talk" with Michael. He always envied his son-in-law. He was good in sports, mechanical things, and so many more things that he had never quite mastered. *Sarah had done well*, he thought.

"You want me to look at it for you?" Michael asked. He started off of the porch.

"No…no…it's all closed up now. Maybe next time."

"Isn't it still under warranty? Why don't you bring it back and have them fix it?" Michael asked.

"Because Joseph hates driving down to the dealer, waiting all day, and then wondering if they scratched it up or not." Anne joined the conversation.

"It is a hassle. I think that they make it that way just to keep their expenses down," Joseph responded.

"What? Now, how does that work?" Anne asked, frowning.

"No one brings in their vehicles, so the dealers don't have to pay for the repairs," Joseph replied, exasperated. He motioned with his arms toward the passenger's door. He wanted to get going.

"Oh, that makes sense…" Anne said, nodding.

"Right…" Joseph smiled.

"So then, no one would return to buy their cars again, and then they'd be out of business," Anne countered.

"There's that irrefutable logic, Michael! Watch it! Your wife inherited it!" Joseph laughed. He loved it when they bantered like this.

"I know," he smiled. "She keeps trying to convince me that we would save money if we bought a new car every other year."

Joseph was startled. Maybe Sarah had inherited a few traits of his, too.

"Come and give Grandma a hug, kids! I'm going to miss my little munchkins!" Anne slowly bent over with her arms outstretched. Laura and Joseph ran over to her.

Joseph watched Anne's face carefully. Despite the broad smile, he knew what she was thinking. After all these years, their minds could have been one and the same. He knew that she knew. This could be the last time. Joseph turned his head, unable to watch. A lump formed in his throat.

"Don't forget Grandpa, kids!" Anne urged.

The kids ran over and repeated the little drama with Joseph. It took all his effort not to break down openly.

"What's wrong, Grandpa?" Laura asked.

"Nothing," he lied. "I'm just going to miss you, that's all."

"Well," the two children said in unison, their hands outstretched. Joseph's little surprise ritual had become more ritual than surprise. From the early years of his fatherhood, he had brought his children small gifts whenever he traveled on business. He carried the tradition forward to the next generation… as a parting gift. But, with everything on his mind, he had forgotten.

"Ummm…let me see," Joseph was thankful that he usually played up a fumbling search for the gifts. This afternoon he needed the time to think of something.

"Grandpa left one of them in my purse, Laura!" Anne interrupted.

"Oh yes, that's right," Joseph picked up her cue. "And there is something for Little Joey right here..." Joseph's fingers numbly identified the objects in his pocket. A Swiss Army knife? No, he's too young. Then, reflecting the late afternoon Bakersfield sun, a shiny Eisenhower silver dollar glistened. It was his "lucky dollar." Joseph had kept it as a souvenir of a hospital visit of his own. Doctor Waller had pronounced him as "fit as a dollar" and had awarded him with the token. That was more years ago than Joseph wanted to remember.

Joseph knelt down to Little Joey's eye level. "You're a very special boy, Joseph. I want you to keep my shiny silver dollar for me. Can you take care of it for me?"

Little Joey looked at the shiny coin with big blue eyes and nodded. Seeking confirmation, Joey glanced toward his mom, who nodded her agreement.

Joseph rose, acutely aware that the small weight in his left pocket was gone. Little Joey ran to show it to his father and mother.

"Joey! Go give Grandpa a hug and a thank you!" Sarah urged. She motioned with her arms.

"Thanks, Grandpa! I love you the bestest!" Joey smiled as he hugged his namesake.

"You're the bestest, Joey!" He quickly turned to his wife. "We better get going."

"Dad's right, Sarah." Anne's eyes met and held

Sarah's, and they stared at each other for a moment, neither of them ready or willing to initiate the good-bye. Finally, Anne leaned over and hugged her daughter. With a whisper that Joseph barely heard she said good-bye.

"Shall we stop for a drink, Anne?" It had been many miles since he had spoken. They were both lost in thought after the emotional goodbye. Anne had not attempted to make conversation. Instead, she simply stared out the window.

"Maybe a little later. I'm not very thirsty or hungry."

"Well...we can stop in Lake of the Woods...at the mini-mart...that's about a half hour away."

"Maybe. We'll see."

Joseph slowed as the traffic in front of him started showing bright red tail lights.

"Oh, nuts! Not an accident," the old man groaned.

"Maybe we should get off the freeway and wait it out. I hate sitting in a car while they clean up traffic," Anne offered.

"Good idea. I'll take the next exit."

"The one with the great window in the men's room?" Anne smiled.

"Yeah...but I don't know what's so great about it."

As they pulled into the handicapped parking space, Anne feigned a sigh of disappointment at the recently repaired window.

"Darn!" Anne chuckled.

"About time!" Joseph countered.

The traffic was tied up for over an hour. Joseph and Anne spent most of the time sitting in the truck stop coffee shop, sipping on sodas. The sun was low on the horizon when Joseph noticed that the cars were beginning to pick up speed.

"Looks like we can hit the road again," he said, reaching for the check.

"I'll just use the restroom quick and then I'll be ready." Anne rose and walked toward the restroom.

Joseph felt the all too common fears well inside him as Anne disappeared into the ladies' room. What if she collapsed in the bathroom here? How would he be able to help her? How would he know? He sat down on the bench outside the ladies' room and waited. It seemed like hours. Two women walked out, obviously upset.

"I can't believe it! On the floor!" an older woman, wearing a large purple muumuu, said.

"You'd think she'd have the dignity to do that somewhere other than on the bathroom floor," her friend responded, equally appalled.

Joseph felt the panic rise sharply. He stood up and began pacing in front of the entry to the ladies' room. He debated. Should he go in? Was that Anne they were talking about? Was something wrong?

Just then a young woman with a baby walked slowly out of the ladies' room. Anne was right behind her, much to Joseph's relief.

"Never let those cackling old geese bother you, honey. You did nothing wrong," Anne reassured the woman. She turned to Joseph. "You look a little flushed, Joseph? Are you okay?"

"I'm fine. What was that all about?"

"Joey, this is Shelly," Anne began the introduction.

"I was just helping that poor young woman with her bustling baby. She was trying to get the diaper changed and the baby was squirming all over just like Paul used to do." Anne's face took on a reminiscent gaze.

"Paul," Joseph repeated his name as a reminder. "I need to call him..."

"Soon, Joey," her eyes were pleading. "Please."

After taking one of the pills that Doctor Waller prescribed, Anne fell asleep quickly in her seat. Joseph was thankful since she had looked so pale lately. Although she wouldn't admit it aloud, he knew she wasn't sleeping well.

As he drove up the steep incline they called the Grapevine, into the mountains near Pine Mountain, a growing pressure began to distract him. "I should have gone to the bathroom," Joseph whispered to himself.

"Where were you when I was in the ladies' room?" Anne asked in a sleepy voice.

"Are you awake?"

"Uh-huh. The swaying of the car woke me up."

"Do you want me to slow down...?" Joseph asked.

"That's okay, I'm fine...but you're obviously not," Anne giggled.

"Hey...a man's got a bigger bladder. I'll make it home."

"Sure. We'll see. You're not the same as you were years ago, old man!"

"In that department I am!" Joseph asserted.

"We'll see. We'll see."

Joseph wondered how long they had bantered back and forth like this. It must have started when they met when he was a college freshman.

"No—I was in sixth grade, so you were a senior in high school," Anne offered.

"Can you read my mind now?"

"You've forgotten. You mumble now and then."

"So, when was the first time we teased like this? Do you remember?"

"It was on the creek during that field trip in Mr. Edwards' sixth grade class." Anne's response was immediate.

"Was it? I remember! You thought I was silly, making a little boat out of twigs."

"No...I thought you were silly making a twig boat

while you were trying to eat a sandwich, and while holding your pocket shut, trying to protect your two cookies!" Anne laughed. So many of her memories were clear snapshots—yet others faded.

"Hey, they were chocolate chip cookies. I wasn't about to lose them!"

"But you did!" Anne giggled again.

"Yeah, right into the creek."

"Remember how we used to call it 'Chocolate Chip Creek' from then on?"

"I also remember how you used to make a 'creek' out of chocolate chip cookies on the kitchen table." The joyous sound of their mutual laughter filled the car.

"But…you still have to go…" Anne poked as she laughed.

"I know…I know." Joseph craned his neck to see around the curve. At that moment the lights of the Frazier Park exit appeared around the bend. "Ahhh… relief ahead…"

"I thought you said you could make it home…" Anne chuckled.

"Did I say that?" Joseph shrugged and put on his left blinker.

Chapter 13

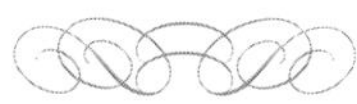

Joseph quietly crept out to the telephone table in the kitchen. It was still too early for Anne to be awake. Usually she slept in until nine o'clock. He looked at the bird clock in the kitchen. *Good*, he thought, *almost a half an hour left*. He picked up the phone and dialed.

"Good morning! This is Computer Teksys..."

"Hello. I'm looking for an employee of your company..."

"...welcome to our automated messaging system..."

"Damn! Doesn't anyone answer the phone anymore?"

"...press 1 now if you have a touch-tone phone..." Joseph pushed the button.

"...thank you..."

"Imagine that. A polite machine!" Joseph said to no one in particular.

"You may dial the extension of your party at any time if you know the number..."

"I *don't* know the number...that's why I'm calling," Joseph argued pointlessly with the recording.

"...or press 1 for customer service..."

"I'm not a customer..."

"...2 for corporate offices..."

"Two! That's it! He works for your corporation, and he has an office!" Joseph pushed the 2 button on his phone.

"...thank you...one moment..."

"Welcome to our central corporate offices..." another machine picked up where the last one had left off.

"Oh, come on, just give me a human being to talk to!" Joseph was frustrated. He glanced at the door, hoping Anne would remain asleep. "That's the problem with this country...machines are taking over!" Joseph pushed the 0 for operator button.

Gentle background music filled his ear.

"Now a concert?" He shook his head. Many minutes passed.

"Good morning, this is the Computer Teksys operator...how may I direct your call?" A polite male voice said.

"I'm trying to find my son. Can you help me?"

"Sir, what company are you looking for? This is a computer services company, not a detective agency..."

"Damn it, I know that! My son works for you guys. Why, I don't know...but he does..."

"Sir, have you tried our automated online employee directory?"

"No...listen...I just want you to connect me to his desk phone. Can you do that? It's somewhere in Orange County, California...I..."

"Hold on...I'll transfer you out to the California operator." The once-polite voice turned curt as he interrupted Joseph.

"But..." Joseph stammered. More music filled his ear...for minutes.

"Computer Teksys San Diego. How may I help you?" This time a female voice came on the line.

"I'm looking for someone. Can you please help me?" Joseph could feel the desperateness in his voice. If only he had known where Anne had kept her address book, this would have been a lot easier. Over the past few years, Anne had started changing her storage locations. He used to always be able to count on her to put everything back in its place, but these days "its place" changed almost weekly.

"What is the last name?"

"Marino. Paul Marino." Joseph spoke clearly into the mouthpiece of the telephone. He could hear the woman punching keys on a computer.

"He's not at this site, sir."

"He's not? Do you know how I could find him?"

"I'm sorry, sir. I cannot give out any information on company employees."

"That is ridiculous." Joseph's voice grew weary as he rubbed the top of his head.

"Have you tried our corporate headquarters in

Maynard, Massachusetts? Maybe they could assist you better."

"Yes, they transferred me to you. Listen, I'm Paul's father—I need to get in touch with my son—it's very important."

"Excuse my ignorance sir, but if you are his father, then shouldn't you already have his phone number?"

"Damn it, I don't! I'm traveling and don't have it with me," he lied. Joseph took a deep breath to regain his composure. "I'm sorry for being so upset, but please listen…his mother is very ill. I'm not as sharp as I used to be and don't have it memorized. Is there anything you can do to help me?" Joseph could hear her shuffling some papers.

"I can relay a message to him, but that's the best I can do."

"Okay," Joseph responded, realizing it was his only choice. He wondered if Paul would return the message. Joseph relayed his name and number. "Can you call him soon? It's very urgent." Joseph looked toward the bedroom to see if Anne was awake yet. There was no movement. "His mother is…" Joseph swallowed heavily, "…dying."

"I'll call him right away," the woman said, her voice softening.

"Thank you. What is your name? You are the only person who has been able to help me."

"Meredith…"

"Thanks, Meredith. I appreciate this." Joseph hung up slowly after saying good-bye.

"Meredith, huh?" Arranging dates at nine-ten in the morning?" Anne smiled. Joseph was startled by Anne's entrance.

"You're awake!"

"Looks like you weren't expecting me to be."

"Oh...that," he said while gesturing toward the phone. "It's a surprise."

Joseph had just finished cleaning the dishes from breakfast when the phone rang. He headed for it, but it stopped after the second ring.

"Who in the world would be calling and hanging up before we got to the phone?" Anne asked, shaking her head.

"Probably those local kids who've been..." Joseph was staring out the window. His mouth fell open and he dropped the dish he was cleaning into the sink.

Bang!

"Joseph! What on earth?"

"The wall! Damn them all! Look at what those hoodlums did to our stone wall!" Anne rose quickly and walked over to the window. They looked out together. The center of the stone wall was completely missing.

"That's it...I'm calling the sheriff," Joseph growled.

"Slow down, honey. Remember your blood pressure!" Anne grabbed her husband's arm.

"I'll show them some blood pressure!" Joseph's face grew redder.

The phone had started to ring again. Joseph froze. Anne walked toward it to answer, and Joseph wanted to jump in front of her, but he couldn't will himself to move. Anne picked up the receiver and cupped her hand over the mouthpiece.

"I'll bet we'll find out who it is that's been crank calling us!" Anne brought the receiver to her ear. "Hello? This is Anne."

"Hello?" Anne repeated shrugging toward Joseph.

Joseph just stood by the sink. When a large smile spread across Anne's face, he instantly knew who it was.

"Pauley! Paul! Oh, how good it is to hear your voice! You don't know how much I've been praying that you'd call!" Anne settled onto the chair nearest the phone. Her gaze shifted slowly from the wall to Joseph.

"He did, did he?" Anne motioned for Joseph to come closer. He shook his head. Anne frowned.

"That explains it!" she answered into the mouthpiece.

Joseph wiped his hands with the dishcloth he was holding.

"Did your father know that?" Anne asked, still smiling. Joseph slowly opened the door and walked onto the porch. As he quietly and gently closed the screen door he stood motionless for a long time, watching his wife smile and gesture into the air.

The wheelbarrow grew exceptionally heavy as Joseph piled more and more stones into it. The rear runners of the barrow were pressing heavily into the grass. Sometimes old fashioned physical labor is what a man needed at times like these.

"Joey?" Anne called from a few feet away. Joseph turned to find Anne's tear-streaked face staring back at him.

"Are you all right?" He put the wheelbarrow down as he turned fully toward her. Anne nodded, reaching for him. Joseph brushed the dirt from his hands. "I'm kinda dirty," he mumbled.

"No, you're as clean as snow…" Anne threw her arms around him.

"What's this for?" Joseph asked, though he already knew the answer.

"You made me very happy this morning. I know how hard it was for you to make that call. It's an answer to my prayer."

If only we could have a few more prayers answered, Joseph thought.

"I have so much to do!" Anne broke free from Joseph and began to bustle back toward the house.

"Take it easy…remember what Doctor Waller said. What's so urgent anyway?" Joseph had a feeling it had something to do with the phone call.

"Nothing…you'll find out…tomorrow!" Anne walked quickly back to the house.

"Anne," Joseph called while entering the house. He heard the shower from the bedroom.

"Annie?" He entered the bathroom admiring Anne's feminine form outlined against the beach scene of the shower curtain.

"Joseph! I'm in the shower!"

"Is it about Paul?" Joseph pulled back the curtain a bit and peeked into the shower.

"Well, part of it." Anne had a content and satisfied look on her face.

"Part of it?" Joseph pursed his lips.

"You have no idea, do you?"

"Anne, c'mon…you know there's a lot of bad blood between Paul and me."

"Yes, from a long time ago." Anne massaged her scalp as she talked.

"Maybe I should call him." Joseph let go of the curtain.

"You can't," Anne stated matter-of-factly.

"Didn't you get his number?"

"Of course, but you still can't call him."

"Why Anne?" Joseph felt a mix of frustration and fear blur his thinking. Anne turned the shower off and looked out through the end of the curtain.

"Please. Please. Just this once…don't spoil this."

"All right, have it your way."

"You'll know tomorrow—I promise." Anne made a cross symbol over her heart with her fingers.

"I'll hold you to that." Joseph left Anne to finish toweling off and walked into the kitchen. On the pad of paper near the phone was a cryptic message.

P+M fl380 10 2k!!!

Just below the odd writing was a phone number. Joseph was half tempted to call the number, but instead he walked outside and began to work, once again, on Anne's wall.

Chapter 14

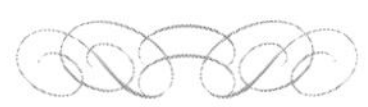

"SO, I'M ABLE TO SHARE ONE MORE SUNRISE WITH you, Old One!" Joseph whispered to the craggily peak of Pine Mountain. The sun had not yet risen over the serrated ridges around the eastern end of the valley. Pine Mountain had a dim, gray look about it. Joseph leaned on his hoe and tried to make out the features of the dominating mountain.

"Why can't I see your ridges...your trees?" Joseph pondered. He loved to go out to the side yard and watch the night melt into day. It was his favorite time of day, and his favorite time of year on Pine Mountain. But he had never noticed how difficult it was to make out details on the mountain. Maybe, he thought, he'd never worried about it. Maybe it was earlier than usual. Maybe his eyes were going. He shivered, but not from the cold. How he feared blindness. More than anything else, he needed to see. A slight breeze rustled a few leaves around Joseph's feet.

"I'm a lot like you are, leaves," Joseph addressed

the small greenish yellow objects gathering at his feet, "...my useful life is over. I just wander with the wind...wondering when it will end." Joseph wondered what someone would think if they overheard the many conversations he had had with the mountain.

"He's coming back today, Old Man!" Joseph barely whispered to the broad shoulders of the looming rock. The wind gusted and scattered the leaves. "You got that right," he answered to the wind. "A tempest is brewing!"

Joseph straightened. There was a distant sound of echoing wind on the side of the old mountain. It was a faint sound, but it danced in Joseph's ears.

"I know how you feel. It stirs a man deep down inside. But you don't know what to say," Joseph shook his head.

A glint of light caressed the peak of the mountain. "Right again. Show your true feelings." Joseph stared at the mountain's peak for a long moment. "This time I will," he said quietly. "There may not be many more chances." The sun began to warm Joseph's face.

"Time to get to work. Got to make the place look worthy of guests!" He tipped his hat toward the mountain and then walked over to the wall. Joseph picked up the hoe and began turning over the dirt around the flowers that lined the driveway. Before long all of the weeds had been pulled, and Joseph leaned back to admire his handiwork.

"Joseph! Come on in! Breakfast!" Anne was calling from the kitchen door.

"What? What are you doing up at this hour? You know what Doctor Waller said."

"I couldn't sleep. There's so much to do!" Anne leaned heavily on the screen door. Joseph gently leaned his hoe against the outside garage wall and walked to meet her. Although her voice sounded full of energy, she looked more tired than ever.

"You don't look too well."

"Just tired," Anne said, shrugging off Joseph's worry. "I was so excited I couldn't sleep well." He watched Anne carefully. "Maybe…I'm a little dizzy…" Joseph got to the door just in time to see Anne lean all her weight on the kitchen counter. He struggled with the door.

"Stupid door," he whispered.

"You still need to fix it…" Anne smiled. The door flung open with a mighty pull from Joseph's right arm.

"What can I do?" His entire body shook visibly as he recognized the panic in his voice.

"My medicine…in my purse…on the phone table…" Anne was having a tough time speaking.

Joseph ran to the phone table and roughly emptied the contents of Anne's purse. Grabbing the pill bottle, he quickly made his way back to Anne.

"Here they are, Anne…Annie?" Her eyes were closed. Joseph reached down and touched her arm. No response. He dropped the pills.

"Annie? Please...just nod...or say anything..." Joseph put his hand under Anne's nose and felt a faint movement of air against his palm. He picked up the pills and clumsily managed to get the lid off. He pulled out a pill and then stopped. How did Doctor Waller tell him to do this? He cursed his memory. Gently, he cupped his hand around Anne's mouth, opening it slowly. "Oh, Annie...I'm sorry...my hands are a mess...but..." he slid the pill between her teeth, and under her tongue. He stood up and reached over to the sink, grabbing a wet washcloth. He began to wash her face, hoping that the cool water would help. After a few minutes she began to stir.

"Uhhhh..."

"Shhh...it's okay, Annie...I'm here..." He wondered how much comfort that statement could possibly bring.

"I'm so tired," Anne said simply. Joseph looked down at his wife. Would it end like this? After fifty years—how could everything just stop? How could *they* stop? Joseph burrowed his hands gently beneath Anne and lifted her into the air.

"What are you doing?" She had little strength to resist.

"Getting you off of the damned floor!" Joseph stood as best he could, and staggered with his limp wife toward the living room.

"Joey...you'll hurt yourself." In the midst of all her pain, Joseph realized she would never quit worrying about him.

"I'm fine," he lied, his face reddening. He caught a glimpse of the nearby couch and lurched toward it. His knee became more and more wobbly. Darn…that old football injury! Carefully, he kneeled down and placed Anne on the couch.

"That's better," she said slowly.

"I'll be right back love. I'm going to call Dr. Waller."

"Her number is…" Anne started.

"…by the phone. I know. I put it there…" Joseph finished her sentence. Suddenly a sharp pain hit him in the back and he crumpled to the floor.

"Joseph…" Anne cried out in a voice just above a whisper.

"It's…all…right…" Joseph was breathing hard. Just then the front door opened. It shut with a slam.

"Who is it?" Joseph rolled over to see who had entered.

"You need help. Let me help you," the young girl offered. Joseph didn't know the girl, but he knew the face. It was the face that had peeked out from behind the tree.

"Please…my wife…" Joseph started.

"She's sitting up over on the couch," the girl said. Joseph looked over and was pleased to see that Anne was indeed sitting. A bit of color had come back to her face. The girl reached behind Joseph's back and helped him to a chair. He let out an audible sigh of relief.

"Thank you! You are a Godsend!"

"No…I came over to talk…I was just worried when I heard that sound of your falling."

"You are wonderful!" Anne offered.

"No! Please…this is hard enough…" The girl bit her lip and stopped talking.

"Hard? What is, honey?" Anne asked quietly, though her mother's intuition had already guessed the essence of this girl's message.

"Wait…wait. Are you two going to, you know, die or something?" The girl was obviously frightened.

"Oh, dear, not yet!" Anne smiled.

"But…"

"When you get a lot older, you can't do the simple things that you did when you were a kid. Like carry someone into the next room." Anne looked disapprovingly at Joseph, but a smile soon spread across her face.

"You're better now?" the girl asked, then sighed.

"Well, somewhat," Joseph replied.

"What's your name?" Anne asked, eager to change the subject.

"Shannon. I live on the next street over. Yellowstone." The girl twirled a lock of hair around her pointer finger.

"You were the one we saw."

"Saw?"

"In the forest," Anne continued, "with the brightly colored vest!"

"When?"

"When my husband blew up and hit the tree with the shovel. You were there, hiding behind a tree."

"Yes," Shannon's nervous voice confirmed. "I felt bad because of what they did."

"They?"

"My boyfriend and that…that…jerk." Shannon vented a little anger.

"What did they do?" Joseph rubbed his back, becoming very interested in the conversation.

"Your stone wall…the paint…" Shannon guiltily stared at her Nike shoes.

"It's okay Shannon. You can tell us," Anne gently assured the young girl. "You're a very special girl for coming and telling us."

"You're not like what Isaiah said you are like…"

"What does he say we're like?"

"He said that you're just like all of the other grownups around here. You hate us."

"Hate you?" Anne was surprised.

"Yeah…hate."

"We don't even know you, honey."

"Nobody wants teens around here. 'Stay out of the pool,' or 'Stay out of the clubhouse.' 'Stay out of the parking lot.' Stay out. That's what you old people want us to do."

"Shannon," Anne spoke for both herself and Joseph, "we certainly don't feel that way toward you. You are the future."

"If that's true, it doesn't look like many people want a future."

"How about something to drink?" Joseph asked, realizing that this could be a lengthy conversation. "I need a drink."

"See…you are like them! Need a drink! Just like my parents and Tim's! They come home late at night and get drunk!" The girl walked backward toward the door as if readying herself for a quick escape.

"My wife and I don't drink alcohol…we haven't in over fifty years."

"But you said you 'need a drink.'"

"There was a different meaning to that once." Joseph felt like centuries separated him and the girl instead of decades.

"Yes, dear. My husband loves lemonade. Drinks it by the barrel full."

"Lemonade?"

"Lemonade. Plain. Well, with a little sugar." Joseph smacked his lips and tried to get up.

"Would you like some, Shannon?" Anne offered.

"Uh, I guess." The girl took a few steps forward. "No alcohol?" She seemed unable to grasp the concept.

"None. Not even at our wedding."

"None? My mom got blasted at hers…I had to drag her into the kitchen that night."

"What?" Anne tried to conceal her surprise.

"Pretty picture, huh?"

"Your mother's wedding? But how…"

"Anne," Joseph interrupted, rolling his eyes. "A second nuptial," he hinted under his breath.

"A third, actually," Shannon offered, bowing her head. "How many have you guys had?"

"You're looking at all of them…right here in this room."

"You two have never been married to anyone else?"

"No one else would have the old goat," Anne winked and smiled.

"Goat…hah! I still have many a woman make a pass at me, I'll have you know!"

"They probably think you have money." Anne's teasing was quickly replaced by a wince.

"Annie…are you…?"

"I'm fine, Joey. Just exhausted, like I told you."

"I'll get the lemonade," Shannon offered.

"The cups are in the sink. Sugar above the stove, sweetie," instructed Joseph. He was surprised at how he felt toward this young girl who had walked in this morning. He felt paternal.

Shannon returned a few moments later, carefully holding three plastic cups. "Do you guys always keep *that* much lemonade in the fridge?"

"No…usually it's more!" Joseph replied, reaching for his glass.

"How old are you, Shannon?"

"Seventeen." She sipped on her drink.

"Are you in school?"

"No…it's summer vacation."

"But in the fall?" Anne continued.

"Yeah…a senior…" Shannon's voice trailed off as she looked at the old woman. "Is she all right, mister?" Shannon motioned toward Anne, who had closed her eyes.

"She's been very sick," Joseph whispered as he studied Anne's face.

"Maybe I could help you—during summer vacation?" Shannon offered.

"That's really nice, but…"

"We accept, Shannon." Anne had opened her eyes and was looking directly at Joseph. "But we must pay you for anything you do."

"What can I do?" Shannon put her empty glass down and rose, eagerness in her voice.

"Can you vacuum?" Anne asked.

"I guess. I've done it once or twice. How hard can it be?"

"Well, there's a start!" Anne smiled before closing her eyes once again.

Chapter 15

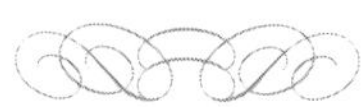

Joseph returned to his stone wall. The weeds had been removed from around the driveway. The front porch was clean. The wall had nagged him for days now. So much to do, and so little time. The old man was startled. Time! He looked up and down the length of the wall, reviewing what had been completed and what needed to be done.

My God, he thought, *it will take me months to finish this! Months! Anne…she had what? Months? Days? Less?* His heart ached as he stared at the job in front of him.

"Mr. Marino?" a voice called from behind him.

"Yes?" Joseph turned to see Shannon standing a few feet away.

"Your wife wants to see you." She fiddled nervously with the many rings on her fingers. "I'm done with the cleaning, too."

Joseph studied her face. It was pretty, actually. Nice almond-shaped eyes, and, when she smiled (even a nervous smile) she had a certain beauty about her. Joseph recalled what Anne had always said about teens…"try to say something nice to them, even if it is only about how clean their nose ring looks!"

"Mr. Marino? Are you okay?"

"Yeah…yes. Sorry. Old people have strange ways, Shannon. I was just admiring your smile. In some ways you remind me of my granddaughter."

"Is she my age?"

"No…oh, no…younger. But we oldies see all of you as young ones, you know." Joseph smiled. "I hope that she is just as pretty as you are now!"

"Do you really think I'm pretty?" Shannon looked surprised, as if no one had ever used that adjective to describe her.

"Sure! You act as if this is the first time you've had anyone compliment you."

"Nobody has ever said that to me before." Shannon smiled a nervous smile.

"Not even your parents?" Joseph didn't want to be nosey, but he found that hard to believe.

"Not that I remember," she said shyly. "I don't see them very much."

"Your boyfriend?"

"He doesn't like all that mushy stuff."

Joseph felt his compassion and paternal instincts surge. In that moment he recognized something special about this girl. He recognized a need, a loneliness, a sadness. He recognized something that maybe, just maybe, he could help rebuild. Joseph squeezed Shannon's shoulder.

"I better go see what Anne wanted. She can get mighty cranky."

Joseph smiled at the girl and then turned toward the house.

"Mr. Marino...?" The old man stopped and turned his head. Shannon hadn't moved. He turned back toward her.

"What is it, Shannon?"

"Can I...I mean..."

Joseph recognized the girl's shyness and fear. What was on her mind was very important. "What is it—you can tell me."

"I mean...well...I've always wanted one." The girl was obviously nervous about the request she was going to make.

"Wanted one? One what?"

"Can I call you Grandpa?" Shannon blurted the words out.

Joseph was stunned. He opened his mouth, but couldn't think of what to say, so instead he simply nodded. As he did so, the fear seemed to fade instantly from Shannon's face. Slowly she walked toward him, extending her arm.

"It would be very nice, Shannon, to have you as my granddaughter. I wonder what my wife would think." Joseph chuckled.

"Grandma won't mind. She said so..." Shannon slipped her hand into the crook of Joseph's arm.

"Shannon tells me that we have a new grandchild!" Joseph chuckled as he stepped onto the porch.

"You always wanted a large family!" Anne winked at Shannon.

"Just like Sarah…I find out after the fact!" Joseph pouted.

"Oh, stop." Anne ran her fingers along her neck.

"You're wearing the necklace." Joseph pointed with his worn index finger.

"You noticed," Anne said, pleased.

"This must be a rare day!"

"It certainly is."

"Still won't tell me, huh?" Anne shook her head in reply. "See, Shannon, she keeps me in the dark. I'll bet all of this just confuses you to no end!"

"Oh, no. I understand, but I swore that I wouldn't say anything."

"You know too?"

Shannon smiled and nodded an affirmative yes. Joseph removed his hat, wiped his brow, and slammed the hat into his leg. "Doggone! Beaten again by the female species. I swear it's a conspiracy!" Joseph returned his hat to his head, turned, and walked off the porch. He stopped about halfway to the stone wall and turned around.

"Anne?"

"What is it?" she called from the porch.

"What did you need me for, anyway?"

"To tell you that the surprise will be here in about fifteen minutes."

Joseph looked at his watch. Past noon! *Where has the time gone*, he thought. He shook his head in resignation, waved, and returned to the stone wall.

Stone after stone was placed on the stone wall. Joseph worked feverishly knowing that there were no more moments to waste. The "somedays and tomorrows" weren't relevant anymore. As he paused to take a swig from his water, he looked up to his friendly mountain.

"Could you just deposit some stones right here on my wall, please? I could really use some help." Joseph wished the mountain could reply.

"I'll help." A man's voice came from behind Joseph. Joseph knew that voice. He froze and his water bottle slipped out of his hand. He stared straight ahead, toward the mountain, unable to will himself to turn around.

"Paul," Joseph whispered. Despite his awareness of the surprise, he felt he had the wind knocked out of him.

"Yes. It's me, Dad." Silence. Joseph still looked straight ahead.

Joseph turned slowly around and found himself staring into the eyes of his son—into the eyes of himself.

"How long has it been?" Joseph whispered over the lump in his throat.

"More than five years." Paul and Joseph stood absorbing each other, their expressions of uncertainly almost matching.

Slowly, Joseph brought his arms up and opened them to his son.

Paul, hesitant at first, reached for his father and the two men embraced.

"Dad," he said quietly. "I don't know how to work out or fix all that hurt from so many years ago…"

Joseph interrupted him. "We don't have to work it out right now…son. I just thank God that you are here now." Joseph closed his eyes, relishing in the joy of being hugged by his only son. When he reopened his eyes, he noticed the rest of the family had collected on the porch and was eagerly watching the reunion.

"Everybody is watching," Joseph said, reluctant to let go of his son. "Your mom has a handkerchief over her mouth. That's her universal 'sad movie look.'" The two men separated, and Paul turned to look at his mom.

"I remember that look. Remember when I wrecked the car?"

"How can I forget that?" Joseph removed his eyes from Anne and scanned the rest of the porch. "What on earth?"

"I have a family now, Dad."

"My…my grandchildren?"

"Two of them. And my wife!"

"And your wife..." Joseph echoed his son's words. He slowly moved toward the porch, staring the whole time at the people in the shadows.

"We're the rest of the surprise," said the pretty young woman. Joseph was speechless, although his expression spoke of more happiness than words ever could.

"That's Eddie...well, Edward...and the other little guy, holding onto the rail and gnawing on some wood is Paul Junior. And this is my wife..."

"We've already met," her very familiar voice interrupted her husband. She stretched out her hand.

"Your voice...I've heard that voice before..." Joseph said finally.

"Maybe this will jar your memory... 'Computer Teksys San Diego...How may I help you?'"

"Meredith?" She nodded and smiled.

"All be damned..." Joseph finally said. "Well—how about some lemonade for all?"

"You haven't changed a bit, Dad," Paul said, and Joseph found himself ever so pleased to hear those words.

Chapter 16

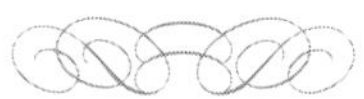

It was strange, Joseph thought, having someone sleeping in the other bedroom. He stopped in the dim hallway and touched the door. It was even stranger that it was his son and his daughter-in-law. Even more incredible was that there was a small grandchild that he never knew he had asleep on the living room couch. And another one asleep with his mother and father.

Joseph crept slowly down the hall. He avoided the loose board outside of the bathroom. But he missed the one by the front door.

"Who is it?" a small boy's voice said.

"Go to sleep, Eddie. It's your grandfather…I'm going outside…" Joseph whispered. He opened the door and turned to quietly latch it. Eddie stood at the door, rubbing his eyes.

"Whatcha doing?"

"Just some chores, that's all. I always get up this early but you look like you need to go back to bed."

"I'm hungry," Eddie kept rubbing his eyes.

"Well…I suppose we can help that. Let's go to the kitchen." Joseph retraced his steps through the front door. He signaled for the boy to follow him, and then he raised his right index finger to his mouth. "Shhh…"

Little Eddie nodded and staggered through the living room behind his newfound grandfather. As they entered the kitchen Joseph clicked the lights on. The old man searched through the cupboards until he came to the one over the refrigerator. There were three brand new boxes of cereal and a note attached to the center one. Joseph squinted as he read it.

Good morning, Joey!

I knew they were coming so I had Megan down at the store deliver these for the children. You will also find a jar of chocolate milk mix, some candy, and a few other things in here. I also knew that you'd be the one to get the kids some breakfast this morning.

I hope that you enjoy my notes…

Love,
Annie

PS: Candy is NOT a breakfast food!

"Where's my breakfast, Grandpa?" Eddie whined as he settled into a chair at the kitchen table. Not just any chair. Joseph noticed which chair. His chair.

"Coming right up. What will it be...Cocoa Crunchies or Corn Booms?" Joseph reached for the boxes.

"Grandpa?" Eddie said with his mouth half full of Cocoa Crunchies.

"Don't talk with your mouth full, son..." Joseph mumbled as he reviewed the second page of the day's newspaper. He had retrieved it from the rear porch while Eddie started his breakfast.

"I'm not your son...I'm your grandson. That's what my mommy told me," Eddie lectured. Joseph lowered the newspaper.

"What else did your mom tell you about me?"

"That you and my daddy had a fight a long time ago." Eddie looked out the back door. The cat meowing at the rear door distracted him.

"That's just Felix. He adopted us a couple of months ago."

"I always wanted a cat."

"Don't you have a pet?"

"My mom said that I am allergic to cats..."

"Oh," Joseph nodded. Eddie continued.

"We had to get up real early yesterday." He took a bite of cereal.

"Really?"

"Yeah. We got to go on a airpain." The boy said while chewing.

"An 'air-pain'?"

"Yeah. Up in the air. We saw water and little cities."

"An airplane."

"That's what I said..." Eddie reached for an orange, but he couldn't quite stretch his arm to the center of the table. Joseph grabbed one and handed it to his grandson.

"So, why did your mom tell you that you were coming up here?"

"'Cause Grandma is really, really sick." Eddie started ripping at the skin of the orange.

"Let me help." Joseph extended his hand. Eddie pulled the orange away.

"I can do it myself!" he exclaimed.

Small bits of orange peel flew around the table, as Eddie clumsily tore the peel off his piece of fruit.

"Your dad used to do it that way, Eddie."

"Uh-huh..." Eddie was concentrating on his orange.

"I want owanje!" a small voice yelled. Joseph lurched forward, spilling his morning juice.

Little Paul Junior was reaching for Eddie's almost-denuded piece of fruit.

"It's mine! Get your own!" Eddie replied. Joseph was wiping the mess off his shirt. Now he remembered why he was happy that his kids had grown up.

"I wanna *owanje*!" Paul Junior screamed.

"Sshhh...Paul...Eddie...hold on..."

Joseph reached for an orange and tore a giant chunk of peel off it. He placed it on a plate next to him, and motioned for Little Paul to sit down. "Here's your own orange!" Paul scanned the orange on the plate.

"I wan *dat* one!" Little Paul said as he pointed to Eddie's half-eaten orange.

"That belongs to your brother…here's a nice new one right here."

"Waaahhh…." Little Paul resumed his cries of frustration.

Joseph was flustered. It had been too long since he had had to deal with *this* sort of sibling problem. Then it dawned on him. He knew what to do. He craned over the table, made a few funny expressions, and began to talk. "How about some candy?" Joseph whispered while looking around behind him.

The two boys immediately took notice of him. Paul thrust a thumb into his mouth seeming to forget the orange.

"What kind of candy?" Eddie asked.

"Chocolate, of course. Would I offer anything less than the perfect candy to my wonderful grandsons?"

"Choc-ote! Choc-ote!" Little Paul started jumping up and down.

Joseph rose and pulled a bag of candy from the upper cupboard. The boys stared as Joseph opened the bag and then extracted four pieces. "Two pieces for each of you."

"Yay! Candy!" The boys jumped up and down. Joseph put his finger to his lips.

"We have to be quiet," Joseph reminded them, trying to forget Anne's note. The boys nodded as they cupped their hands over their mouths.

The sun seemed extraordinarily hot that afternoon. Joseph had returned to his pressing labor…the stone wall. The boys had started the morning out helping him but retired to the television for cartoons after about fifteen minutes.

"Well, what do you think, Old One? My son came back after all these years. I hardly know what to say to him. So much has happened. How do I undo what was done so many years ago?" Joseph pleaded with the granite slopes of the mountain as he removed his hat.

The wind lazily drifted through the pine trees.

"What do you think of my grandsons? What will become of them, Old One?" he continued while wiping the brim of his hat.

The wind picked up his hat and it landed on top of the unfinished wall.

"They are the next layer, huh?!" Joseph shook his head and smiled.

He grabbed his hat and returned it to his head. His aching arms reached out onto the pile of raw stones and picked out a nice flat one. He tried to fit it on the stone that the hat was resting on. It wobbled and would not sit right. Joseph picked up his old hammer and whacked at the stone, trying to remove a small burr on the bottom. He stopped and stared at the stone and where he wanted to place it.

"Have I failed, Old One? I've made so many mistakes..." Joseph whispered.

"So have I, Dad." Paul was standing right beside him.

Joseph was startled. "I was just mumbling..."

"I do it, too, sometimes." Paul stared at the mountain with his father. Paul sensed his father's discomfort and changed the subject. "How bad is she?"

Joseph turned and looked at his son's profile. He realized that Anne's medical situation was a day-to-day issue for him, but Paul had just been hit with it. He wished he had more practice talking to Paul. He wished he knew how to tell him. "I'll tell you what they told me, son." The wind kicked up again. "It's not good. The last set of tests showed even more damage." Joseph swallowed hard.

"Uh-huh..." Paul barely acknowledged his father.

"I'm sorry...I forget sometimes...I'm so wrapped up in this. It's the heart..."

"I kind of figured. What happened? I didn't want to ask Mom."

"It happened right behind us. On the stone path. I was talking to her and she collapsed." Joseph looked at the path where she had fallen, wishing this was one of the memories that would fade away.

"Heart attack?"

"Yes. A bad one. Doctor Waller said that what I did that day saved her life."

"It's been tough on you, too, Dad." Paul touched his father's shoulder. Joseph nodded and looked at the stone wall. "How long have they given her?"

Joseph looked up at the peak of Pine Mountain trying to borrow some of its strength. He drew in a deep breath. "She is living on borrowed time, Paul. They don't know. We've had a few scares. And they're getting worse." Joseph whispered.

"Why the wall, Dad?"

"Hmmm?" Joseph queried at the change of subjects.

"If these could be the last days, why are you spending them on this wall?"

"Your mother has been pestering me for years for this."

"Why?" Paul's hand traced one of the heavy rocks.

"When we were kids, her family had a stone wall. She loved that stone wall. I don't fully understand it myself."

"Dad...if she hasn't got much time left...and there is so much to do..."

"I know! Paul! I damn well know!" Joseph felt the angry blood rise in his neck.

"Hey...I didn't mean to..." Paul put his hands up in defense.

"I'm sorry son." Joseph felt instant guilt for snapping at his son. "I'm just really sensitive about how I've messed things up."

"Messed things up?"

"Yeah. I never seem to be able to finish anything. I promise and don't deliver. The wall. The stupid squeaky door. The slats in the chair on the porch. And…." Joseph tensed and stopped.

"And?"

"You. I've completely messed up my relationship with you. Damn it, Paul. I missed your wedding. The birth of your kids. More than five years wasted… because of my stubbornness." Joseph gestured toward the house.

"We have both made mistakes, Dad. Do you remember the lemonade yesterday?"

"Lemonade?" Joseph was confused.

"Yeah. Meredith got a big laugh out of how you and I keep gallons of lemonade around. She thinks I'm a little clone…" Paul had a faint smile.

"No…you're your own man, son."

"Yes, I am. But I'm a lot like you sometimes. Meredith and I have gone to counseling recently. I've found out that I'm the cause of our chafing. I'm controlling and bullheaded. Sound familiar?"

"Must be those stupid genes." Joseph shook his head.

"We are both at fault, Dad. Two headstrong men messed things up—it wasn't just you. Do you even remember what started it?"

"Ohhhh…yeah. A certain situation with a car…"

"The accident? Do you think it goes back *that* far?" Paul was surprised.

"No...even further. But that is when the gloves came off. We started bare-fisting verbally."

Paul slowly nodded.

"So...what can I do to make up, son?"

"You've already done it. You reached out. We still have to work so many things out, but Meredith told me about the phone call you made that day."

"Your mother wanted this most of all—she wanted us to have each other when she is..." Joseph's voice drifted off, and Paul didn't choose to finish his sentence.

Chapter 17

The sun had not quite crested the mountains to the east, but Joseph could tell that it would happen any time now. He looked out the kitchen window and saw the gleaming slopes of the pinnacle of Pine Mountain. It would be a warm day, he thought. He scrubbed his hands thoroughly. He wanted to make sure his grandsons had clean bowls for their cereal.

"Do you mind a little company?" The sound of Anne's voice startled him.

"How about having breakfast with me this morning?" Joseph invited, noticing that her skin looked paler than usual—almost white.

"How about waffles?" Anne asked.

"Do you want me to make them?"

"No—I need to wake up anyway." Anne rubbed her left arm. "I didn't sleep well last night."

"Does your arm hurt?"

"I think I slept on it wrong. I am hungry, though." Anne stepped toward the stove.

"Please—let me fix this one." He led her to the table.

"This ought to be a treat," Anne said sarcastically, still rubbing her arm.

"Hot waffles...coming up." Joseph scrounged through the cupboards. Sheepishly he glanced back over his soldier. "The waffle pan?"

"Left side, down on the bottom, where other heavy items are," Anne pointed. Another few moments passed and Joseph rustled through the cupboards. Again he glanced over his shoulder.

"Bisquick?"

"Second cupboard to the left of the glasses." Anne crossed her arms over her chest, obviously amused.

"Let's see..." Joseph said aloud. "Milk?" Anne rolled her eyes.

Joseph assembled the batter in a large bowl. "Uh... where's the mixer?" He turned with embarrassment.

"Oh, no...hand mix it...much better results."

"If you insist." He brought the bowl over to the kitchen table and began to turn the batter over and over.

"You made my day yesterday, Joey," Anne whispered. The wooden spoon clanked against the bowl.

"You deserved it. You have been patient enough." Joseph got a glint of white beneath Anne's robe. "You're wearing the pearls?" Normally, she kept them in her special teakwood box. In all the years of their marriage, he hadn't seen her wear them but a dozen times.

"I just wanted to feel them near me." Anne fingered the strand. "You know how I love them."

"They are the most unusual pearls I've ever seen." Joseph returned to stirring the mix. "Unusual" wasn't the word that described how he felt inside. "Cheap" was closer to it, but Anne strongly objected to the use of that word in context with the pearls.

"Thanks to you."

"Heh! Yeah, right. I planned it that way!" Joseph was defensive. How was he to know that pearls came in different shades?

"No...I like them...I do! Each one has its own personality, and I can tell which one stands for what..." Anne pleaded.

"You've always said that, but...well I can see how much they mean to you...I used to think you wouldn't wear them because they were all a little different."

"They are my life. They are my history, my memories." Anne reached out and touched her husband's hand.

"Yeah, but I could've learned how to pick pearls...a few times I considered swapping them for a matching set." Joseph shook his head as he stirred a bit more vigorously.

"No...I would never trade these in. Look at them, Joey." Joseph watched her remove the strand and hold it in an outstretched palm. She was pointing at the darkest one. "Have you ever noticed how the different shades of the pearls match the events of our lives?" Joseph shrugged. He'd never thought about that. He'd just always seen them as different, no more, no less.

"I just saw them as a collection of odd pearls..."

"But when I see these dark ones, I feel strong emotions..." Anne gently stroked a few of the pearls on one side.

"So, the darker they are the worse the memory?"

"No...no...the darker they are the more searing, the more memorable the memory."

"That's not why I picked them that way..."

"I know...that's the beauty of the necklace. You were unaware of what you were doing. I knew what it meant back then."

"You knew I was picking dark pearls for strong emotions?"

"Oh, no..."

"What do you mean, then?" Joseph shook his head in confusion. Wrinkles appeared on his brow.

"Look at these two pearls. The first ones you ever got me."

"Oh, I remember them. I had to buy cheap ones. They were flawed." Joseph felt a twinge of guilt. He stressed the word "flawed."

"They were, but they aren't any more."

"Oh? Something's changed?"

"Early in our marriage we had little money for this sort of thing. You had to buy the flawed ones. The ones with a tinge of darkness in them."

"Yeah, thanks for reminding me...for the next fifty years I was trying to find pearls that were better, but I have always had to live with the first few..."

Joseph tossed his head around. He had a frown on his face.

"Our most memorable events were early in our marriage..." Anne began.

"Yeah, they sure were!" Joseph raised his head and looked out the window. The shadows were lifting from Pine Mountain. The trees in the yard swayed in the morning breeze.

"Remember what you gave me the first one for?" Anne rubbed her husband's left shoulder.

"Do I! Who can forget? Our first anniversary!" Joseph turned to look at Anne. He slowed his beating of the mix in the bowl.

"You sold your trumpet for it."

"Never could play that thing anyway!" Joseph smiled.

"We had no money for gifts that year, but you wanted to give me something." Joseph winced as he remembered the abject poverty of their first couple of years together.

"We have come a long way," Joseph whispered.

"Do you remember anything else about that pearl?" Anne tilted her head and put her arm through Joseph's.

It was strange, he thought. The years seemed to melt away. He could clearly see her face in his mind as she used to be. Her face was so pink; her eyes so blue. He closed his eyes and remembered the smell of her hair that autumn day. "The car broke down! I was late for dinner!" Joseph slowed his beating of the batter.

"Yes. I had worked for two hours making spaghetti, meatballs, and garlic bread. I even used the last candle from our wedding and that old checkered tablecloth."

"Hah! I remember not being able to get the grease out from under my fingernails. Every time I took a bite I had to be reminded of the day's fiasco!"

"That was the day we decided that a decent car was a priority in our family."

"God, that seems like yesterday!"

So, the dark marks on this pearl represent the grease…and so much more…" Anne replied.

"More? All I can remember was the grease." Joseph smiled.

"Like, how 'in the dark' we really were about our relationship."

"Oh, were we ever," Joseph nodded.

"I remember how I hated how you never flossed your teeth!"

"Me? I can't stand going two days without doing that!"

"Not for our first year!" Anne smiled broadly, accentuating her teeth.

"Hey, don't rub it in! So, the white of the pearl could stand for dental floss?" Joseph chuckled.

"And the wedding candle! But every pearl is like this to me. Remember this one…from when Paul was born…"

"Yeah, I can't forget *that* night! A power outage on that night, of all nights."

"Remember how white the hospital lights had seemed after driving in the pitch-black city?" Anne leaned in her chair.

"So…the black is for the power outage…"

"…and the white is for the hospital! You're getting the idea!"

"Black was for how I felt when I got the bill!" Joseph stirred the batter more firmly.

"And white was the gown they gave us to wrap little Paul in."

"I think the mix is ready now," Joseph said, breaking them from their memories.

"You've finished with all the ingredients. Time to cook!" Anne responded.

"Oh…" Joseph returned his focus to the bowl in front of him. A third of the batter had spilled or splashed beyond the bowl's edge.

One rock on top of another. One stretched into fifty. Fifty stretched into hundreds. The wall continued to grow. Joseph stopped to wipe his forehead.

"Dad?" Paul said from Joseph's left side.

"Come out to help?" Joseph gestured toward the growing wall.

"I'd like to, but I've got to get back to San Diego. We have a plane to catch at LAX."

Joseph wiped the sweat off his arms as he looked over at his only son. There was a tense silence.

"I won't fight you this time, Paul. You're a grown man now. I tried to control you too far into your adult years. My heart says 'tell him to roll up his sleeves and help out, get a later flight,' but I'll take the high road. I'm proud of you, son." Joseph's voice trailed off to a whisper.

"Dad…I want to try to…how should I say it?"

"Straight out? Just say it. Let's hold nothing back."

"I want to try and work things out, but I need time. I was afraid of you so many years ago. It doesn't go away that fast."

"What do you mean?" The back of Joseph's neck tensed.

"Dad, I know that you want to make up, for Mom…"

"And for me, son."

"Please, let me finish." Paul replied after which Joseph threw his hands up into the air.

"Sorry…"

"We need to take it slow. We need to build a new relationship, one that throws out the communication problems that we used to have."

"They're gone. My word!" Joseph raised his right hand.

"No, Dad, they're not. Not just because we say so."

He looked past Paul and saw Anne standing on the porch. He literally bit his inside cheek. "I… understand. Slow and easy." Joseph took a deep breath. These were not two traits he possessed and he wondered where his son had picked them up. Definitely had to be Anne.

"Look…I've got to go."

"Yeah. Gotta go." Joseph felt nervous and fidgety. He looked down at the ground.

"The kids are ready. Come and say good-bye…" Paul turned to walk away.

"Paul," Joseph said quickly.

"Yeah?"

"Believe me…I know we've had a lot of pain, but…"

"But what?"

"I know I don't say it much, but…I love you very much. You are my only son. That means a lot to me."

Paul stopped and looked at his father, then at the ground. "I meant it. I do wish I could stay and help you, Dad."

"I wish you could, too."

Chapter 18

"It's late, Joey. Let's get to bed," Anne whispered to her husband, lying on the opposite side of the bed. It was cool that evening. The window was open a bit, allowing for the cool breeze to refresh. Joseph's light was the last one on.

"I'm having a tough time settling down."

"What's going on?"

"It's Paul. It hurts, Anne. It really hurts."

Anne stroked her husband's back gently. "You did so well this time, sweetheart. You really reached out to him."

"All the wasted years, Annie. He's my hope, my life. And I wasted so many years fighting with him because I'm a stubborn, selfish man. I was always too busy or too bothered by some ridiculous thing he did."

"Shhh…just be grateful that you will waste no more years."

"Remember those parents in the store, with the teenagers?"

"Shhh...yes, I remember..."

"It hurts that they're doing the same thing...it repeats, generation after generation." Joseph turned to look at Anne. She was still wearing the pearls in bed. "Maybe I'm just like them."

"Maybe we all are in some way or another," Anne said simply.

"The pearls Anne, you forgot to take them off."

"I don't want to take them off anymore."

"They look good on you." Joseph kissed her on the forehead. "Sweet dreams, Annie." He paused before he turned out the light. Something about the cross on the wall caught his eye. It was the wind, gently moving it.

God...watch over my family... Joseph prayed.

He turned out the light but lay in the dark watching the curtain sway with the breeze. The minutes turned into long hours as he lay there listening to the clock, watching the light and the breeze play on the cross on the wall. Listening to Anne's breathing. Despite a few minutes where he had drifted into sleep, he had lain awake caught in a whirlwind of emotions and memories.

Joseph slid out from under the sheets and quietly tiptoed toward the bathroom. When he finished he retraced his steps and slid under the covers, being careful not to wake Anne up. He noticed the sheet had been pulled toward his side. Probably did it when he left, he thought. Joseph slowly reached across and pulled the sheet up to Anne's shoulder. The pearls shone in the dark. She looked so beautiful wearing them. He brushed against her cheek. She was cold. Maybe, he thought, he should shut the window for her.

He had just closed the window when it hit him. *She was cold.* Joseph spun around, clicking the switch of the antique lamp. "Annie?" he said loudly enough for her to hear—but quietly enough so that he would not startle her.

She did not startle.

This time he shouted. "Annie! Annie!"

He ran to her side of the bed and reached a frail hand toward her neck.

"Annie?" It was half statement, half question. An eerie silence filled the room.

Chapter 19

Paul, Sarah, Meredith, and Michael were waiting at the car with all of the children. Every now and then Joseph looked past the freshly smoothed earth to see the remainder of his family. He felt strange. Normally his mind was racing with thoughts, but now he just felt numb. He thought only of the wind. He didn't know if he should get up and walk back to the cars or just sit there and stare at the temporary wooden grave marker. The decision seemed one too difficult to make. The wind blew, a soft whistle.

"Annie," he whispered.

Again the wind blew.

"Annie…"

"Dad?"

"Huh?" Joseph looked around, but couldn't find the source of the voice.

"Dad…over here." A soft, feminine voice said. Joseph felt a gentle stroking on his left shoulder.

"Annie?" he startled.

"Dad…it's me. Sarah."

"Sarah?"

"It's all right, Dad. You're going to be fine."

"Fine?"

"Come on. Let's get you home. You're awfully tired."

"Tired." Joseph stared straight ahead. He, at Sarah's urging and with her help, started to get up. Two other arms supported his right side.

"Huh?" Joseph said as he looked to his right.

"It's me, Dad. Paul. We're here for you."

"Annie…" Joseph repeated.

"Shhh…hold on, Dad," Sarah whispered. "Let's get you home." They slowly led him down the slight slope, away from the shade of that beautiful pine tree. One thought came through Joseph's mind clearly: Leaving the cemetery, after burying your wife of fifty years, was the loneliest, most terrifying time of a man's life.

Joseph struggled to the car, finding it difficult to focus.

"Why don't you take dad and I'll take Meredith and the kids? I think he needs some quiet time right now," Sarah said.

"I think you're right. Maybe Michael and I can get him to take his pills."

"He needs them now. He hasn't slept in three days."

Joseph heard the two talk as if he wasn't even there. In many ways, he wasn't.

Michael took Joseph's right arm from Sarah.

"Doctor Waller gave us some pills for you, before she left."

"Pills?" Joseph simply echoed whatever he heard.

"She said you need some sleep. Can you take this?" Joseph looked into Sarah's palm and saw a little yellow pill.

"I can do it." He placed the pill in his mouth. He remembered placing the pill under Anne's tongue. He forced the memory out of his mind and returned to blankness.

Joseph woke up to the sun shining across his room. The window was open and the cool morning breeze was brushing against his cheek.

"What a nightmare," he said, rubbing his eyes to rouse himself. He noticed that he was wearing his socks. He never went to bed with his socks on.

"Annie...did I get undressed last night?" he asked. There was no answer, but he heard her voice down the hall. How could she have beaten him to rise, he wondered. For fifty years, he had always gotten up first. Sleeping with his socks? His mind swirled with confusion.

"Must be in the kitchen," he mumbled, reaching for his robe.

"Annie...do you remember me getting undressed last night?" he asked as he entered the light-filled room.

"Dad? You're awake! We were wondering how long you would sleep!"

"Sarah?" And then he remembered the ride in the car, the yellow pill, the soft earth. He remembered that the nightmare was real. Joseph brushed his shirt pocket while trying to focus. He felt something and gently pulled it from his pocket.

"What is it, Dad?"

"Pearls…our marriage pearls," he whispered.

Part Two

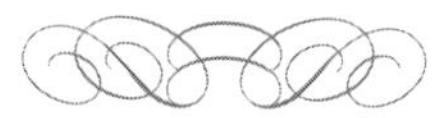

The Pearls

Chapter 20

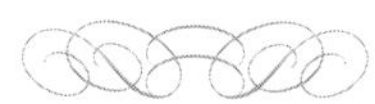

THE FIRST RAIN OF AUTUMN WAS MORE LIKE a gentle drizzle that year. It was early, too. The temperature had fallen gradually. There was no snowstorm to announce the cold times ahead, just a soft, falling dew from the clouds, settling everywhere. Drab gray clouds.

The leaves fell, as they do every year, and covered over the outdoor works of humanity and nature. Darkness came earlier in the day. It seemed as if the final chapter was being written in this cycle of life.

The wall was still there, unfinished. The old man hated to look at it. It had been weeks since he had gone out back.

"For once I'm glad to see the leaves all over. I don't have to look at that reminder of my laziness," Joseph mumbled, rubbing his uncombed hair.

He wandered, mostly. In the twilight time before dark he would pace and turn every light in the house on. He hated this time of day.

For a while he sat in the living room. He listened to the grandfather clock in the corner tick. He tried listening to his old music, but it just brought back memories of…

"Annie…" He mumbled. He rubbed the top of his head again. Noises came and went. A car. The sound of a bird. Banging…

"Mr. Marino? Grandpa? Are you okay? Can you hear me?"

"Huh? What? Who is it?" Joseph rose slowly, letting his hands linger on the arms of the chair.

"It's me, Grandpa…Shannon," said the shadowy figure in the doorway.

"Shannon? Oh…Shannon! Hold on a minute…" Joseph ran his fingers through his hair and straightened his shirt.

"What's wrong with your lights?" she asked.

"Wrong…nothing's wrong…why…I just forgot to turn some on." Joseph clicked on the floor lamp on his way to the screen door.

"It's cold and wet. You shouldn't leave the door open, you'll get sick!" Shannon scolded.

"Oh, sure…pick on an old man!" Joseph offered the faintest of smiles.

"I'm just worried about you. You've been so…I don't know…so lost…"

"Lost? No…look, I'm right here!" He pointed to the floor trying to make light of the situation.

"You're still hurting," Shannon quietly said.

"You're right. I just feel so…well, you said it, lost. Annie was somebody special, Shannon. I feel so alone.

I had lived my life with her—we were one and the same person. Half of me is gone, and I'm not sure I like the half that's left."

"Here…I brought you something!" Shannon handed over a large picnic basket. It had a red and white checkered cloth over it.

"What is it?"

"Open it!"

"Tupperware dishes? Food! Oh, I can't have you doing this…you've done so much already." Joseph began to close the basket.

"No…it's for you. Please. You have to eat." Shannon pointed to Joseph's loose pants.

"Funny," Joseph said, although he wasn't smiling. "All those years I tried to lose that weight and now…" Joseph threw up his hands. He looked at the basket and then at Shannon. Her eyes were pleading. Her eyes could always melt him. They were like the almond eyes of his long-ago cat. He relented.

"Anything for you. What do you have?" Joseph reopened the basket and started rifling through the contents.

"Let's take it in to the kitchen. I'll make you a proper dinner." Shannon pulled the basket away and walked across the living room.

"No…wait…" Joseph reached out for Shannon's arm but missed.

Shannon walked into the kitchen and turned the light on. A gasp escaped her. "What happened here?"

"I've been meaning to clean up. It's just so hard to get around to it." Joseph looked down at the floor. If Anne saw how he was living, how he looked—

"It's not so bad. Here, we can have it fixed up in ten minutes. I'll just put the dinner in the fridge."

They cleaned the dishes and straightened the counters. It wasn't terribly messy, just enough to disgust a teenager.

"There...let me see...napkins..." Shannon went about the business of setting the table.

"What? I thought that all you teenagers were messier than this old man."

"Not me. It really bugs my mother. She hates cleaning up," Shannon said while dishing out potato salad and cucumbers in vinegar.

"What is this...? How did you know...?" Joseph was astonished. She was laying out some of his favorite picnic dishes.

"Just wash up...I'll warm up the meatball sandwiches." Shannon walked over to the microwave oven with a bag.

"Meatball sandwiches! And I suppose that there's a summer salad in that big Tupperware dish there..." Joseph pointed to the other side of the table.

"I guess...I don't know what it's called...it's tomatoes, cucumbers, onion, celery...a little of that dark lettuce... oil, vinegar, pepper..." Shannon grabbed a hot pad.

"Summer salad! Where did you get the recipe for all of this...?" Joseph was amazed.

"Grandma...Mrs. Marino."

Joseph stared at Shannon and slowly moved toward his usual chair.

"Anne?" he whispered.

"Yeah...she asked me to do this someday. I didn't know when or if I should push—but I saw how down you look...so, I thought...hey, why not? Besides she gave me some money to pay for the food."

"When did she..." Joseph began.

"Remember those days when I came over to help clean up?"

"Yeah."

"That's when." The smell of warming Italian meatballs wafted across the room.

"Ohh...that smells like a bit of heaven..." Joseph closed his eyes and took a deep breath.

Shannon pulled the sandwich from the oven and gently placed it on Joseph's plate.

"Here it is. And you like Romano cheese on it, don't you?"

"Anne again?" Joseph smiled.

"Again." Shannon nodded.

Joseph treasured every bite of his sandwich, every cucumber that he bit into, and every bite of his favorite summer salad. He hadn't eaten this much in months.

"How is it?" Shannon inquired.

"How is it? Well...I have to try a few more bites to be sure," Joseph teased, "but it seems okay..." The first real smile since Anne's death crossed his face.

"How is that boyfriend of yours…what's his name?" Joseph changed the subject. He was feeling too emotional, too uncomfortable.

"Tim? Well…okay, when he stays away from Isaiah."

"He's the orange-haired troublemaker?"

"That's putting it lightly! If he shows up when Tim and I are hanging around together, I leave." Shannon began to clean up the dishes.

Joseph walked over to the sink and picked up a hand towel.

"I'll dry."

"Dry? What do you mean?"

"Dry. I'll wipe the dishes with the rag…"

"What about the dishwasher?" Shannon pointed to the appliance near the sink, below the counter.

"We used to use it once in a while—when we first got married and hated washing dishes. Over the years we realized that it was God's way of giving the two of us some time together. Sometimes we even used to light some candles when we did it…silly, I know…" Joseph picked up another plate.

"That's so romantic." Shannon smiled.

"You think so? I thought teenagers thought romance is limousines and fancy dresses."

"Not me. I guess I'm different."

"I'll say that you are." They finished the last of the dishes, and Joseph started packing up the Tupperware for Shannon's trip home.

"Those are for you to keep," Shannon said, stopping him.

"Mine?"

"Grandma even let me borrow them for you…my mother doesn't have any of this. We usually eat something that comes from takeout or the microwave." Shannon pulled on her sweater.

"Wait…I'll drive you. It's getting nasty out there," Joseph offered. He looked around at the kitchen. It was clean, the way Anne used to have it.

"You are a wonder, Shannon!"

"Are you sure you can drive me? I can walk."

"Never! I wouldn't have it!" Joseph scrounged around in his pockets, looking for his keys.

"I'll wait in the living room, then." Shannon replied.

"Uhhh…my keys must be on the couch." Joseph patted his pockets.

He found them in the fold of the couch, and the two headed for the door.

"Grandpa?"

"What?"

"I put something on the table by the lamp for you." Shannon pointed across the room, to Joseph's favorite chair. There was a small box and an envelope there. He turned to get it.

"No…wait…when you get back…" Shannon urged.

Joseph stopped and looked at Shannon.

"Annie?"

Shannon nodded.

"She told me to say something if you argued…it was something like…'just this time, Joseph…please…don't wreck this…'" Shannon smiled.

Joseph felt a lump in his throat and nodded. He turned back to look at the card and then pointed toward the door.

It was very quiet when he returned. The clock ticked on the wall. He slowly opened the door, holding tightly to the doorknob. His eyes were immediately drawn to the objects on the table by his chair. He shut the door and locked the deadbolt.

Slowly, so very slowly, he walked toward his chair and sat down. For the longest time he stared at the envelope. It was a pink-colored envelope, the kind that Anne used to use all the time.

He was afraid to touch it. Afraid to look inside. He stood up and thought he would take a shower. He started taking off his sweater.

"Ahh…enough of this…"

He stopped. Again he sat down and stared at the envelope.

His trembling hand stretched out toward it, and he gently took it into his hand. He noticed the small box by the light.

Very gingerly he pulled open the envelope and looked inside. He pulled out the paper that was carefully tucked inside…

Dear Joey,

Because you are reading this note, I have gone home to heaven. I gave this to Shannon and asked her to give it to you if…or, I guess, when, something happens to me. I have been watching you these last few weeks, and I've noticed how you've changed so much. Every morning I've watched you get up and quietly leave our bedroom.

Yes, I was awake. And yes, I had to give this to Shannon. I wanted someone you cared about to give this to you. I felt that you would be terribly lonely and in need of a smile when you read this.

How was the meatball sandwich? The salad? Everything else? When you've finished reading this, there is a surprise in the refrigerator. I know you'll like it. Do you remember how I used to sit on the porch and write? Well, I wasn't writing in my diary! I wracked my brain for days trying to figure out what I could do for you. You've done so much for me these last few weeks. I came up with this.

All around the house are notes that I've written to you, Joey. I have wondered what it would be like to be alone after more than a half of a century. Perhaps, this is a way I can stay with you.

I have a few requests for you. Simple things, really...Would you finish my stone wall? Be the parent that Shannon desperately needs? Could you help kids like her? I know your heart, Joey. You are a warm, caring man.

And then there are Sarah and Paul. What you did with our son gave me the peace to go home to heaven. You answered my deepest prayer. Please reach out to them. They hurt, too, right now.

Strange...I wont know how this kooky plan of mine will work out. Well, not until I see you again...on the other side. I'll be there for you, Joey, the man I've always loved...on God's Chocolate Chip Creek! You'll recognize me!

Last thing...I love you. There's a little something in the box on the table. You'll understand.

With my love forever,
Annie

Joseph let the tears flow freely. He had not cried since the funeral. He had locked his heart, his soul, his thoughts into a little box inside his body—scared to open the lid and examine them closely. Now, at Annie's thoughtfulness, the box opened.

He moved the note to his left hand and reached for the small box next to the lamp. Inside was a small Swedish flag and, under that, a small stone. Beneath the two items was a simple note:

I always wanted a stone wall, as much as you wanted to go to Sweden...

"I understand, Annie." Joseph looked up at the ceiling. "God, how I miss you! If it's the last thing I do, that wall will be finished. Annie...when I get there with you, first thing I'm going to say is 'the wall is finished!'"

Chapter 21

THE COLD, DAMP AIR OF AUTUMN SLAPPED at Joseph when he opened the door to the backyard the next morning. It was before the first appearance of the sun. He flipped on the outside light, and immediately the leaves seemed to glow with the dew all over them. There it was, just at the edge of the light. The stone wall.

He worked hard through the dawn and into the middle of the day. Every hour or so he had to stop and wipe his brow. Catching his breath was getting more difficult as he aged, he noticed.

He would load a wheelbarrow with stones from the rapidly diminishing pile, then the load would be pushed to the working section of the wall.

After hammering the rough edges off, he'd set the stone on top of the one below. Sometimes the stone would fit just right. Sometimes it took a lot of hammering to get it to settle in the natural hollow. Other times he had to go back to the pile and find a better piece.

Joseph looked at his watch and was stunned to see that it was after twelve o'clock. He felt the grumbling in his stomach. He needed to sit down for a while.

After a lunch of summer salad bread, and butter, and Anne's special treat, an éclair, he trudged out to the wall once again. He looked down at his hands, now swollen and scraped. They looked like the hands of an old man, he thought.

The handles of the wheelbarrow were made of wood and had the rough feel of age. He worked his way toward the pile of stones with the old wheelbarrow. When he was almost there, he slowed. There was nothing left but gravel and dirt.

Time to make a run to the creek bottom for some more rocks, he thought. Many years before he had built a large cart to haul stones from the creek for the project. It was made of heavy pine and had a redwood base. It had been sturdy years ago, but the seasons of neglect had taken their toll. It was still reliable, but the quirks of age were setting in. The front right wheel was warped, so the cart wobbled slightly, and Joseph knew not to put rocks over the right rear wheel. The frame under the floor of the wagon had split.

The old man freed the cart from the weeds that had grown around it and then went into his shed to get some oil for the wheels. Something caught his eye. It was a familiar streak of yellow: the last side of the shed that had never been painted.

The oiled cart squeaked and creaked as it made its

way down into the creek bottom. Joseph took it slow and easy. An old man was in no shape to argue with a heavy, gravity-driven cart. He looked around for his usual way out of the bottom land…a gentle slope up the same side a little further down.

The gurgling creek was one of the benefits of coming down here. So many times Joseph and Anne had walked these paths. So many times they had played in the water.

So long ago.

"Well, one rock is as good as any…" Joseph said as he stopped the cart and started sorting through the available building material. One by one he loaded the cart beside him. Most were damp and moss covered.

The water seemed to speak to him…voices from the past tickled his ears as he loaded. Occasionally he would stop, still bent over, and listen. He would swear that something from a long, long time ago was calling him.

As he loaded one large stone his foot slipped. He tried to catch himself, but the stone kept him off balance. His right foot slipped forward, and he landed in the water on his rear end.

The gurgling waters mocked him. This was another time, he thought. So long ago. Shadows became children. But the water was still cold.

Joseph smiled in spite of the ache in his lower backside. He thought he could see the wide, toothy grin of his long ago friend, Larry Yates, reaching out with a young hand. He sat in the cool water and allowed his thoughts to return to that summer, long ago, in Maine.

"C'mon, Joe! Try that fall again!"

"Yeah, you looked like my Aunt Betty when she fell into the pond with her Sunday finest on! We laughed for weeks!" shouted Petey Barnes, pushing his ever-present lock of hair out of his face.

Are you all right, Joey? a pretty voice sounded from his left. The old man turned his head to the left, straining to see that gentle face. A simple bush greeted him in return.

"I'm fine, Annie." the old man mumbled, still staring into the empty bushes and rubbing his lower back. He strained to remember how pretty she had looked that day; her hair seemed to glow from the sunlight streaming through the trees behind her. Her eyes were almond shaped, and brown. She looked so caring and worried that day, crouched down with her arm extended. He knew he could see her. He so much wanted to see her.

"God, how I miss you, Annie…oh, what I'd pay just to see you for one day, to hear your voice again… to touch your face. Oh, Annie!" Joseph cried out as he grabbed and slapped at the cold, clear water. Only the windy echo of his own words returned to him.

The old man thrust his right sleeve into his mouth and bit down hard with anger. The wool coat tasted wet and bitter.

The cart was full enough, Joseph thought. He stopped for a moment to look back at the creek.

"Well, Annie…is there a Chocolate Chip Creek… in heaven…?"

The water gurgled by, as it always does in the wet autumn.

A muffled sound distracted the old man. He turned and peered into the dark recesses of the forest. He saw nothing out of the ordinary.

It was getting dark. The sun was leaving the valley below Pine Mountain, and the shadows were long. Joseph felt a momentary panic. He didn't bring a flashlight and there was a lot of distance to cover.

Joseph decided to lighten the load of the cart and come back for a second load in the morning. He left a pile of stones near an outcropping of rock at the creek's edge. It was a convenient place because he could wash his hands and face in the creek when he was finished.

It didn't take long to dump a third of the cart's load. Joseph decided that the little wooden wagon was now light enough to allow him to get home quickly, before it got too dark.

"Heyyyy….!" A muffled voice called from the woods. Joseph turned to look toward the sound. He saw nothing but trees and brush.

"Hello? Is somebody there?" Joseph called. There was no answer. It was strange, he thought. He'd heard that voice before…somewhere. He stayed next to the creek, squinting, trying to see what or who was there.

Joseph shook his head and decided that he was imagining things. His mind had been playing many tricks on him. Sometimes he thought he heard Anne in the shower or saw her fleeting image. Suppressing his thoughts, he picked up the handle to the cart and started to pull.

"Yea-hah!" a voice called through the trees. Joseph stopped for a moment and looked again through the trees. The voice sounded much closer now. He cupped his hand around his mouth.

"Who's there? Who is it?" he called.

The trees swayed in the gathering wind.

Once again Joseph shook his head. Time to get home. He pulled harder, and the wagon began to move away from the muddy bank of the creek.

"Hey…old man…!" a male voice shouted.

Joseph stopped and looked toward the voice. He saw no one. *Stupid teenagers*, he thought. He returned to the task of getting the rear wheel over a large rock.

Laughter filtered through the trees. Joseph turned again toward the sounds. Something moving caught the corner of his eye, but not soon enough.

Crack! Joseph felt a sharp crash of pain on his forehead, near his ear. The momentum of the impact knocked him off balance, and he tumbled into the creek.

Joseph grabbed at his head, but sharp pain drove his hand away. The water rushed over his shoulder and knee. The world was spinning around and blurry.

"I'm going to get his wallet."

"C'mon, man! You've really messed him up… let's go!"

Joseph felt something tug at his waist. He tried to turn over but couldn't move. The sound of footsteps trailed off.

"He's dead," one boy yelled, panic gripping his voice. "Damn," he said in shock. "Isaiah…you killed him!" the boy said in horror. His voice resonated of the terror of a game that had gone too far.

"Shaddup, come on. Let's get out of here." Isaiah's voice held the faintest bit of matching fear as he glanced from left to right.

Joseph tried to move, but the pain was unbearable. Something warm and dark red flowed into his face, stinging his eye. Joseph moaned.

The voices became more faint, and the sounds of the rushing water filled Joseph's ears.

"Help…" the old man called with what little volume he could muster. Panic accompanied his growing dizziness. With the pain of every movement his vision became more blurred, and the dizziness increased. His breathing became labored.

Darkness descended over the old man by the creek.

"Hey...can you hear me...hey?" A voice erupted from the darkness. Joseph stirred and opened one eye. No matter how much he willed it to, the other wouldn't open. With his one-eye vision, he saw only mud and leaves. Joseph let out a weak moan.

"Lay still," commanded the man. "You've taken quite a blow to the head there."

"Where...who are..." Joseph mumbled.

"Shhh, don't move. I found you laying here. Did you get the license plate of the truck that must've hit you? I've got to get you out of the water." The man grabbed Joseph's arms and began to pull slowly but was interrupted by a yelp from Joseph.

"Okay, okay," he reassured Joseph. "I won't try that again. I'm going to run up to the dirt road and see if someone is up there. I need to get some help," the man replied.

The sound of footsteps crushing leaves filled Joseph's ears. He struggled and turned to look up toward the sky. It was bright. It was morning. With his right hand, he touched his forehead and winced in pain. He brought his fingers in front of his eyes; they were covered with dirt and dried blood.

The man returned shortly, with the aid of another. "You stay here," he instructed. "I'll go over to the Bonner's house and call the ambulance."

Bonner. Joseph knew that name for some reason. Bonner. He tried to remember in spite of the blurriness. It was Shannon's stepfather's name!

"Shannon," Joseph whispered.

"He must know them. That's Bonner's kid's name. Who is he?"

"I don't know. What's your name?" asked the one man as he leaned forward to catch any soft-spoken words.

"Marino. Joseph." A memory of someone pulling at his waist returned. "Wallet…my wallet…"

"Hold on, let me look…" One of the men pulled at Joseph's pocket. "Nothing in there, Mr. Marino… maybe it fell out…" The man walked around Joseph, scanning the near ground. "Here it is! By this broken up old cart!" The man returned.

"Broken cart?" Joseph managed to prop himself up on his good elbow.

"Whoa…take it slow!" The man handed back the wallet.

"My cart!" He slid down to the ground again, the familiar feeling of defeat surrounding him.

"It took quite a beating, all right! What happened here?"

"I don't know. Somebody in the trees…" Joseph touched his forehead again. It was throbbing. He had to shut his eyes.

"Somebody bushwhacked you?"

"I guess so. Was everything taken from my wallet?"

"It seems like everything's there. No money, though."

"They took my money."

"How much was in there?"

"I don't know. Maybe thirty dollars."

"They did this to you over thirty dollars?" The man knelt down beside Joseph.

"What time is it?" The old man asked.

"It's almost eight-thirty."

"I've been here since last night!"

"Grandpa! Mr. Marino!" A girl's voice burst into the scene.

"Shannon?"

"I ran right over when I heard them call the sheriff. Are you hurt?"

"I'm in some pain, but I'll probably live."

"Who did this to you? What happened?" Joseph wondered how many times he would be asked these questions.

"Some teenagers...last night." He rubbed his cheek. It was covered with mud. From a distance a siren grew louder.

"Here comes the sheriff, Joseph. You're going to be fine now," the man assured. The siren pounded against Joseph's ears and sent waves of pain through his head. Soon he could hear several sets of feet pounding through the woods.

"I'll find out who did this," Shannon vowed as she rubbed her Grandpa's brow.

"No, Shannon. Let the sheriff handle this."

The sheriff led the new arrivals, a man in a blue uniform stood just at his side.

"Mr. Marino! What in the world happened to you?"

Joseph repeated his answer, his head still throbbing in pain.

Chapter 22

"This will only take a few minutes, Mr. Marino." The deputy unfolded his notebook.

"What else do you need to know? I told you everything that I remember when we did this yesterday." Joseph laid back in his hospital bed. He had talked more in the last two days than he had since the time of Anne's death.

"I just need to clarify a few things and ask a couple of questions," the deputy said patiently. "Sometimes our memory clears up after a few days."

"What is it this time?"

"The voices you heard. Tell me about them again." The deputy sat down next to the bed.

"They were male. Sounded like teenagers."

"Did you hear any names? Any identifying words or remarks?" The deputy was writing.

"No." Joseph looked toward the ceiling like he was trying to look backward in time. "One boy did call out a name, what was it..." His fingers absentmindedly traced the bandage on his forehead. "Isaac...no... Isaiah!" Joseph said, now confident.

"Anything about him that you remember?"

"Too much," Joseph said, remembering his grocery store run-in.

"You know him?"

"Unfortunately. He has orange hair. Shannon could tell you his last name."

"Yes, we've talked to Shannon and the pieces are definitely coming together. Tell me about the other voice."

"It was a husky voice."

"Well from that and what Shannon said, it was probably Tim—her boyfriend. Well, this just about wraps it up." The deputy started to rise.

"So what happens now? Do you have to talk to the boys or something?" Joseph wondered how Shannon was handling all of this.

"No, that won't be necessary. Tim already came over to our office the other day and told us the whole story. Since it matches what you have told me, we pretty much have all we need."

"Tim? He confessed?" Joseph was surprised.

"Well, his girlfriend had something to do with it." The deputy returned the notebook to the vest pocket of his jacket.

"What about Isaiah...he's the one that did it, I think."

"We're looking for him right now. I'm sure we'll get him, sooner or later. We know who his family is, if you could call them that, and where he lives. It's a matter of time." The deputy zipped his jacket up.

"Before you go," Joseph paused.

"Yeah?"

"What'll happen to them? I mean, they're just kids."

"They'll probably do some time in the juvenile facility. Tim's seventeen."

"And Isaiah?"

"Same age…same situation. It's really up to the judge."

"They did this, but I can't stop thinking…" Joseph looked out the window.

"Thinking what?"

"Have you ever seen how these kids live?"

"Well, I guess so. I have to deal with them all the time. They're always causing problems in the cafe or in the store." The deputy changed his voice to a whisper, "If you ask me, this is a blessing in disguise to get some of them in lockup instead of harassing our community."

"How can we blame them completely for this kind of behavior when they're growing up alone?" Joseph stunned himself as he heard the words come out of his mouth. He sounded like Anne.

"That's not my job, Mr. Marino. Believe me, I'd really prefer that the parents would deal with them, and not me."

"So, what's next?" Joseph asked. The deputy stopped at the doorway and turned around.

"You'll be seeing them in court."

Joseph turned and looked out the window at the haze of the city and sank back into his hospital bed, alone with his thoughts.

Chapter 23

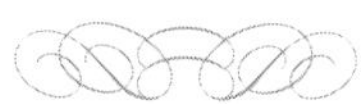

"Well as long as you have someone who can stay with you for a couple of weeks to help, you are free to go. Do you think your son or daughter could come in?" Doctor Harman studied the old man's chart.

"My daughter has stopped in…" Joseph paused, realizing how odd it felt not to have Paul visit or call, "but there is no way she could get away for a few weeks."

"I'd feel a whole lot better releasing you today if I knew someone would be there. You'll still have the occasional bout of dizziness."

"But I'm doing fine. I've got a headache, but I've had quite a number of those in my seventy-eight years," Joseph said with a weary pleading in his voice. He was tired of the sterile room. Acutely aware that his days on earth were not limitless, he hated spending any of them inside the hospital.

"I want to check your pupils. You have a concussion, Mr. Marino, and you've had very few of those in your life. Let's have another…"

Joseph fell back to the soft padding of the hospital bed. Doctor Harman thrust his left arm under the old man's shoulders just in the nick of time, preventing a nasty impact.

"Uhh…I'm…I mean…" Joseph mumbled.

"Ssshhh…just stay quiet. As I was saying, you'll have to slow down for a while. No more rock collecting for you for some time." The doctor handed Joseph a small black plastic wand. "Cover your right eye," Doctor Harman instructed.

"See any signs of intelligence in there, Doc?"

"Not much, but there appears to be a bit back in the corner of your brain, right next to that candy machine."

"Candy machine?" Joseph was confused.

"Yes…candy machine. It's the thing that keeps someone going. The hope of a reward."

"Can you tell what's in my candy machine?" Joseph shot back, with a sardonic half-grin on his face. "I'd sure like to know what my favorite candy bar is!"

"You've got the same candy that anybody else has; here, I'll check inside it. Cover up the other eye." The doctor asked politely, with a touch of curiosity on his tongue. Joseph complied and switched the hand-held eye patch to his other eye.

"Well?"

"Just as I thought…M and M's!" Doctor Harman smiled.

"What?"

"M and M's. Mother and marriage." The doctor started to return his instruments to their case.

"Mother and marriage? What the heck are you talking about?" Once again, Joseph was touching his bandages.

"Leave the linen alone," the doctor quickly corrected him. "Poking and scratching at your head will only bring on more bleeding and an infection!"

"What are you getting at with this M and M's business?" Joseph returned the doctor to his earlier statement.

"Everyone desperately needs all-accepting love and companionship. Mother and Marriage…M and M's! Relationships. Children. You're no different, Joseph." Doctor Harman sat down on his swivel stool and wheeled over to the short counter desk.

"But I've had all of that. A great mother and a great wife. Two children who I'm proud of. My candy machine is full," Joseph said confidently.

"It was, that's true," the doctor paused. "But, you have to keep restocking it. You've let the inventory drop." The doctor scribbled some notes in Joseph's bulging chart.

"I came in here for a patch-up, and now I'm getting counseling." Joseph tried to make light of the situation but he knew there was a lot of truth in the man's words.

"You're a lonely, hurting man, Joseph."

"What can you expect at my age, with my situation? I have a lot to be thankful for. Paul's a computer guy down in San Diego. Sarah has her own business here in Bakersfield. In fact, Bakersfield Memorial, this very hospital, is her client," Joseph said with obvious pride.

"What? She works at this hospital and she hasn't been in to see you all week?" the doctor shot back.

"She has other clients, too. Two kids, a hectic job and...and...damn. Who am I trying to convince? I see her four times a year. I miss her more than I can say. And Paul, well, I see him about once every five or six years." Joseph stared at the imitation oil painting hanging on the wall.

"Joe...please. I didn't want to kick you at a time like this. What I meant to say was that, well, I've been watching you from my office window up on Pine Mountain, and I always see you walking up Mil Potrero. Alone. Over the many Fridays I've spent up in the mountains recently, I've never seen you with anyone else. Your only companion seems to be that broken-down wagon you pull." The doctor ended his statement, but he looked as if he wanted to say more. Joseph looked away. The doctor bowed his head, giving Joseph a bit of emotional privacy.

"It was a cart. I used it to haul stones. Thanks for your care, and for your help, Doctor. How do I check out?" the old man said, as if to a complete stranger. The doctor put down the chart, sat quietly for a few moments, and then looked into Joseph's eyes.

"Joseph, please. I want to help. I've never considered my job to be one of simply mending broken flesh. I wanted to be a teacher, to help kids. My father pushed me into medical school. I love medicine, but my real rewards are found in the smiles of my patients. You have a kind smile, Joseph. A warm, caring smile. But I see it so rarely anymore." Harman's eyes seemed too intense for Joseph.

"I was a high school teacher," Joseph offered. "Up until Anne and I decided to retire." Saying her name aloud still brought back the pain of that night.

"How long has she been gone?"

"Too long. Over three months," Joseph whispered.

"You miss her terribly, I can see."

"Terribly. More than terribly. I think Paul and Sarah don't want to visit with me because, well, because I'm not the same anymore. They know it, I know it—but I can't change it." Joseph threw up his hands.

"Are you sure that's why they stay away?"

"Doc," Joseph said as he reached for his shirt. He was determined to leave, no matter what the doctor said. "To tell you the truth, I'm not sure of anything anymore."

"You've given all you could for them. Surely you could call one of them and ask them to stay a while," Harman said, pushing a bit harder.

"I'll try, but I think it's a waste of time. They learned how to be busy from the best. Me. So many times I was too busy for them. Turn around is fair play, isn't that what they say?" There was bitterness in Joseph's voice.

"Maybe this can be the opportunity to turn things

around. Call someone." The doctor pointed at the nearby phone.

"I'll tell you what, I'll call my daughter if it will get me out of here quicker. No offense, Doc." Joseph reached for the phone and entered the number. Silence filled the room as he waited for someone to answer at the other end of the line.

"Hello?" a young one said.

"Hi, Laura? This is Grandpa!"

"Grandpa! Are you feeling better now?" a happy, girlish voice responded.

"As good as new," he lied.

"Where are you? Are you still in the hospital?"

"I'm still here, but I think if I give the Doc some chocolate, he will let me go home today."

"D'ya want me to get my mother?"

"Thanks Laura." Joseph held the line as the girl yelled "*Moooommmm.*"

He could tell that Laura had put down the receiver and was running down the bright hallway he remembered fondly...the one with garden windows at each end. He could tell because he heard the sounds of her shoes clapping on the tile he had put down years ago for his daughter. His thoughts drifted back to that week. Anne brought the tile over when he needed more. Sometimes a cold soda was on top of the stack of tiles she held. He strained to see her face from that day, but just like his memory, the images of her face were fading. He wondered if there would be a day when he couldn't picture her at all. The thought terrified him.

"Dad? Are you there? Hello? Dad?" an older female voice asked.

"Hi Sarah." Joseph tried to recover quickly.

"What's up?"

"I'm trying to get out of the hospital today, but Doctor Harmon insists that I have someone stay with me before he will sign the release papers." Joseph paused; he hated being so dependent on another person. The only person he had ever been dependent on was Anne. "It would be a couple of weeks."

"I wish I could Dad," Sarah said, somewhat distracted. Joseph could hear the kids calling for her attention in the background. "There is no way I could get off from work, and Michael is going to be traveling so I have to be home with the kids," Sarah sounded apologetic. "I could pick you up today, though," Sarah paused. "You could stay here for a few days, but you would be alone part of the day while I am working."

"I would like to see the kids. I can live with that." The doctor was listening in on Joseph's call, and he conveniently did not repeat aloud the fact that he would be unaccompanied part of the day.

"What time are you being discharged?" Sarah asked, only paying half attention to the call. She was obviously focused on the children running underfoot.

"Hold on." Joseph covered the mouthpiece and turned to Doctor Harman. "Well, a few days at my daughter's place is the best I'm going to get. How much longer until I can go?"

"Two hours. Can you stay at her house for a week or two?"

"Probably." Joseph lied again before continuing his call. "You can pick me up in two hours."

"See you then." Sarah quickly hung up the phone.

"Bye," Joseph replied slowly although Sarah was already gone. He repeated the word as he replaced the handset. He felt a strange sense of loneliness.

"Joseph—can I ask you something?" Doctor Harmon interrupted his thoughts.

"What is it?"

"You know a lot of people up there on Pine Mountain call you the 'Stone Man,' don't you? What have you been doing all this time with those rocks?"

"The 'Stone Man'?" Joseph repeated the words, liking the sound of them. "I've been called a lot worse."

"I have to admit—the rumors have you a bit crazy, lugging rocks all the time. I know better. But I confess, I do wonder what on earth you are doing."

"Building a wall, pure and simple. I enjoy working with my hands. I like to build things. It's cheap therapy, I guess." Joseph gestured with his arms out wide.

Chapter 24

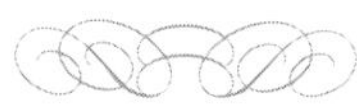

Joseph slowly unlocked the door to his cabin. It seemed strange coming back from the hospital with Sarah's family. So many times he had driven the long strip of Highway 99 with Anne. He wondered how he could feel so lonely inside a minivan full of family.

"Are you sure you'll be all right, Dad?" Sarah asked as she put the bright yellow duffel bag down at the front door.

"Of course I will. You picked up some groceries for me. I think that I still have electricity…I paid the last bill…" Joseph lifted his eyebrows. Sarah moved closer to her father. She lowered her voice.

"You know what I mean. Those teenagers who did this to you. What about them?"

"The sheriff will handle them. He knows who they are."

"Oh great." Sarah frowned. "You told the sheriff who those kids are? They'll be after you for snitching on them, Dad!"

"I didn't 'snitch.' I told the truth. What choice did I have?" Joseph returned the keys to his right front pocket, then he tried the door. It opened with a squeak, as it always had.

"You should get a dog. A pit bull or a rott. They'll take care of those hoodlums."

"Maybe a dog would be nice. It does get kind of lonesome out here sometimes." Joseph liked the thought of a warm presence to greet him.

"Well, I'm glad to see you still have some sense." Sarah turned and walked back to her car, instructing Michael to take the groceries in.

"Just set them there, Mike." Joseph was the only person Michael allowed to use that name. He set down the groceries and looked up.

"Joseph, I was thinking, maybe Joey and I could stay up here for a couple of days. Sarah could drive back on Monday and..."

"I have to work on Monday," Sarah interrupted. "My supervisor is already unhappy."

"Then I can take the day off," Michael offered. "There's nothing *that* pressing." Michael's voice tapered down to a whisper when he was able to get a good look at his wife's expression.

"The kids Michael...we really need to spend some time with them. They haven't seen you in almost a week."

Michael shook his head reluctantly.

"Yeah. I just hate to see you up here all alone, especially after what you've been through." Mike grabbed Joseph's upper arm and quickly pulled away when Joseph let out a cry.

"Sorry…I couldn't remember which arm was hurt." Michael grimaced an empathetic pain.

"Well, you had a fifty-fifty chance, and you blew it. Don't take too much money to Las Vegas…you can't seem to beat good odds…" Joseph tried to smile. "I have an idea," Joseph offered. "Why don't you two grab lunch across the street, and I'll make sandwiches for the munchkins."

Sarah looked at Michael.

"My treat," Joseph urged, pulling a twenty out of his pocket.

"Sounds like a deal to me." Michael reached for the money. Joseph was grateful—he wasn't looking forward to the familiar silence that would come once they left.

Sarah helped the little ones out of the van. They had been asleep and were trying to wake up by rubbing their eyes.

"Come on, kids…Grandpa's going to make you sandwiches," Sarah said cheerfully.

Joseph smiled at Michael. "I knew she'd come around."

"So, what'll you kids have for lunch?" Joseph asked, rubbing his hands together beneath the old sink's warm water.

"Cake!" Laura shouted.

"Ice cream!" Joey added.

"I don't know if your Mom would be too happy about that."

"Come on, Grandpa, just this once..." Laura jumped up and down. "We won't tell."

"I'll tell you what. You eat one of my special sandwiches, and then you can have all the ice cream you can eat!" Joseph turned toward the counter and reached for the bread.

"What kind of sandwich?" Laura asked.

"You like peanut butter and jelly, don't you?" Joseph pulled the ingredients from the refrigerator.

"Yeah...but that's boring."

"Not the way I make it." Joseph pulled out one piece of bread, cut it into quarters and spread peanut butter on two of the pieces. On the other pieces he dabbed a little jelly. He pressed the two together and then reached for the old cookie cutters that had seen many a Christmas. It was a trick Anne had taught him. They had used it often to make sandwiches for their own children. He chose a very small heart shape and gently pushed it through the soft bread. "Voila!" he announced.

"Cool!" Laura yelled in amazement.

"Coo..." Eddie tried to echo.

Joseph smiled as the two little ones each grabbed a mini sandwich. In two bites, they were both done.

"Now can we have ice cream, Grandpa?" Joey asked.

"Well...let's see. Did you have a sandwich?" Joseph winked.

"Yes!" Both children shouted at once. Joseph opened the freezer and placed two very large scoops into bowls.

"That sure is a big scoop, Grandpa!" Laura exclaimed.

"That's right, but how many scoops did you get?" he asked.

"One," Laura smiled.

"So...you had a sandwich and one scoop of ice cream, right?"

"Right," the kids said in unison.

"Grandpa?" Shannon shouted from the rear porch. Joseph turned from watching the children do battle with the mountain of ice cream in front of them.

"Shannon! How have you been?" He rose and walked toward the door.

"I'm fine—more importantly, how are you? When did you get out of the hospital?" Shannon fidgeted, rubbing her hands up and down her pant legs.

"Just a few days ago," he said quickly. "What's going on? You look nervous."

"I'm worried," she said simply.

"About what for Heaven's sake?"

"Aren't you mad?"

"Mad? At you?"

"Yeah." Shannon looked down.

"Why? You haven't done anything to hurt me?"

"But…Tim. He did."

"So when did you become Tim?" Joseph managed a weak smile. He opened the screen door and gestured with his head for her to come in. Shannon flashed a relieved smile.

"Want some ice cream? Better hurry…they're eating me out of house and home!" He gestured toward the kitchen table.

"Chocolate?" Shannon asked.

"Neapolitan. Chocolate, vanilla, and strawberry—two gallons of it." Shannon slowly walked past Joseph, into the kitchen. She stopped when she noticed that he was holding his arm next to his side unnaturally.

"Your arm…is it broken?"

"It had a hairline fracture and some sprains. It will be fine in a couple of weeks. Nothing to worry about…" Joseph stretched his arm as much as he could, trying to minimize the wound.

"I'm so glad you are all right," she said softly. She wrapped her arms tightly around him. "I'm so sorry."

Joseph found comfort in the girl's warmth. Before he broke down, he diverted her attention. "You better get some ice cream before it's gone."

"…and the trial is next week. Tim's mom is really mad at him." Shannon blurted in between bites. She had been bringing Joseph up to date on the latest news.

"Next week?"

"Yeah. Didn't they tell you?"

"They probably didn't know I was at my daughter's placc," Joseph shrugged.

"What will you do?" Shannon asked.

"I'll do whatever the court asks of me. I'll tell the judge what happened."

The girl put her spoon down slowly and sat back. She looked out the window.

"I have to, Shannon." Joseph knew she was trying to be strong but was torn between her love for him and her love for Tim.

"I know. It's just that I wish Tim had never met that idiot. Things used to be so different."

"Grandpa," Joey interrupted, "she said a bad word!" His small hand pointed an accusatory finger.

"You're right, Joey. Shannon…bad girl!" The old man feigned a slap on her arm. Shannon smiled.

"Sorry, Joey…I shouldn't say that word."

"I thought you big kids knew all about what was right…" Laura offered.

"Hah! I thought that you little kids knew!" Shannon responded.

"Wait a minute…none of you know?" Joseph looked surprised.

"You do, Grandpa!" Joey announced proudly.

"That's not true Joey…even I make my share of mistakes."

"We're back," Sarah announced from the living room.

"So soon," Joseph rose from the table. "I didn't hear you come in."

"Of course not. The screen door is wide open, stuck against the chair."

"No wonder I felt a breeze…" Joseph shrugged.

"Ice cream?" Sarah looked from Joseph to the kids.

"We had a sandwich first, Mom!" Laura smiled reassuringly.

"Let me guess…you had a tiny little sandwich." Sarah knowingly turned to her father. He smiled faintly.

Joseph walked up to the passenger's side of the minivan and gently rubbed Sarah's arm.

"Don't be too hard on them, Sarah. It was my idea. You know that."

"I know, Dad. It's not the ice cream that I'm upset about."

"What is it?"

"I'm just afraid that I am losing you, too."

"Me? Nah…I'm a tough old bird. It takes more than a rock in the head to get me. Got to get me in my soft spot…" The old man smiled.

Sarah grabbed her father's arm. "I remember always grabbing you like this when I was scared."

"Like the time I pulled you out of the swimming pool in that motel years ago?" Joseph patted his daughter's arm.

"Like that," Sarah smiled. A tear found its way down her cream-colored cheek.

"Love is like that, honey. For the rest of time I'll always love you like you were my little girl." Joseph kissed her softly and wiped the tear from her cheek.

"Can I walk you home, Shannon?"

"I'd like that," she replied. They had just finished cleaning the last remnants of ice cream from the kitchen table.

"Why are you so quiet?" Joseph asked as they walked along the roadside.

"My family is such a mess compared to yours, Grandpa. It just makes me think."

"About what?"

"I wish I could have grown up like Laura is."

Joseph looked up at the mountain towering over the community. He took a deep breath.

"I wish that I could have fixed that for you, Shannon. Look up at the mountain a second." He stopped on the side of the road. Shannon stopped and looked up.

"I've seen it a million times."

"But have you looked at it. Really looked? There's a difference."

"It's just a mountain."

"How big are you compared to that mountain?"

"Me? I'm not even six feet tall."

"Can you tear down that mountain, Shannon? With a spoon?"

"No, that's ridiculous. What type of question is that?"

"Do you worry about not being able to tear it down?"

"What? I don't even think about it...why should I even want to?"

"Some people don't like mountains. Mrs. Fowler likes the plains better. She's from Iowa."

"So?"

"She's always telling people that she wished she could flatten that old mountain."

"That's stupid. Why doesn't she just move to Iowa?"

"Because her husband likes that mountain. He wants to live here."

"So?" Shannon shook her head and raised her palms.

"Do you find something you like from having that mountain around?"

"I guess...It is pretty with snow on it. It gives us cool water in summer."

"Ah-ha! Something good from it! Mrs. Fowler always complains that it boxes us in and made it tough to get out in the winter. See what I'm getting at?"

"Not really."

"You've had a rough childhood, there is no doubt about that."

"Yeah," Shannon agreed.

"I know you hurt because of it, but..."

"...but I can get something out of it, is that it?" Shannon began to draw pictures in the sand by the road. Joseph nodded.

"What could you learn from what you've gone through?" Joseph touched her upper arm.

"That what a kid really wants is a good mom and dad?" Shannon asked tentatively. Joseph raised his eyebrows.

"You are a bright one!" He smiled as he reached out and took her arm, before continuing the walk toward her house.

Chapter 25

JOSEPH OPENED THE CLOSET DOOR AND PULLED out his favorite tweed jacket, the one with the patches sewn in the elbows. He stopped and remembered when Anne had given it to him as a Christmas present. Ever so gently he stroked the lapel.

"It seems like everything I touch reminds me of you, Annie." Joseph whispered. He picked up his glasses case from the table in the hall and slid it into the inside vest pocket, but something was resisting the sliding of the case. He pulled it out and reached inside. He felt around and discovered a piece of paper…no… an envelope. He pulled it out and warmth surrounded him. It was another of Anne's little stationery envelopes. The word "Joseph" was written across the front in Anne's handwriting. A little heart was on the bottom left corner.

He turned the envelope over. On the back was some writing he couldn't make out. Quickly, he put his glasses on, bringing the script into focus. It was a doodle of Anne's initials. A. M. She used to do that on her love letters to him, so many years ago. Of course, the last letter wasn't "M" back then.

Dear Joey,

I never did thank you for saving my life in the backyard a couple of weeks ago, so I decided to write this to you.

I know that I dont have much time left. But because of you I have some time left. Because of you, I can see my children one more time and tell them that I love them. Because of you, I can sit and enjoy the beauty of Pine Mountain. I can breathe in the clean air and see how blue the sky is...one more time.

You've given me another chance. More important than anything, I can spend another day at your side; another day with my soul mate. I know it's hard knowing that any day now I may be gone...but we can let go of all of the things that are meaningless and really live. Because of you, I can find the peace of focusing on my faith and my family...and be happy.

I dont know...I'm writing these notes wondering if you'll think that I've lost it. Maybe I'm crazy.

Keep looking, "man that I love." There will be more notes from me to you…I just hope that they touch you how I wish to touch you—with love…

Dont think I'm too crazy…

I love you.
Annie

Joseph walked slowly back to his room and opened the little handmade wooden box on Anne's dresser. Lovingly, he picked up the first letter and held them both close to his chest.

"I'll always keep you near me," he whispered softly, before tucking the envelopes into his inside pocket.

"The State calls Joseph Marino," the bailiff announced from the side of the judge's bench. Joseph rose slowly, taking liberty with his age. He made his way to the area in front of the judge.

"Joseph Marino?" the man asked. Joseph nodded.

"Please place your left hand on the Bible and raise your right hand."

"Like this?" Joseph asked nervously.

"Do you swear to tell the truth, the whole truth, and nothing but the truth, so help you God?"

"I do," Joseph affirmed.

"Please take a seat," he pointed at the witness stand.

The prosecuting attorney walked toward him and stopped about seven feet away.

"Please state your name and occupation, for the record."

"Joseph Marino, retired."

"Retired from what profession?"

"Teaching. I was a teacher," Joseph quietly said.

"Tell us what happened that afternoon by the creek, Mr. Marino."

Once again, hopefully for the last time, Joseph told his story.

Joseph quietly sat in the back of the courtroom, awaiting the entrance of the judge. It had been a tough couple of days, but it was almost over. He turned to look at the other side of the courtroom. There weren't many people observing the trial. The two boys who had assaulted him were out in the hall with their parents, or people whom Joseph assumed were their parents. He noticed a girl sitting with her mother on the opposite bench. He did a double take.

"Shannon?" Joseph asked. She was so dressed up. She looked so…so…grown up. She smiled when their eyes met, but they were quickly interrupted by the people in the hall who filed back into the courtroom. The boys walked slowly toward the front.

"All rise! The court is back in session!" The crowd

stood in silence. Judge Ashley walked quickly from the doorway to the bench. The bailiff approached the bench and began whispering to the judge.

Joseph looked down, wondering what Anne would do if she were the judge. These were the times when he missed her the most, when important decisions had to be made.

A crazy thought ran through Joseph's mind. He felt the warmth of Anne as a strong presence. He knew what she would do.

"Would the defendant Isaiah Moulton please rise?" Joseph shook his head. "In this matter that the State has brought before this bench, I find the following..." The judge shuffled some papers.

"Count one. Aggravated assault. I find the defendant guilty as charged. Count two. Robbery. I find the defendant guilty as charged. Sentencing will be done at one-thirty, after lunch." The judge shuffled more paper.

"Timothy Johnston. Please rise." Timothy meekly did as he was told.

"Count one. Accomplice to aggravated assault. I find the defendant guilty as charged. Count two. Robbery. I find the defendant guilty as charged. Your sentencing will be at one-thirty as well. Bailiff, take these two into custody pending sentencing." They were led out a door to the right of the judge's bench.

"This court is adjourned until one-thirty," the judge announced, his gavel striking hard.

Joseph looked over at Shannon, who stared down at her interlaced hands, a single tear rolling down her soft cheek. He longed to comfort her but felt awkward. Joseph's paternal love outweighed the awkwardness. He waited until the courtroom was mostly deserted and then approached her.

"Shannon," Joseph whispered. He rested a hand on her shoulder.

"What do you want?" Her voice was upset, but not accusing.

"I'm sorry."

"Me too."

"I wish that things could be different." Joseph took a seat beside the young girl.

"Tim's lawyer says that he could be in detention for a few years."

"I know. It's a high price to pay—but he has to be accountable for his decision. You understand that, don't you?"

Shannon stared ahead blankly. Then she slowly unclenched one hand and rubbed her lower abdomen. Joseph raised his eyebrows.

"Shannon?" he asked. "Do you want to get something to eat?"

She nodded simply, tears welling in her eyes.

Joseph scanned the dining area for an empty table; he found one toward the back.

"There's one..." They walked quickly toward it. Joseph pulled out a chair for Shannon; she hesitated.

"An old-fashioned habit of an old man. Go ahead and sit."

Joseph took the seat across from her and unfurled a napkin. Shannon watched, then followed his example.

"I'm not all that hungry," Shannon began.

"Well, you look like you haven't eaten in three days. I know how tough these emotional things can be on one's appetite." The old man smiled and pulled out one of Anne's letters from his pocket. Shannon smiled.

"You found another letter from Grandma?"

"Yep. This morning." He set the envelope on the table. "Here comes the waitress. What'll you have?"

"Not much. Really, I feel sick."

"How about soup and crackers?"

"Are you two ready to order?" the waitress asked.

"I think so. My granddaughter will have some of your cream of celery soup and some crackers."

"And you, sir?"

"Uh...a turkey and cheese sandwich...on rye."

"Anything to drink?"

"I'll have a root beer, and Shannon will have... is milk okay?" Joseph turned toward Shannon. She nodded.

"I'll be back with your drinks." The waitress left.

"How far along, Shannon?" Joseph finally asked while lining up his silverware.

"What do you mean?" she asked, a confused look on her face.

"Oh... I see," Joseph's heart felt heavy. "You haven't told anyone or been to the doctor, have you?"

"I..." Shannon stammered, looking for words.

"You're afraid. I understand. Especially considering what is going on today." Shannon nodded.

"My mother would be furious—and Tim's family, they have gone through enough."

"You can talk to me Shannon. Go ahead, try and say it."

"All right...please...don't say anything...please..." Shannon pleaded.

"About what?" Joseph prodded.

"You know. I'm...going to have a..." Shannon stalled.

"Ice cream sundae?"

"A baby!" she said, obviously flustered. But the relief with voicing the words felt incredible.

Joseph reached over and touched her hand. "There's nothing wrong with being pregnant."

"Please—don't say that word!"

"Well, face it, Shannon, you are."

"Do you see why I'm so upset?"

"Yes. I presume that Tim is the father. And he's going to jail." Shannon nodded.

"I don't know what to do."

"You have to tell your mother. How can you hide this from her?" He pointed at her stomach.

"I'll get an abortion."

Joseph tried to conceal his surprise at how easily those words tumbled from Shannon's mouth.

"I can't raise a kid," she said, defending her position.

"What about adoption?" Shannon didn't reply.

"Shannon," Joseph leaned forward. "Do you love Tim?"

Shannon stared down at her stomach for a long moment before raising her eyes to meet his. She nodded yes.

Joseph took a sip of his root beer, wishing that life could be easier for the precious girl in front of him.

"We'd better get back. It's one-twenty!" Joseph blurted when he noticed the clock on the cafeteria wall. He quickly rose and pulled out his wallet. Shannon got up slowly.

"I'm not sure I can handle this, Grandpa."

"You will. And you'll sit with me."

Joseph, followed by Shannon, found his usual seat. Shannon's mother was not in the courtroom.

"All rise..." The bailiff announced the entry of the judge.

"I would like to hear arguments and recommendations for sentencing prior to my decision." The prosecutor rose to speak first.

"Pssst...Shannon...remember...it's his job to make Tim look like the bad guy," Joseph leaned over and whispered to her.

"Your honor, these two are not boys, they are men. They are criminals. They attacked a defenseless old man and tried to kill him. They robbed him and left him for dead. This should not be treated lightly, Your Honor. Make the punishment fit this crime. They must pay." After a long argument, and statements from the defense attorney, the judge nodded, and put his hand up.

"Mr. Marino?" The judge scanned the audience gallery.

"Yes, Your Honor." Joseph rose from his seat. He hadn't prepared for this. All eyes turned toward him as he began to play with his coat button.

"What is your opinion, Mr. Marino? This court is very sensitive to the rights and needs of the victims. What do you feel justice would look like in this matter?"

The button popped off Joseph's jacket into his hand. He looked at the judge and opened his mouth, but was unable to speak. He dropped the button into his inner vest pocket. His hand touched the envelope… the envelope from Anne. When he spoke, he felt the words were Anne's—not his.

"Maybe I'm old, or crazy, but it doesn't seem right to send these boys to prison as punishment. I'm sorry if I'm out of line, but Your Honor…" Joseph was almost stuttering. He looked down at Shannon. She had a surprised look on her face.

"Go on, I want to hear what you think." The judge, like most of the courtroom, listened intently.

"Well, Your Honor…" Joseph touched the letter in his pocket, garnering courage from Anne's words.

"I need help to finish my stone wall. I promised my wife, before she died, that I'd get it finished. Now that I'm injured it will be tough to do." He paused briefly to glance around the courtroom. Confused looks covered the observers' faces. "Perhaps they can help me out? They could fix my wagon and help me with my wall."

The two boys looked at each other in disbelief.

"You may have something here, Mr. Marino. I've seen too many kids who aren't accountable for what they have broken."

"I'm just guessing that it might help us all," Joseph shrugged.

"I hereby sentence both defendants to two years of probation and three hundred hours of community service working for Mr. Joseph Marino. They will report to the sheriff's deputy on a weekly basis. Any failure to do their community service and they will end up back here in front of me."

"This court is adjourned until tomorrow morning at nine o'clock."

Shannon reached up and grabbed Joseph's hand. She was crying. Tim walked slowly toward his newfound mentor, his mouth still open. Isaiah remained at the lawyer's table, shaking his head.

"Grandpa…you did this for Tim? For me?"

"And for the baby. He, or she, needs a mother and

a father." Joseph smiled and extended a hand to meet Tim's offer to shake.

"Thank you, Mr. Marino. I'm really sorry..."

"I appreciate hearing that, Tim. I believe my wife and I made the right decision."

"Your wife?" Shannon was surprised.

"I have a feeling she had a hand in this," Joseph said, tapping his coat pocket.

Chapter 26

THE STARS WERE STILL OUT EARLY THAT FALL morning. Joseph took a moment to study the night sky. He often wished he had taken a few more astronomy classes over the years. Mars and Venus were easy to make out, and, of course, the Big Dipper, but so many of the other celestial objects remained a mystery. Joseph pulled the collar of his coat up closer to his neck as he stepped off of the rear porch. It had been difficult to sleep, so he had decided to get up and get things arranged before his new assistants arrived for the first day of work.

What a turn of events, he thought. Once he had silently cursed these boys and now they would be helping him finish the wall. Anne's wall. The judge had sentenced them both to two years of probation with weekly appointments to check in.

Joseph finished staking out the sections of the wall. A small redwood stake was placed at every point where the wall had to make a turn, or change direction to overcome a difficult slope.

The plan was not well thought out, Joseph realized after he had spoken up in court. Perhaps he had spoken too soon in his eagerness to ease Shannon's pain. What made him think they would respect his house—or him—after what they had done in the past? He pictured them standing on his front porch. The thought made him shudder.

Joseph had created a list of rules for this "community service." He typed them up the night before and made four copies. One copy was hung on the refrigerator, two were for the boys, and one was for him. He had drawn three lines across the bottom of his copy to allow for each person's signature.

The list was simple, he thought, and to the point. It had been his experience as a teacher that teenagers needed simple, straightforward rules and someone consistent in enforcing them. The white paper simply stated:

Rules of the House

1. Respect each other, the property, and yourself.
2. Do not use any room other than the living room, kitchen, or bathroom in the hall.
3. No smoking, tobacco, drugs, alcohol, or swearing.
4. Everyone helps with making meals and cleaning up.
5. Put tools away neatly when finished with them.

The sun would be coming up soon, Joseph thought as he picked up his tools. "Here goes nothing," he said under his breath.

Joseph heard a knock on the front door. Quickly, Joseph wiped his hands, tucked in his shirt, and checked his hair in the reflection of the toaster before he went into the living room. "Hold on…I'm coming," Joseph called out as he checked the clock in the living room. Seven o'clock. Too early for the boys to be here yet. Joseph opened the front door. There was a neatly dressed woman and Tim was standing behind her.

"You're early; I wasn't expecting you until eight." Joseph opened the door wider.

"I know he is supposed to be here at eight, but I have to leave for work now, and I wanted to make sure that he got here." The woman was obviously nervous. She fidgeted with her car keys. "Would seven be okay?" she asked with a soft voice.

"That's fine," he assured her.

"Stay out of trouble while I'm gone." The woman's voice changed dramatically when she turned to address her son.

"Mom…I'm not going…"

"Yeah, I've heard that before," she said under her breath. "That's how you got into this mess. You told me you weren't going to hang out with that Isaiah character."

"Mom…I'm not anymore…why don't…" Tim looked young and vulnerable under his mother's harsh words. He glanced up at Joseph, shame and embarrassment clouding his eyes.

"That's enough. Listen, Mr. Marino…thanks for getting him off of the hook. He doesn't deserve this, but I appreciate it."

"No problem…I know that jail would be…" Joseph started.

"Embarrassing," she interrupted. "Yes. I would have been humiliated." The woman rubbed her upper arm. "I appreciate you thinking of me." Tim turned away from the conversation and stared at the mountain.

"Actually, I thought it would have been hard…"

"Hard! You're darn right it would have been hard," she interrupted again. "Driving to the jail for visits. Of course, I'd have to visit. What would people think if I didn't? Yes, this is much better." She turned back toward her son.

"Don't screw this up!" she directed with a pointed finger.

"Ma'am, I don't think you understand. I meant…" Joseph felt her interruption coming before he could finish his sentence.

"You're right; I don't understand. I've given this kid everything. I work my finger to the bone so that he can have his video games, his expensive tennis shoes." She began counting the items on her fingers. She caught a glimpse of her watch.

"Look at the time! I've really got to go…Mr. Marino, I've appreciated our talk this morning!" She stretched out an open hand toward Joseph.

"Um…my pleasure." Joseph looked at Tim and raised his eyebrows.

The woman walked off quickly toward her car. It was a new one. It still had the paper plates one gets at the car dealership. Tim just nodded when his mother waved at him.

"Sorry, Mr. Marino. She's like that with everybody."

"Does she ever hear anyone?" Joseph asked.

"Not me. All she ever does is complain about how I never appreciate anything she does for me."

"Do you?"

"I guess not. Why should I? She never listens to me."

"What's in the bag, Tim?" Joseph pointed to Tim's left hand. The two had gone inside and sat on opposite sides of the kitchen table.

"Oh…breakfast. I hope you don't mind. We went to the cafe and my mother got something to go for me."

"Let me see it." Joseph signaled for the bag. Tim handed it over and Joseph looked inside.

"Cold egg sandwich on toast! How appealing…" Joseph rolled his eyes.

"That's better than my normal choice."

"Which is?" Joseph didn't think he wanted to know.

"A couple of Toaster Tarts."

"Okay Tim," he said gently. "For starters, you will need a real breakfast if you're going to do some real work for me. From now on, you come at seven and we will eat together." Joseph wondered how he could be so kind to this boy who had assaulted him a few short weeks ago. Even now, there was something different about him. When he talked to him and saw him without the walls he had built around his heart, he didn't seem so tough. In fact, Joseph thought, he seemed like a little boy.

"You won't tell my mother, will you?" Tim asked nervously.

"Not if you don't want me to. Why?"

"She doesn't like me taking anything on charity."

"Charity? We'll call this 'wages.' Meals are included with this job."

"I like that." Tim smiled tentatively.

"So how about scrambled eggs and bacon?" Joseph leaned over from the refrigerator, looking at Tim from behind the door handle.

"That sounds great."

"How many?" Joseph held two eggs up.

"I dunno…I've never made them before. Ten?" Tim guessed.

"Ten! I know you're big and hungry…but ten would feed five people! How about starting with two?" Joseph asked and Tim nodded.

"I'll tell you what. I'll cook the whole pound of bacon. Besides, I love the stuff myself." He smiled as he brought the frying pan out of the cupboard and turned on the stove. Within minutes the kitchen was filled with the tantalizing smells of bacon frying and eggs being turned over.

"Do you like orange juice?" Joseph asked while turning over some bacon.

"Sure." Tim sat up.

"In the refrigerator…I've been defrosting some. Can you dump it into a pitcher?"

"Okay." Tim walked over to the refrigerator, opened it, and started looking around. "Look at all of this real food in here!"

Joseph glanced over his shoulder. "What do you keep in your fridge? Dogs?"

"Not much. Beer for Jack and some wine for my Mom. Sometimes we have real food, like peanut butter." Tim forced a smile.

"Who's Jack?" Joseph decided to pry a bit.

"Jack's my mother's husband."

"So what do you eat for dinner?" Joseph turned the bacon strip nearest the edge.

"My mom usually leaves me some money for the diner." Tim found the orange juice and pulled it out. "Other times I bum off of friends. Shannon usually makes me a sandwich at her house." Tim stopped quickly. "But don't tell her mom."

"Don't worry, I won't. You and Shannon are pretty close, huh?" Joseph pulled a plate from the upper cupboard. It was an old, cracked one. He stopped, looked at Tim, and put it back. He pulled out some of the newer ones.

"Yeah, I guess." Tim blushed a little.

"What're you embarrassed about? You like her… she likes you." Joseph set the plates on the counter and scraped the eggs onto one of them. He plopped seven pieces of bacon next to the eggs. He slid the remainder of the bacon onto the other plate.

"I dunno…I guess I'm just not used to talking about this stuff." Tim shrugged as he stirred the juice.

"You don't talk to your Dad?" Joseph acted casual, wanting to know more without scaring him off. He grabbed some silverware and set it softly next to the plates.

"Nah. He took off when I was a kid."

"What about your stepfather?"

"He's not my step-anything." His voice took an angry and defensive tone. A shiver ran through Joseph. "Like I told you, he's my mother's husband."

Joseph decided not to push any further. For now.

Bang, bang. The sound came from the back porch.

"It sounds like we have more company." Joseph expected Isaiah, but Shannon stood in the doorway.

"Come on in." He ushered Shannon to the kitchen.

"Hey Tim," she said. Tim blushed and moved his arm in a small, elbow-at-the-side type of wave. "What's that smell?"

"Mr. Marino made me breakfast," Tim offered. Shannon turned to Joseph and smiled. She looked back to Tim and suddenly had the feeling that she was interrupting something.

"Is something going on?" Shannon asked.

"Not much," Tim said. "Just guy talk."

Bang, bang. Another sound…from the living room.

Joseph rose again, knowing that only Isaiah was left. Apprehension filled him.

Bang.

"Hold on…I'm coming…" Joseph picked up the pace.

Bang, bang. The knocking continued.

"Stop already," Joseph said, opening the door. He feigned a smile. "You must be Isaiah."

"Yeah…and you're Mother Goose." Isaiah looked at Joseph's outstretched hand and wiped his right hand on the sleeve of his jacket.

Joseph slowly pulled his arm in. He felt anger rising but decided to not let it get the best of him.

"That's me. Come in for some eggs?"

"What?" Isaiah shook his head in disbelief.

"Eggs! Mother Goose! Get it?" Joseph responded.

"Too weird, man…"

"Me? Oh, no…I'm the 'Stone Man'!" Joseph puffed out his chest, as if he were a comic strip superhero. Isaiah just shook his head.

Chapter 27

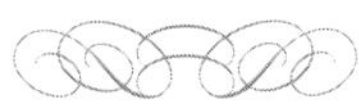

"NOW...LET ME SHOW YOU WHAT'S GOING on around here." Joseph started as they stepped off of the porch. Joseph was in the lead and moving quickly.

"Not much, dude!" Isaiah whispered just loud enough for Tim to hear and then started laughing. He turned and looked at Tim, hoping that he had struck a nerve of laughter in his friend.

"That's enough, Isaiah..." Tim said quietly.

"What? You talkin' to me? Are you telling me to 'shut up'?" Isaiah turned and squared off in front of Tim.

"Leave it alone, man..." Tim put his arms up, with the palms facing toward Isaiah.

"You're dogging on me, and you want me to back off? What kinda fool d'ya think I am?" Isaiah's volume was going up, making his British accent more obvious.

"Come on man, let off. We just got out of this mess. Stay cool."

"Is that what you are?" Isaiah mocked. "Mr. Cool?"

"Hey...you're the idiot that threw the rock and got us in this mess in the first place." Tim stood his ground.

"And you're the twerp that had to squeal to the sheriff," Isaiah mocked him in a childish voice.

"Boys, we have work to do so stop with the macho stuff."

"Shut up, old man. This turkey and I have something to settle!" Isaiah continued to stare at Tim. He moved forward.

"Don't talk to him like that," Tim said, quickly coming to the man's defense. Tim squeezed his fingers into a fist. Joseph slowed, not knowing how to handle the situation.

"Will you two stop?"" Shannon tried to push the two of them apart.

"Gotta have the cow rescue you, huh?" Isaiah sneered.

"Leave her alone!" Tim growled. Joseph reached for Tim's arm.

"Looks like you didn't! Got her knocked up, didn't ya?" Isaiah pointed at Shannon's abdomen. Tim quickly looked at Joseph, but there was no doubt, he had heard.

"Last time I try talking to you," Tim yelled as he threw a punch at Isaiah. It landed on the side of his orange head. Isaiah tumbled to the ground and came back up ready to swing.

"That's enough!" Joseph yelled. The tone in his voice even startled him. With a raw energy he hadn't felt in a long time, he pushed his way between the two boys. "What the hell are you doing?" he said, staring into Isaiah eyes.

"What are you talking about?" the boy asked. He hadn't been prepared for any rebuttal from the old man.

"I got you out of that mess with the court. One call and you're back in."

Isaiah took two steps back and held his hands up. "You saw him...he threw the first punch, Marino..." Isaiah pointed at Tim.

"Said the rattlesnake to the calf." Joseph shook his head.

"Wha...?" Isaiah looked confused.

"He may have thrown the first punch, but it was you who set the bait." Joseph grabbed him by the collar. "I have had it with you. You've hurt me, Shannon, my beloved Annie. You are on thin ice—and just about to break it." Although Joseph was much older, he was at least six inches taller and fifty pounds heavier than the orange-haired boy.

"Bravo! That sure does answer one of my questions." A male voice came from behind Joseph. He turned to find a deputy walking toward him.

"Oh...deputy...I didn't see you..." Joseph was flustered and afraid he'd gone too far. He released his hold.

"That's okay, I saw you, and what a show it was! Everybody down at the station would have paid good money to watch that performance. When you said you wanted to do this I was worried that you wouldn't be able to handle this spoiled punk." The deputy pointed toward Isaiah.

"Frankly, I was too," Joseph admitted out of Isaiah's earshot. "But I think we have an understanding now."

"I came over to make sure this guy wasn't giving you any trouble. It seems that you can handle any trouble that he can dish out," he smiled.

"You're not gonna arrest him, Rock Cop?" Isaiah was angry.

"Arrest him? For what? Stopping a fight between teenagers? No way."

"'Rock Cop'? What's that?" Joseph asked.

"Some of 'em call me that. They know I don't take any crap."

"I'm not going to take any, either, deputy...Isaiah either plays the game my way, or it's the highway," Joseph answered.

"The highway to the detention center." The deputy stared intently at Isaiah. "In my opinion, right where he belongs." Isaiah spat on the ground.

"I was about to explain how my project worked," Joseph pointed to the unfinished stone wall.

"Go ahead. I'm sure you have their attention now," said the deputy.

"So you find a stone that is about the right size and shape, then place it on the wall—kind of like this,"

Joseph demonstrated. "If it wobbles or slides, you try to flatten it to fit, by using the hammer." Joseph picked up a hammer and whacked at the underside of the flattened rock. He then placed it back on the wall. "See? Much better. Remember...each rock has to be fit properly. If it isn't then the ones above it will be loose, and the whole section of the wall could come down. Try a couple of different ones...until you find the right one."

"Let's have one of them try, Mr. Marino." The deputy pointed at the boys.

"Tim?" Joseph handed the hammer to him.

Tim walked over to the pile of stones and picked one out. He placed it on the wall and it wobbled dramatically when he checked its steadiness.

"Try another one, son," Joseph encouraged. Tim searched through the stones available and made a second choice. It was far less wobbly.

"It worked!" Tim smiled. He picked it up again and whacked a small piece off of the bottom. When he reseated it, the rock was steady.

"Great! You've got it!" Joseph said with pride.

"I'll leave you alone with them now, Mr. Marino. I think you can handle it."

Together, they turned to watch the three teens picking through the stones, sorting by size. Isaiah was lagging behind the other two.

"They'll be fine," Joseph assured him. "What's the problem with Isaiah, anyway?"

"He's racist, spoiled, and angry—that about covers it." The deputy paused before lowering his voice. "If you think he's bad, you oughta meet his father." He let out a low whistle.

"What's he like?"

"Racist, spoiled, and angry. The father infected the son."

"The mother?" Joseph inquired.

"Left years ago. Took off one night, I guess. They fought like cats and dogs." The deputy looked up to the mountain above.

"She left her child with a father like that?"

"She was piece of work, I tell you." The deputy seemed to enjoy sharing his town knowledge. "She probably slept with every guy on the hill!"

"Not every guy," Joseph clarified.

"Well, of course," the deputy said quickly.

Joseph stood on the little rise above the stone wall. The deputy had headed back toward town, and Joseph now admired the kids. It was an amazing sight, three teens stacking stones. Tim and Shannon worked diligently enough, but Isaiah always seemed to lag behind, taking more breaks than the other two.

Suddenly Shannon stopped, leaning on the fence. Tim was at her side, quickly helping her settle on a half-finished segment of the wall, one peppered with reddish-colored rocks.

Joseph made his way toward the couple. Tim grew quiet as he approached. He took a seat on Shannon's opposite side.

"I'm sorry about that," Tim offered about the earlier confrontation.

"I'm not worried about that," Joseph said. "But I am worried about Shannon."

"Don't go worrying about me, Grandpa."

"It's too late. I am worried, and Tim should be too."

Tim shuffled his feet in the dirt. "I am," he said quietly. "But I don't know what to do."

"The first thing is to get Shannon to a doctor."

"But," Tim pleaded. "The town is so small—our parents will find out."

"I'm sorry Tim," said the old man. "But the baby and Shannon are more important."

Tim nodded. He knew the old man was right.

"It's settled then. We'll make an appointment and you two will go in together and learn about your options."

Isaiah was slowly approaching them and Joseph quickly changed topics. "Drinks anyone?" he asked as he rose.

"Yeah…vodka and orange juice…" sneered Isaiah.

"Gotcha! Root beer it is!" Joseph stood up and went to the kitchen.

Joseph watched through the kitchen window while he

opened the root beer bottles. Tim had his arm around Shannon and was brushing away a wisp of her hair with his fingertips. Joseph froze for a long moment. Tim's touch, somewhat clumsy, reminded him of his own. Shannon's nervousness brought back Anne's memory. Before he became lost in thought, he quickly grabbed the bottles and headed back toward the wall.

"Who wants a drink?" Joseph offered the bottles. Tim and Shannon quickly grabbed one each. Isaiah lazily walked over and flippantly threw his arm around and swiped the bottle from Joseph's hand.

"Very good! You have talent, Isaiah!" Isaiah walked off, his permanent sneer mounted on his face.

"Why do you talk to him like that?" Shannon asked curiously, between sips of her drink. She had never received anything but respect from the old man.

"Like what?" Joseph replied. He was turning the root beer bottle around, reading the label.

"You act as if everything he says is a joke."

"Isn't it? How can anyone take *him* seriously!" Joseph smiled. Tim and Shannon returned the expression.

"He's as hardheaded as these stones," Tim said in a monotone, staring at Isaiah.

"I wonder what made him like that?" Shannon asked before taking a sip of her soda.

"What makes anyone hard-hearted? Fear. Pain," Joseph whispered.

"Hard-hearted?" Shannon asked.

"Yeah. I have this theory. If someone has been hurt a lot, they build a hardened crust around their emotions. They keep people away…no one gets close and they can't get hurt anymore," Joseph answered.

"And they spend the rest of their lives lonely," Shannon added.

"Like stones…" Tim finished.

"We're a lot like stones, too," Joseph took a long drink.

"How is that?" Shannon asked.

"Look at the way one stone is nested inside of the one below it." Joseph pointed to the wall.

"Yeah? So?" Tim asked.

"Each of us is like a stone. We ride on top of whatever our parents build as a foundation for us. Like this…" Joseph began to wiggle the top stone. The three under it moved as well.

"The higher the stone, the more the wiggling," Tim observed.

"Right. You are the top one, your mother is the one under you…and so on," Joseph continued.

"So, a long time ago something happened that made my family wobble?" Shannon asked.

"You could say that," Joseph answered.

"Will I be even worse?" Shannon looked worried.

"Not necessarily," Joseph said. "Look at the set of stones over here. Notice how this one," Joseph prodded one, "is wobbly, but the ones above it are solid?"

"How does that happen?" Tim asked.

"Each rock overlays the one below it, to the side. It can use one near it as a support, even if it isn't the 'parent' stone."

"So we just need the stones?" Tim asked.

"Exactly. Look for a rock to lean on. Find someone you can relate to, talk to, and count on. Someone older, who's been there before." In his heart, Joseph hoped he could be that person for the two teens before him.

"Count on an adult?" Tim questioned. "The only old thing I can count on helping me is my car."

"Some of the time," Shannon clarified, resting her head on his shoulder. She smiled.

"Okay, most of the time." Tim rolled his eyes.

"Kind of like my old coat here. It's something I've counted on for years. I know where everything is, and every little strange quirk about the coat. My eyeglasses go here, in the inner pocket..." Joseph reached into his pocket, stopping suddenly.

"Another one?" Shannon whispered.

"I think so," Joseph replied.

"Another what?" Tim asked.

"Grandma...uh...Mrs. Marino...left notes all around for him...before she...uh..."

"Before she passed away," Joseph whispered as he slowly pulled the paper from his pocket. He kept looking straight ahead.

"It's the same kind of envelope, Grandpa..." Shannon observed. "Open it!"

"Here goes." Joseph slowly and gently pulled at the corner. Silently, he read.

Hello, Joey!

I put this one in your coat because I knew it would be on your back in the early fall, when you are outside. Is it October? I hope that you are working on my wall.

There is one other thing I want to ask of you. So many times you asked me to climb Pine Mountain. Do it someday. I feel so guilty that I never said yes.

Thank you, again, for calling Paul for me. I know that you and he can heal your relationship.

I'll always love you, honey.

Annie

Joseph cleared his throat.

"Are you OK, Grandpa? Is it tough to read?"

"Uh…yeah…" Joseph found it difficult to speak. He handed Shannon the note. Tim leaned over and read it with her.

"She sure could count on your coat, Mr. Marino!" Tim whispered.

"Yes," Joseph said, his voice barely audible.

"Maybe you're the rock we need, Mr. Marino." Joseph turned to look at the two teens. Tim had his head down and was drawing circles in the dirt.

"This shaky old thing?" Joseph smiled.

"This solid as a rock old thing," Shannon corrected.

"Hey, when are we gonna finish this?" Isaiah yelled as he walked toward the group. "I thought we were supposed to be working."

"You're right, Isaiah! For once, you're right. We need to get back at it..." Joseph struggled to his feet.

"Yeah. There are a lot of stones around here that need a home..." Tim added.

Chapter 28

"GOOD TO SEE YOU HERE BRIGHT AND EARLY!" Joseph used the stone wall to help him stand. He gently tossed two stones to the ground.

"Well, two of us are here," Tim replied.

"Where's Isaiah?" Joseph asked as he wiped his hands on his sleeve.

"Who knows? Maybe, if we're lucky, he's decided to not show up again." Shannon threw her hair back.

"Hmmm..." Joseph looked around. There was no sign of the other boy.

"I'm hungry," Tim exclaimed.

"Of course you are. That's a constant!" Joseph joked.

"Yeah...but..." Tim swept his arm around toward the kitchen.

"Getting spoiled, huh?" Joseph smiled.

"I guess," Tim said, smiling.

"Well, you deserve it," Joseph led them toward the kitchen.

"Look at this! He had it all planned!" Tim exclaimed as he opened the kitchen door. In front of him was a table set with a cloth and china!

"Grandpa...what is this?" Shannon asked.

"I thought you two could help me out. I'm used to a special breakfast on October eleventh."

"Why?" Tim asked.

"It's our... or it was—our anniversary." He continued quickly, "So I can't eat all alone on my anniversary."

"Of course we'll stay," Shannon responded for them both. "This is wonderful."

"How do you like French toast?" Joseph asked, heading for the refrigerator.

"Love it!" Tim responded quickly.

"Is that what you used to have on your anniversary every year?" Shannon asked.

Joseph nodded. "Every year...for over fifty..."

"Is there anything I can do?" Tim asked. He had gotten used to helping Joseph prepare the breakfast.

"Not a thing. It was the one time of year I used to serve her. You two sit down. I need only the special centerpiece..." Joseph reached into the cupboard over the refrigerator and pulled out an aged box.

"What's the centerpiece?" Shannon turned to see.

"Our wedding cake top. Two ducks...a male and a female." Joseph opened the box. He began lifting up the centerpiece, his hand stopping short.

"What is it?" the teens asked in unison.

"Another note..." Joseph whispered.

Happy Anniversary, Joey!

I knew you'd still have our ducks on the table in the morning. I'm sad that I cant be there this time. If you look at the male duck, he's sporting a lipstick kiss. It's for you. I'll be watching you and loving you—today and always.

Love, Annie

"Put the ducks here in the middle, Grandpa!"

"Nowhere else, Shannon!" The ducks took their spot in the place of honor. One of them had a big red kiss mark on the side.

"She is leaving quite a mark, isn't she Grandpa?"

"I would say." Joseph smiled at the centerpiece, then at the teens. Not only had she left behind the notes, she had left behind hope for the two children in front of them.

"What are you thinking?" asked Tim, noticing the furrow of Joseph's brow.

"I'm just amazed at how many of the things we leave behind are often those we don't plan or foresee.

"What have you left behind Grandpa? What didn't you foresee?"

"Too many things, honey," Joseph wearily shook his head. "I worked my rear end off years ago, thinking I'd give my kids a better life. But the price was I was never home. They grew distant from me. The one thing I wanted I couldn't really have. The love of my son." Joseph's fingers traced the mallard's back.

"You talk like you don't have any more chances," Shannon commented. "You can do something now."

"Yeah," echoed Tim. "If we can have another chance after what we did, surely you can, too."

"I'm trying. I've been trying to work the courage up to call him. But every time I just turn away. I just don't know what to say."

"How about what you just said to me?"

"You're a bright girl, Shannon." He smiled, knowing she was right.

"So, what're the plans for today, Mr. Marino?" Tim leaned back and rubbed his stomach. The French toast had left him comfortably full.

"We need more stones for the wall." Joseph finished a glass of orange juice.

"So we go down to the creek and get some?"

"Nope. No way to get them back here."

"So we rent a truck?"

"Of course not!"

"So...how do we get the stones back here?"

"With the cart!" Joseph stood up and began clearing the dishes.

"The one we broke?" Tim said quietly.

"The same one. Also the one you'll fix." Joseph took the ducks and carefully placed them back in the box. When the two teens weren't looking, he quickly brushed his lips over the duck.

"I miss you, Annie..." he whispered faintly.

"I'll get some lemonade...I'm dying of thirst!" Shannon offered. The three had just returned from their scavenger hunt to find the cart. It had further disintegrated with time and it was all they could do to lug it, and its parts, back to home base.

Tim and Joseph stared at the gnarled mess. "Well, we'll have to start with those two pieces of wood and that main bolt," Joseph pointed. "It's bent."

"Do you have the parts?" Tim asked.

"Nah...we'll have to get them down at the hardware store."

"I'll go with you. I'm pretty good in a hardware store, you know."

"I'll bet you are!" Joseph was beginning to like this young man.

"I fixed my mother's sink once."

"Well today we will see how good you are at cart repair!"

Chapter 29

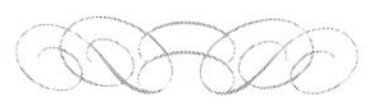

"Mr. Marino," said the store clerk. "It's good to see you. Certainly been awhile."

"Hi, Maggie," Joseph smiled faintly. He had never much cared for the pounds of gossip Maggie was always so eager to share.

"So," she said, sliding around the counter. "Did you hear about..." she stopped short.

"What is it?" Joseph asked only half-interested as he was studying some small screwdriver bits.

"It's some of those...teens," Maggie spoke quietly, gesturing toward the back of the store. Joseph turned to look. He didn't see anyone else in the store.

"In the paint section," Maggie said, wondering if what she heard was true and the old man was really losing it.

Joseph followed Maggie's gaze to where Shannon and Tim were looking at a paint can.

"Them? They're good kids...they just need some guidance." Joseph smiled.

"Are you kidding? Have you seen the one that they hang out with? That one with the orange hair?" Maggie grit her teeth. "They're all a pain in the behind."

"Actually, that particular one is a pain in the neck." Joseph smiled softly as he stroked his head.

"Huh?" Maggie turned back toward her customer.

"Nothing, Maggie, just cut them some slack."

"Slack? Just like they cut me slack when they leave soda cups and trash all over my porch? Every morning I have to clean up from the night before."

"Have you ever heard the story of the young bull elephants in the national park in South Africa, Maggie?" Joseph picked up a bolt.

"No…about what elephants?" Maggie looked confused.

"Bull elephants. They turned some rogue young elephants loose in a park. They tore the place up."

"Exactly. See what I mean. Bull elephants. Those…" she pointed toward Tim and Shannon, "teens are tearing this town up."

"Know how they fixed it?" Joseph questioned the sales clerk.

"Shot all of them?" she offered.

Joseph rolled his eyes. "Nope. They introduced older bull elephants. They started hanging around with the young ones. Within days the rampage had ended."

"So they should follow their parents," Maggie concluded her own moral from Joseph's tale.

"It's hard to follow someone who's not there, Maggie."

Joseph threw the bolt down on the counter.

"Not there? They're the parents."

"Oh…yeah. From midnight to six in the morning."

"So these kids aren't grateful? Parents have to work to make a living."

"Sure. And pay for expensive new cars." Joseph suddenly felt claustrophobic in the store. "I'll just take this bolt and that wood. I can't get anything else here."

"Listen," Maggie punched the register keys. "These days people have got to work. Jobs are demanding."

"Like I didn't have to work in my day?" Joseph smiled and shook his head.

"No…it's just…different."

"How?" Joseph pulled out a five-dollar bill.

"Things cost more now."

"And we made less then. So?"

"You don't understand." Maggie shook her head. "Look, I spend as much quality time with my kids as anybody else."

"That's what scares me. I hear that line all the time. It's not about quality. It's about caring. Quality is for products." Joseph gestured to the store around him. "Caring is for people."

"But I care…" Maggie offered in her own defense.

"Yeah," Joseph commented. "How much do I owe you?" Joseph didn't meet her eyes as he handed over the money.

The old man gently pushed his hand forward, across his bald head. The water pooled in front of his pinkie finger, then ran into his face. He wiped the inside of his hat, then looked up.

"Ah, the Old Mountain calls to me again," Joseph said as he slipped the small bag from the hardware store into his coat pocket. The sudden burst of sunlight reflecting off the mountain caught him unprepared. He squinted in the crisp autumn sunlight.

"What's that, Grandpa?" Shannon hesitantly asked.

"This mountain and I have had quite a relationship over the decades," Joseph relayed to the two teens.

"A relationship?" With a mountain?" Tim chuckled. Shannon turned and frowned at her boyfriend.

"Well, it just seems strange," Tim defended.

"A lot of things seem strange when we don't understand them," Joseph offered.

"Well how is this for strange," Tim started, "I made some money this week and I want to buy you both lunch." Tim beamed as he held up a twenty-dollar bill.

"I've never turned down a free meal!" Joseph's pride matched that of the boy.

"Where shall we sit, Master Timothy?" Joseph grinned as he swept his arm around the almost empty room.

"Uh, I like the one in the back of the other room,

by the window." Tim answered, obviously uncomfortable at being treated so "royally."

"Then that's the place!"

"Hello, Mr. Marino!" an older woman called out.

"Guten tag, Frau Edie!" Joseph responded. He removed his hat and bowed, European style. He then began to walk toward the back room.

"Don't try your German on me, Marino! You have a lot to learn!" Edie, the owner, followed close behind.

"But, Edie! I am such a faithful student," Joseph feigned a complaint.

"Faithful eater, ya. Student? Nein!"

"Tim...do I work hard or not?"

Tim shrugged.

"See...the boy knows the truth!" Edie teased.

"He works harder on that wall than any of us, Edie," Shannon defended the old man.

"Are you still working on that silly wall up there on Bryce Court?" Edie smiled as she handed out the menus.

"It'll be finished this year, Edie. Just you watch." Joseph turned his attention to the menu.

"Ya! This year! Should I pick my flag now or later?" Edie asked Joseph.

"I mean it this time," Joseph said, trying to sound determined but feeling more like the little boy who cried wolf.

"Look, kids...we have a running bet. Each year that Joseph pronounces it to be completed, and it isn't, he has had to buy me a new small flag of some country.

In a couple of more years I will have all of Europe!" Edie pointed to a shelf full of flags high on the wall, behind some travel posters.

"What's the big one under the little ones for?" Tim asked.

"Ah...that's my side of the bet. He gets that one if he ever finishes." Edie laughed softly as she wrote down their orders.

"It's a pretty one. What country is it?" Shannon asked.

"Sweden," Joseph interjected without looking up from his menu.

Chapter 30

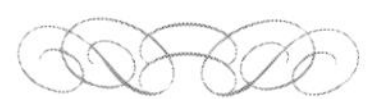

"THE TRICK IS TO USE A LOCKING WASHER. THAT holds it on a lot longer," Joseph said as he pointed at the right rear wheel of the cart. He was squatting, holding the back end.

"How does that help?" Tim asked.

"It's simple, really. The washer keeps pressure on the nut as it wedges against the back of the threads… here." The old man pointed at the bolt he had just installed. He always felt a certain pride, and a joy, in explaining mechanical things.

"How did you learn about this stuff, Mr. Marino?" Tim pushed his hat back.

"Well, a lot of places, really. My father, mostly. When I was in high school, I had a great shop teacher." Joseph wiped the mud off his hands with a rag that he pulled from his rear pocket.

"Hey…don't look now…it looks like we have company!" Tim pointed behind Joseph, toward the road. The old man turned to look just as a police truck pulled into the driveway.

They watched as the sheriff's deputy stepped out of the vehicle and went around to the other side. He opened the passenger door and Isaiah stepped out.

"I wonder what this is about," Tim started.

"I don't. He's supposed to be here. Obviously, the deputy caught him somewhere else." Joseph brushed off his pants as he rose.

"I see you found our 'lost sheep.'" Joseph commented as the deputy moved forward with a firm grip on Isaiah.

"Yeah, causing trouble down at the store. He said you sent him down there to pick up some drinks. I wanted to check with you before I hauled him away for probation violations. He was supposed to be working here." The deputy pointed at the boy's wrists. They were handcuffed. Joseph tried to look into Isaiah's down-turned face and then turned toward the deputy.

"Where are the drinks? Do you have them in the truck?" Joseph gestured toward the driveway.

"Drinks? You sent him to get drinks?" The deputy was obviously surprised.

"It took him long enough to get back." Joseph was staring at Isaiah.

"Whaa...?" Isaiah whispered.

"Drinks, son. Did you get my lemonade?" Joseph's eyebrows rose.

"I didn't have time..." Isaiah stammered.

"Listen, Mr. Marino, you don't have to play this game with me. I've been watching this one. You've cut him a lot of slack. The other one's been showing up…but…"

"I call him when I need him, deputy. That's all. Isn't that the main requirement of the deal with the judge? That they help me when I need it?"

"All that I'm saying is that you don't have to cover for this one. I nailed him red-handed. He was trying to walk out with a bottle of wine."

"White zinfandel, I hope? I wanted to celebrate the finish of the wall by breaking a bottle of wine on it…" Joseph smiled.

"It wasn't…and he wasn't old enough to buy alcohol…" the deputy added.

"Oh, well. What does he know about wine? Old enough? Well, I told him to ask the clerk to put a bottle aside for me. I guess he just wanted to make sure that he got it, and…"

"Okay—I've heard enough," said the deputy, definitely unconvinced. "But…" the deputy unlatched the handcuffs, "…this is it. One more problem and I'm taking him in, with or without your stories."

"Seems fair to me, right, Isaiah?" Joseph's look hardened as he stared at Isaiah.

"Yeah, right…whatever you say…" The deputy shook his head as Isaiah offered his indifferent reply.

"I'll be watching you like a mountain bobcat watches a gray-tailed rabbit, son," the deputy whispered to Isaiah, in a voice barely audible to the old man.

"I bet…" Isaiah rifled back and then stopped mid-sentence.

"I'm sure I'll be back here, Mr. Marino." The deputy was addressing Joseph, but staring square into Isaiah's eyes. The boy returned the scowl.

"Don't worry deputy, I'll take care of him." Joseph was also staring at Isaiah. Isaiah chuckled at the withdrawing law officer, but sobered quickly when he came face to face with the image of an angry Joseph.

Isaiah rubbed his wrists. A chuckle escaped him as he watched the deputy drive off.

"Funny? You think everything is funny?"

"Yeah. Funny. This is nuthin'."

"You call this nothing? Do you know what they'd do to you in jail? You'd be the bottom of the pile."

"I'm not scared of nothing," Isaiah shot back. "This is nothing compared to what I've lived through."

"So that's it," Joseph chided. "Now you're Mr. Tough Guy?"

"Look," Isaiah grew angry. "You couldn't handle half of what I've been through, so don't come talking your high and mighty stuff around me."

Joseph jumped across the open space between him and the boy. He grabbed Isaiah's arm.

"I've been through a lot more than you know," Joseph said in a low voice. An iron grip held his arm.

"So you're old lady died." Isaiah dismissed the man's pain. "We all die."

Joseph's grip grew tighter, and it was all he could do to keep his other hand from finding the boy's neck.

Instead, he picked up a wrench and tossed it to the boy. "Here...tighten the bolts and nuts on the railings of the cart. Now!" Isaiah stared at the tool.

"What's a matter? Never had to work with your hands before?" Joseph growled, his patience long gone.

"Back off," Isaiah responded.

"As soon as you start tightening! You don't seem to respond well to freedom or kind words, so I'll give you what you're probably familiar with: anger!" Joseph continued.

Tim backed toward the shed, wanting to distance himself from the explosions that emitted like fireworks between the two men. Shannon stood a few feet away from Tim, her back turned to the drama of Joseph and Isaiah.

"Tim, I think I felt the baby move," she announced breathlessly.

"Baby?" Isaiah stopped his work on the cart.

"What?" Shannon turned toward Joseph and Isaiah.

"Hey...get back to it, Isaiah!" Joseph reprimanded the boy repairing the cart.

"Well what'ya know—the cow got herself knocked up." A vicious laugh escaped Isaiah.

"Shut your damned mouth." Tim took one step toward the other boy.

"You gonna do it for me? You don't have it in you," Isaiah dared before turning back to his tightening. Tim rushed over to Isaiah and took a wild swing. It missed. Isaiah rose quickly and rushed the boy, plunging his shoulder deep into Tim's gut. Tim tumbled to the ground. Shannon screamed, and Isaiah turned toward her.

Rising, Tim grabbed one of the pieces of lumber beside the cart and swung it at the distracted Isaiah. With a solid crack, it connected to the side of Isaiah's skull.

"Are you okay, Shannon?" Tim stepped over Isaiah, to Shannon's side. Shannon nodded, her hands clasped over her mouth, holding back screams.

Tim turned to follow her terror-stricken gaze. She was staring at Isaiah, listless on the ground.

"My God," Tim whispered. "Did I kill him?" He took a step closer to his once-considered friend.

Joseph ushered Tim to stay back as he approached Isaiah. The old man leaned over slowly, reaching for the injured boy's neck. He sighed relief when he found the pulse.

"Shannon—get me some water. Tim, find a blanket," Joseph barked out orders. He repeated the orders, breaking through the teens' shock. Slowly the two moved away, back toward the house. Isaiah began to moan.

"Stay down, Isaiah," urged Joseph. "You're hurt."

The boy brought his hand to the side of his head. A small amount of blood dripped from his ear. He let out another moan as he tried to push himself into a sitting position.

"D'ya hear me? Stay down!" Joseph commanded. Isaiah continued to struggle and made it to his knees.

"Shut up, you old bat…" Isaiah cursed, holding

his head. Isaiah used the nearby tree to brace himself. Joseph stood back, his arms halfway extended, ready to catch the boy if he fell.

"Isaiah, come on…" Joseph's tone softened. "This isn't the time to play tough guy; you're hurt."

"Damn you, get away from me," the angry teen shouted. "If you had just let me be, this wouldn't have happened." Isaiah began to stagger toward the road. Joseph walked slowly toward him.

"Son, don't be stubborn," Joseph urged. "Please, let me help you." Joseph closed his eyes. The scene felt familiar—how he wanted to reach out to this boy—and yet was rebuked.

"Get away or I'll knock you down cold, old man!" Isaiah made a fist and shook it at Joseph. Joseph backed away.

"All right…just…you need to have that bleeding looked at…"

"Get away I said."

Joseph stopped when Isaiah repeated his threat and slowly backed away. Joseph watched the boy weave his way through the woods. Shannon and Tim ran up with a blanket and a pitcher of water.

"Where'd he go?" Tim asked.

"He was angry and not thinking right." Joseph replied, still staring into the forest.

"So, what else is new?" Tim asked sarcastically.

"He's hurt. I'm worried. Maybe I should follow him. Just to make sure…" Joseph's voice trailed off.

"Make sure? Make sure that he gets another shot at you with a rock in the woods?" Tim replied.

Joseph looked up at the mountain. No matter how he wanted to, he couldn't save everyone. He thanked God that he had at least been able to help the two teenagers. Joseph turned back toward Tim. "Are you okay?"

"Yeah, just scraped up my back, that's all."

"Right," Joseph said absentmindedly, unable to get his mind off Isaiah.

"There! All bandaged up!" Shannon admired her work on the old man's arm. Joseph wondered if the poor limb would ever be allowed enough rest to heal.

"Looks professional," Joseph complimented, examining Shannon's handiwork.

"Oh...I found something in your first-aid box..." Shannon turned to search the bathroom countertop.

"Let me guess...an old fishing lure? I lost one about two years ago. One of my favorites. I had to pull it out of my thumb, so..." Joseph turned toward Shannon, who was handing him an envelope. Joseph's voice trailed off at the familiar and welcome sight of the pink envelope.

"Annie..." he mumbled.

"Open it, Grandpa...go ahead," Shannon whispered.

"Yeah...go ahead, Mr. Marino," Tim encouraged Joseph from the hall door.

Joseph smiled at the familiar sight of Anne's beautiful writing.

Dear Joey,

Two of the hardest problems to deal with when one is dying are forgiveness and healing.

I'm not worried about me forgiving you...I already have. You've more than made up for all of the mistakes and fights you've created. I don't hold anything against you.

I was worried that I had forgotten why I had married you all those years ago. But the last few months I have remembered every reason why...and I still feel the same. You restored the joy of being alive to my heart.

I am worried that you would not forgive me for all that I have done to hurt you over the years. There is so much to ask forgiveness for and never enough time for amends.

Please forgive me for anything I have done to hurt you. I love you with all my heart and soul.

Love, Annie

Joseph's hands trembled slightly, trying to hold the letter steady.

"She was always like this, you know." Joseph wiped his eyes with the back of his hand.

"Like what, Grandpa?" Shannon's voice was soft and warm.

"Always sneaking up on me," Joseph smiled fondly.

"You have to tell your parents about the baby." Joseph stared at the teens across the table.

"Why is this suddenly so important?" Tim asked, worry etched in his face.

"Would you rather that they hear it from Isaiah?"

"Why would he say..." Tim's voice trailed off.

"Yeah...you see why. He's got something on you two now. And a reason to use it. Don't think he won't, either."

"You're right. He obviously doesn't care if he hurts us," Shannon agreed.

"Today, you two," Joseph insisted. "Not tomorrow."

How he wished Anne were here now to help him, to help the kids—to help them all.

Chapter 31

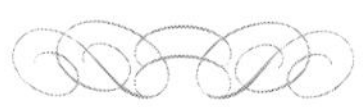

"CAREFUL, GRANDPA! YOU'LL BREAK YOUR button!" Shannon quietly said as she touched his fidgeting hand. With her other hand she pulled on her seat belt, snapping it in place.

"I can't tell you how many times I've done that in my life..." Joseph shook his head as he released the shirt.

"I know. I've seen you." Shannon smiled. "And I've seen Grandma sew many of them back on."

Joseph found something in her smile. Maybe it was the way her mouth turned up at the corner, or maybe it was the softness in her eyes. Something about her reminded him of Anne. It seemed like only yesterday that Anne was sitting on the other side of the car, telling him that they would be expecting a little one.

There had been many models of cars driven since that day long ago, but this car, the car they were riding in, was that special car of the past. The mist of memories swallowed him. The old, large steering wheel of that Buick materialized in front of him.

"Joey…can you believe it? A baby!" Anne was rubbing her stomach.

"Uh…yeah…" Joseph responded.

"What's wrong? You seem nervous…" Annie reached across for her husband's hand.

"Well…" Joseph started, then faltered.

"Go ahead. what is it?"

"I'm not sure I can pay for him…uh, her… uh…it?"

Anne smiled. She gently tapped his hand. "You can call the baby 'Davy Crockett' if you want to…it doesn't matter right now. What matters is that you're scared."

"I guess. I mean, what do I know about raising kids?" Joseph began pulling, and pulling hard, on his shirt's top button.

"You'll break it," Annie whispered.

Reality broke in as the haze vanished.

"Grandpa? You're pulling that button again," Shannon commented.

Joseph willed his hand to stop.

"We'd better get over to my house. I want to get this over with." Shannon sighed as she turned to look out the side window.

"Yeah…I'm not feeling like this is going to be a lot of fun…" Tim added from the back seat.

Joseph fumbled in his pocket and found his keys. After inserting them into the ignition, his eye was caught by a bit of motion to his left. It was the squirrels…scampering up the aspen.

"Mr. and Mrs. Fuzzball!" Joseph smiled as he announced the arrival of his little friends.

"Who?" Tim asked straining to see who was there.

"Well, not really 'who'…more like 'what'…" Joseph grinned as the squirrels scampered up the side of the tree.

Joseph recognized Shannon's fear. Her hands were shaking…the same way that Anne's once did. She fumbled as she opened the screen door. It was strange, Joseph thought, how he had been to this house only once before despite how close he and Shannon had become. The daylight was just beginning to dim, but he could tell that not much was going on inside.

"Mom?" the girl called into the shadowy house.

"I wonder if she's home," Tim asked quietly, hoping she wasn't. He had only made it up to the second step on the front porch when Joseph signaled him forward.

"She's home," Shannon said over her shoulder to the two men behind her. "Come on in," she ushered. "You can wait in the living room while I get my mother." The three made their way inside together. Joseph took off his old work hat and turned to look at Tim. He still had his hat on.

"Tim…your hat," Joseph urged in a strong whisper, pointing to the boy's head.

"But it's my lucky one." Tim rubbed the brim.

"Hats off when indoors, Tim."

"Oh..." He shrugged, slowly pulling his hat from his head.

Joseph slowly scanned the living room. It was a bit on the messy side, but he had seen worse.

"Mom?"

Joseph could hear Shannon's voice far down the hallway.

"Oh...pictures!" Joseph exclaimed when he saw a number of glossy objects in frames in the corner of the room. He sauntered over, with Tim following close behind.

"Those are Shannon..." Tim pointed to the right side of the wall.

"Cute little kid!" Joseph remarked, taking in the memories encased beneath the glass. One picture seemed too familiar to him. A little girl in a white church dress. So much like Sarah...so many years ago. Joseph made a mental note to call her. It had been too long. He had gotten so caught up in the wall...and... he shook his head at his own excuses.

"Hey, that cross on the wall says your name, Mr. Marino." Tim pointed to a silver toned cross.

"My name?" Joseph squinted in the dim light. He recognized the cross. It did have his name on it. Anne's name, too.

"Well, I'll be..." Joseph whispered.

"Was it yours?" Tim asked.

"Yeah, maybe...but I still have mine in my bedroom." Joseph was confused.

"Admiring our collection of religious artifacts, I presume?" an older woman's voice interrupted. Joseph turned quickly and bumped into the table lamp next to him.

"Whoa...I'm sorry! I'm a klutz sometimes..." The old man steadied the lamp.

"Yeah...I can see..." the woman remarked with a smirk.

"Mom! He was just surprised," Shannon scolded.

"Sure. Look Mr..."

"Marino," Joseph offered.

"I am right in the middle of something in the other room. What is it you want?"

"Me? I came because of Shannon." Joseph pointed past the woman as Shannon stepped forward.

"Mom, I have to tell you something, and Grand... er, I mean, Mr. Marino, came with me to try and help."

"What's *he* doing here?" Shannon's mother nodded toward Tim, with obvious disgust. Tim kept his eyes cast toward the floor.

"We're both here to help Shannon," Joseph said on his behalf.

"So tell me already," the woman exclaimed.

"Can we sit down?" Joseph found the woman's lack of manners disturbing.

"Sure...take a load off...stay a while," she said sarcastically, pointing to the couch. Joseph looked at the newspaper-covered couch. He decided to stack the papers on the coffee table.

"My name is Joseph Marino." He dropped the papers onto the table and extended his hand. Shannon's mother waited and then stretched out hers.

"I'm Barbara...Barb, really." Her smile was forced and fleeting. Joseph eased onto the couch, one hand bracing his back.

"I didn't want to interrupt your evening, but we have something important to talk about," Joseph began.

"Yeah?" Barb asked with a gruff voice.

Joseph looked over at Shannon, hoping that she would begin. Her mother didn't give her a chance.

"Hey, listen, if that kid broke anything of yours, you'll have to get her to pay for it," Barb said defensively.

"No, actually she's been very good about..."

"Then she's taken something? Crap, she's always into some kind of trouble!" Barb glared at her daughter.

"Please, will you just listen!" Joseph growled. Barb's eyes narrowed as she stared at the old man.

"I'm listening. What is it?" She reached for a package of cigarettes on the table.

"Please don't do that," Joseph urged.

"Hey, this is my house. Those clean-air Nazis can't tell me what to do in my own house." She began to flick a lighter.

"It's not healthy for an expectant mother...and her

baby!" Shannon blurted out. She ran to the other side of the room and stared out the window.

Tim walked over and put his arm around her shoulder. Joseph could tell by the rhythmic motion of her shoulders that she was crying. Barb had dropped her cigarette. Her mouth was open.

"What the hell? What are you talking about?" she asked through clenched teeth. The woman rose to her feet.

"She's expecting. I've been talking with her for about a month now. I've wanted her to come and tell you…but…" Joseph stood up.

"You knew?" Barb's anger turned on Joseph.

"I did, and I've been trying to…" Joseph felt trapped.

"You knew? And you didn't come and tell me?" Barb yelled.

"I thought that it would be best if she…" Joseph felt his own anger rise.

"…if she told me? You expected that lying tramp to tell me?" Barb pointed at Shannon.

"Watch your mouth," Joseph said firmly. "She's just a young girl and she's confused…"

"I'll say she's confused! She has the nerve to hop into bed with some guy."

"Mom! It was Tim! Only Tim!" Shannon offered in her own defense.

"Tim! You son of a…" Shannon's mother strode toward the young man.

Joseph stepped in front of her, blocking her path.

"Get out, you old bastard!" she screamed.

"Barb…calm down…" Joseph tried a quieter tone of voice.

"You get the hell out of my house before I call the police! Do you understand?" She continued her tirade. Her left fist was clenched as she reached for the phone with the other hand. Joseph stared back at her. For a few moments all that could be heard were Shannon's sobs. He turned and watched Shannon continue her rhythmic shaking.

"I'll leave," he said through clenched teeth.

"And take that worthless kid with you!" She pointed at Tim. Joseph took three steps, stopped, turned, and opened his mouth.

"Barb…"

"Get out! Now!"

Joseph gestured with his head toward the door; Tim nodded. He looked back at Shannon, who waved him away.

It seemed too quiet outside, or maybe it was the intense yelling inside that had made everything else seem quiet. Joseph could hear the gravel under his shoes as he made his way to the car. He hated leaving Shannon within those four walls. Barb's voice echoed from behind him.

"…you are to *never* go over there again, do you understand?"

After fumbling with the keys, he managed to get the car door open. Joseph turned to look back.

"Tim...I'll drive you to your..." Joseph stopped. Tim was gone.

The clouds moved in early that night. Joseph found it difficult to locate his house key. He had forgotten, as he had many times in the past, to turn on the porch light in anticipation of returning after dark.

Once in the house he immediately settled in his favorite old chair. It was quiet. The ticking of the clock in the corner was the only thing that existed to keep him company.

Joseph shook his head and pulled himself out of his chair.

"I'm not going to just sit," he said determinedly. He looked down the bedroom hallway and saw a strange light. He straightened and his eyes strained to see.

"Who's there?" he called out. There was no answer. He slowly made his way to the entry closet. He pulled out an old baseball bat and brought it to his shoulder. Walking slowly down the hall, he checked in every room and studied every shadow. His bedroom door was last.

A loud crash came from behind the closed door. Joseph pulled back. It sounded as if the bedroom window had fallen and broken. He carefully considered his options. Who was he kidding, he wondered. He had nothing to lose.

He choked up on the bat, wet his lips, and tightened his leg muscles. He jumped into the doorway, letting out a primal scream. Quickly, he moved through the bedroom and flicked on the light, the bat high, ready to strike.

No one was there. The window had been broken. The lamp shade lay separate from the lamp. He stood for a long minute, gasping for breath while studying the room. Everything was lit up in an eerie stark light.

His clothing was strewn around the room. From his closet two boxes had been pulled, and the cloth within one of them had been yanked out and thrown all around the floor. His heart sank. It was his flag collection.

The old man knelt by the box of flags and touched the fabric. Slowly he picked up each flag and lovingly studied each one. Carefully, he refolded his prized possessions. He placed Denmark, Norway, and Iceland back in the security of the box. The French flag was torn, and Joseph caressed the pieces between his callused fingers. Gently, he set all the pieces on the nightstand. Joseph looked around. Where was it? Sweden…the flag of Sweden was gone. The one Anne had so carefully packaged for him.

Another shard of glass crashed to the floor from the window, adding to the carpet of broken sparkles.

"The jewelry box!" he whispered, pushing to

his feet. Slowly he walked over to the dresser. The teakwood box was open. Joseph quickly scanned the contents. One item was missing.

"Annie...your pearls..." Joseph whispered.

Chapter 32

Only the darkness seemed unbroken the next morning. Joseph rose early as he always did and went out to start breakfast. As he looked into the refrigerator he reflected on the evening before. A strange thought struck him. How many would be eating with him?

Joseph shut the door and went to the side window. He stared up the road, waiting to see the two young people he had come to depend on.

Nothing.

The lights from a passing car quickened his heart, but it kept going. The darkness returned. Dawn brought nothing new. His stomach growled, and he poured a quick bowl of cereal. Every sound from the front prompted him to stand and turn. He squinted out the side window for a sign.

Nothing.

He picked up the phone an hour or so later and called Sarah. He needed to hear a familiar voice.

"Hello?" the woman's voice on the other end said.

"Sarah, it's Dad. How are you this morning?" Joseph felt his heart race.

"To tell you the truth, busy. I've got to get the kids ready for school. Is there something you're calling for specifically?" A child was crying in the background.

"No...I just wanted to talk..." Joseph recoiled slightly at the agitation in Sarah's voice.

"Hey...Joey! Leave your sister alone! Do you hear me? Sorry, Dad. It's kind of crazy around here."

"Hey...I remember. I was a parent once, too, you know!" The old man forced a laugh. "How about next Sunday? I can call you after church. All right?"

"I'll be here."

"Next Sunday, then."

"Okay...I've gotta go...talk to you soon." Sarah hung up the phone.

"But...well, bye, then..." Joseph looked at the earpiece and then slowly hung up the receiver. He picked it up again, and dialed long distance.

"Hello?"

"Meredith?" Joseph smiled.

"Yes! Mr. Marino!"

"You don't have to call me that," he responded.

"All right then...how about what I used to call my father? Pop!"

"That works for me." Joseph was beginning to feel better.

"Oh, hold on..." he could tell that Meredith covered the mouthpiece of the receiver. When Meredith came back on the line her voice was strained. "I've got to get going."

"Big day?"

"No, Paul just left—so I need to get back to the kids."

"What's Paul up to today?" Joseph asked, wanting to keep the conversation going.

"He's been angry for weeks now," Meredith sighed. She hesitated a moment. "He wasn't happy that I was talking to you..."

"Why?" Joseph felt his heavy heart return.

"His birthday," she said simply.

"His birthday! Oh, God! I forgot! I've been so busy!" Joseph felt his heart drop inside.

"I'll try to get him to call you. But you know how he can be. Sometimes he gets so stubborn..."

"Yeah...I understand." A long silence lingered between them.

"Are you okay?" Meredith asked, politely.

"Fine. Just, well... I'm fine!" Joseph smiled a fake smile, then chastised himself for doing that over the phone. No one could see him fake a smile.

"I've really got to go," she offered meekly. "Take care of yourself."

Joseph hung up the phone and buried his face in his hands. He was alone. On the porch he watched as a few school-age children went by on their way to the bus stop near the club house. None of them acknowledged his presence. He turned his head and stared at the still unfinished stone wall.

"I promised it would be finished and I'm going to get it done," he said as he stepped off the porch and toward the repaired cart resting by his shed. The old man tugged at the cart and began the long trek up the mountain for stones.

Each time he reached for a stone in the creek bed his hands were greeted with cold, sticky mud. The water was low this time of year. It was late autumn, and the snows of winter were threatening. A cold wind compelled him to pull his coat's lapels closer together.

Heavy breathing forced Joseph to find a place to rest; he was tiring more easily nowadays. A sunny patch of light reflecting on a rock by the bank beckoned him.

It was when he sat down, when he was not busy, that the old pains inside crept to the surface. When there was work to be done he could avoid the suffering from the soul, but when his body demanded rest, his emotions went to work.

At first he just closed his eyes and basked in the reflecting sunlight. It was strange, he thought, how he didn't crave warmth and sunlight when he was younger but had for the last twenty years or so.

The forest didn't seem to provide its usual guidance and inspiration today. It was so very quiet. The wind was shallow and occasional. There was nothing to do but look inward.

"God...I feel so alone and worthless..." Joseph whispered as he looked into the sky. His throat felt tighter and tighter as he fought back the feelings that were escaping as the gruff dam of hard work collapsed. His words began to sound like a prayer.

"God, I don't really know what to pray for... and it's been a long time since we've talked. I feel so empty, and without hope. I'm out of gas, Lord. All I want now is to finish the wall I promised Annie. Then I want to be done. I want to be with her. I've messed up so much in my life. All I can really ask for is the strength to get that wall finished. At least I can say I did *something* right in this miserable life."

Joseph sighed and closed his eyes.

"Why can't I do the right thing? All of my life it's been the same. Annie...she was so patient." Joseph covered his face with his hands. The image of Shannon came into his mind. He laid back on the rock.

"I really tried to do what was right...and look what happens. Someone threatens to call the police. That girl needs acceptance, and she gets nothing but obscenities and anger." The stillness around him remained as he hunted the skyline for a sigh, a clue—anything.

"God, I am so empty. Please help me." Joseph stared up at the sky, his sobs quieting as the wind rose. The old man opened his eyes and saw the treetops swaying in their own dance.

The sparkles of the late afternoon sun on the water caught his eye. He rose slowly and gently moved a stone that was next to his head. He found himself mesmerized by the sparkles of the light.

"It's so beautiful," Joseph whispered. He sat up on the large boulder and watched the scene unfold around him: an earthly opera. The waters of the stream played the part of the orchestra, and the sunlight provided the dancers. Every now and then a crescendo of wind highlighted the symphony in the clearing by the creek.

A warm feeling flooded Joseph. There was a simple happiness in his soul. It was a happiness that he had not known for many months. The water, trees, and sunlight gave him a joy that he remembered from childhood. The memories flooded his mind.

"I won! Hey, Annie! I won!" Joseph giggled wiping his tears away with the back of his hand. He looked around, to see if anyone was watching him. Thoughts raced through his mind. It was crazy! Was this what it was like to be crazy?

"Annie! I remember one day long ago! We teased about who would live longer! I won!" Joseph raised his face to the sky and smiled.

Slowly he returned to his perch on the boulder. He stared at the shimmering, glistening water. It felt like messages were hidden for him to decode in every breath of nature.

As the sun lowered, the bouncing lights from the

creek dwindled and the air became colder. Joseph buttoned the top of his coat.

"Mr. Marino?" The voice startled the old man on the rock.

"Huh? What?" Joseph turned around.

"It's me…Tim…" His words trailed off.

"Am I glad to see you!" Joseph straightened himself out and slid down to the leaf-covered ground below.

"Well, at least someone is." Tim looked down and kicked a stone lying at his feet. Joseph felt an upwelling of compassion for the boy.

"Son, we've been kicked around, but I care about you. I think you care about me."

Tim nodded.

"I don't know why, but I know that none of this is important. How much we care for each other is all that matters." Joseph wished he could explain his newfound peace without sounding crazy.

"Yeah, but I care for Shannon, and I can't see her again." Tim's loneliness could be heard in his hollow voice.

"You'll see her again, Tim."

"I don't know…her mother was really mad…and sometimes I just want to hit that old lady. She doesn't care about Shannon!" Tim kicked a boulder with all his might.

"Slow down Tim. We don't need any more angry people in this world."

"But Mr. Marino." Tim's exasperation grew as he

threw his arms toward the sky, inviting an answer. "I just don't know what to do."

"This will work itself out."

"I've had people tell me that my whole life," Tim replied. "And it's just not true."

"Maybe you just can't see it now," Joseph offered.

"Can't see what?"

"Just because things aren't working out how *you* want them to, doesn't mean they aren't working out."

"What do you mean?" Tim looked resigned as he perched himself on a boulder opposite Joseph.

"Sometimes you have to trust that there may be reasons that you don't understand. I think that sometimes the Universe has plans for us that we don't recognize."

"But why do people have to be so mean…so angry?" Tim's eyes stared pleadingly at Joseph.

"Do you see that mud over there, on the other side?" Joseph pointed.

"Yeah," Tim hesitantly replied.

"Why does the water pound against that mud?"

"Uhh…because it's there…" Tim sounded unsure.

"Exactly!" Joseph turned and looked at the water.

"So, she just yelled at us because we were there?" Tim sounded more sure of himself.

"Sounds reasonably unreasonable to me," Joseph smiled.

"Kinda like how my brother comes home and kicks the dog when the bullies are picking on him?"

"I think so. Shannon's mom is gone a lot, and it

sounds like her job is really stressful. What do you think she'd be like when she got home?"

"Like what we saw last night?"

"Right!"

"Just like my parents, too." Tim looked down.

"Just like a lot of us, Tim."

"I don't know. I just don't know what to do..."

"Tim...have you thought about what you're going to do with your life?"

"A little. I guess I'll get a job." Tim scraped the mud with the toe of his boot.

"No...no...what do you *want* to do? I'm worried that you'll just be pulled into the same trap your parents are caught in. Paying bills, hating life, taking it out on the kids..."

"I don't know. Nobody ever asked me that before. All my mother says is 'get a job and get out.'"

"But you must have dreamt of something."

"I really don't know," Tim answered.

"What do you like to do?" Joseph prodded gently. "What excites you?"

"Well, Shannon." Tim smiled.

"Besides that!" Joseph returned with a knowing smile.

"I like airplanes."

"Great! There's a start. Something to do with airplanes..."

"I like to fix things and take them apart." Tim picked up the pace.

"Well, now we have something to work with! How about building aircraft, or fixing them?"

"That would be cool! Do you really think somebody like me could do that?" Tim was sounding downright excited.

"Of course! Why not?"

"I'll tell you a story." Tim changed into the role of storyteller and Joseph waited intently. "Look at these rocks." Tim kicked a pile of four or five.

"Yeah?"

"Which one would you pick to put on the top of your stone wall?"

"I guess…this one." Joseph pointed with his foot at a clean, smooth stone.

"Well, what if I'm this one, over here." Tim pointed at another one, a stone that was rough and dirty. Joseph saw the point the boy was driving at.

"I'd say we need to clean that one off and smooth it out first!" Joseph smiled.

"What does that mean?" Tim was unsure of the answer. It seemed that he expected a different answer.

"You need some educational polish and some 'attitude cleaning,' then you can be used in an important place."

"So my 'rock' just needs a little more work and education?"

"…and the right attitude."

"And then I could have some dreams."

"No. Then you could make your dreams come

true. I think you already have the dreams. You're just afraid to admit that you have them."

"What about you, Mr. Marino? Do you have dreams?"

Joseph was caught off-guard by his question. He hadn't thought about his dreams for a long time. In fact, he realized he had fallen into the same trap that Tim had found himself in. Joseph turned slowly toward Tim.

"I guess so," he whispered.

"What are they?" Tim prodded.

"I guess, well, I've always wanted to climb up to the top of Mount Pinos."

"Why haven't you?"

"I don't really know. I'm scared of high places, I guess."

"Anything else?"

Joseph felt his heart race. The dreams of childhood came crashing home again. There he was, so many years ago, at the creek with little Annie, dreaming of a life together with her; how they'd have kids, how they would...

"Travel. I've always wanted to go to Sweden!"

"So...what's stopping you?"

"I am."

Joseph turned toward the graceful mountain rising above him. It called out to him. He looked back at Tim, and then at the water. He felt his blood racing as he thought of the possibilities.

"Sweden! I could!"

"And I could build airplanes!" Tim followed.

"Maybe I need to start moving again, toward a dream," Joseph pondered.

"Me, too. I've never had anyone tell me that I could have a dream come true."

"Will you help me?" Joseph asked.

"If you'll help me. What can I do?"

"Let's plan an expedition to the top." Joseph pointed to the towering, windswept peak above.

"Let's do it!" Tim smiled.

Chapter 33

"I THINK WE CAN FINISH THIS WALL WITHIN A WEEK, Tim," Joseph commented as he pulled his work gloves on. Joseph felt the pressure of the season. He also felt the joy of having someone over for breakfast again.

"Probably. I hate to say it, but I'm sure tired of hauling rocks, Mr. Marino." Tim rubbed his upper arms. He reached over to move the cart closer to the construction area.

"Just think...a lot of people in Bakersfield and LA pay to get the workout you're getting here for free." The old man chuckled. The sound of a breeze rushing down the slopes of the Mount Pinos canyon distracted him.

"Calling me again, Old One?" Joseph whispered.

"What's that?" Tim turned.

"Oh...not much. For almost forty years I've wondered about that mountain. Something about it calls to me. It's an emotional thing that I can't explain."

"You're so emotional, Mr. Marino." Tim straightened himself and rubbed his arms again. Joseph walked toward the cart.

"You say that like it's a bad thing."

"I'm just not used to it—you know, showing your emotions." The two men reached for a stone in tandem.

"I'm just true to myself, Tim. That happens when you get older."

"What do you mean?"

"I used to try and play the role of 'tough guy,' but it wasn't me. My dad hated when I showed any weakness, so for a long time, I shut out my emotions." Joseph paused before continuing. "Eventually, that comes back to haunt you. I was so angry. I learned I was angry because I was locking all the things I wanted to give to the world inside of myself."

Tim scraped another stone along the bottom of the cart. Joseph winced at the sound.

"Ohhh...I hate that sound..." Joseph gently placed the stone he was carrying on the growing pile of rough rocks at the end of the wall.

"How did you change?"

"The secret is feeling good about who you really are. Your strengths and your weaknesses. Not a pride thing. Just seeing that you are worth something." Joseph looked up at the mountain again. A thought crossed his mind. He had lost sight of his 'Self Trick,' as he called it. For the first time in his life he had forgotten his First Rule: try to feel better about yourself.

"It's hard to see anything good in me," Tim scoffed.

"That's because no one has ever told you about your good points."

"Yeah, that's because there aren't any."

"I know someone who would disagree with you, Tim."

"Yeah, I know. You would." Tim rubbed his palm.

"Hurt your hand?" Joseph pointed at Tim's palm.

"A little. It's not too bad. Thanks for caring..."

"I do, son. But I'm not the only one." Joseph's voice went up in pitch as his smile grew.

"Oh?" Tim looked confused.

"Shannon must've found something worthwhile in you," Joseph suggested.

"I can't imagine what," Tim mumbled.

"Don't put yourself down, there are plenty of people who will do that for you." Joseph picked up another stone.

"So why do I do it?"

"Do what?" Joseph asked.

"If I'm going to quit saying and thinking bad things about myself, don't I have to know why I do it in the first place?"

"Everyone has their own reasons," Joseph said quickly.

"What were yours?"

Joseph resituated himself on the edge of the wall. "Mine were the same as a lot of kids. I grew up with an abusive father who was an alcoholic."

"You too, huh?"

"There are a lot of us, Tim." Joseph had long suspected that Tim's father had hurt him in some way. He had seen him once, when he dropped off Tim on a Saturday. The anger in his eyes was evident.

"My father used to beat me when he drank," Tim said flatly. Joseph knew the tone, it was the tone he had often used to distance himself from the pain. "I remember going to bed and trying to lie so quietly… trying to disappear before he came home." The angst on Tim's face tore at Joseph's heart.

"I used to lock my bedroom door with a device I invented…just longing to feel safe when I slept," Joseph offered, longing to relate to the young boy, longing to let him know that it would be okay. Joseph continued, "He tried to choke me to death, kill me with a vodka bottle, and break my neck by throwing me down a flight of stairs. The list goes on." Joseph squinted as the sun broke out from behind a cloud.

"And you're not crazy?" Tim whispered.

"Well, that's a matter for debate. I don't know how sane it is to stand in the mud and stack old rocks on top of each other. Or a lot of the other weird things I've done in my life. But you're right, Tim, I'm not crazy…I've led a very full and rich life."

"What other crazy things did you do?"

"Oh, my neighbors used to think I was wacky for flying a different flag each day of the year from my flagpole. If I liked a flag I flew it! It was a dream from a long time ago. I guess it still would make me happy." Joseph grew quiet.

"Is that what's over behind the shed…a flagpole?"

"Hah! There's been so much going on the last year. I took it down to oil the pulley." Joseph started walking toward the shed.

"Well, did you get around to oiling it?" Tim followed.

"I don't think I ever did." Joseph felt a bit embarrassed.

"Are you thinking of putting it up?"

"Why not? Better now than never!" Joseph stepped into the shed and searched the shelves.

"Can I help?"

"Yeah…I'm looking for a shoe box with some nylon rope and pulleys."

"So…you haven't told me. What was your secret?" Tim asked again as he searched through boxes, tools, and miscellaneous stored items.

"Huh? Oh, my secret. I call it the 'Self Trick.'"

"'Self Trick?'"

"Yeah." Joseph stared into the box. An envelope was on top of the wound-up nylon cord. A familiar pink-colored envelope.

"Tim, I do something that's really nothing more than a lie." Joseph gently touched the paper object with his cleanest finger. He pulled it out of the box and put it into his jacket pocket.

"A lie?"

"Yeah. I really just trick myself. I talk myself into believing that I'm something that I'm not."

"I don't get it..."

"As I said, it's embarrassing. If I'm feeling like I'm a 'nobody,' I pretend that I'm a 'somebody.' I tell myself that I won a prize or something or that I'm the retired former president of the United States," Joseph blushed.

"Why?"

"When there's nothing down inside that I can feel good about, I make up something from the outside. After a while, you begin to gain those qualities inside."

"Thanks Mr. Marino." Tim was going to step forward and hug him and then thought better of it. "Shall we put up a flag pole?" he said instead.

"Why not?" Joseph smiled broadly.

They left the shed and picked up the worn twenty-five-foot pole. Joseph led the way to a crumbling cement square in the middle of the lawn. Dead leaves covered much of the base area, but they were able to quickly clean it off. Together they bolted and oiled the pulley, placed it on the top of the pole, and threaded the cord.

"Let's put her up!" Together, with Joseph holding the bottom and Tim the top, they raised the pole. Tim inched slowly down the length of the pole until he nearly met up with Joseph. Together they stood directly over the hole in the ground that was ready to receive the base of the pole. They slid it in.

"Do you have any flags?" Tim asked.

"Sure! A whole box of…" Joseph cringed. He had forgotten about the robbery.

"What's wrong?"

"I guess I could get one…" Joseph replied, ignoring Tim's question. He looked toward the back of the house where his bedroom window was.

"Let's put up your favorite! What country is that?"

"Well…Sweden or Denmark…"

"Let's do Sweden, since you talked about that being a dream."

"I can't Tim. Someone broke into my house the other night and stole the Swedish flag. Out of all the flags, they'd have to pick that one," Joseph shook his head.

"Isaiah," Tim said simply.

"I've thought of that, but how would he know which one was my favorite?"

"Maybe he heard you talk about Sweden. I know he heard you talking about the flag collection."

"I guess it could've been, but I'm surprised he'd know which flag was Sweden."

"Oh, Mr. Marino…I hate to tell you…"

"Tell me what?"

"He used to make fun of how you wanted to go to Sweden. He's been there and knows what the flag looks like."

"Oh." Joseph looked down at his dirty hands.

"How about Denmark?"

"Yeah...I could put up the Dannebrog..." Joseph smiled. He knew he still had it.

"Danna...what?"

"Dannebrog...the Danish flag. It's their name for it." Joseph led the way into the house. A few minutes later they were back at the pole. The red flag with the white Scandinavian cross was soon being clipped to the pole. The red and white Dannebrog flapped gently in the afternoon breeze that day, in beautiful contrast to the deep, rich blue of the Pine Mountain sky.

Chapter 34

"LET'S GO, TIM. FINISH UP…WE'VE GOT TO GET working on the wall." Joseph urged as he wiped his breakfast plate.

"You're in a big hurry this morning…" Tim said through a mouthful of oatmeal. Joseph turned and furrowed his eyebrows.

"I need to pick up something important," the old man said in a matter-of-fact tone.

"Really," Tim looked curious. "What?"

"It's a surprise."

"Why didn't you say so?" Tim took a last bite and dropped his spoon into the bowl. "Ready," he announced.

"Hello, Mr. Marino. Well at least we got one package for you today; your other one still hasn't arrived." The pretty blonde woman greeted Joseph as he approached the postal counter.

"One is better than none." Joseph smiled. Joseph

liked her. She was one of the few in town who seemed to ask questions out of sincerity. So many others seemed to just be hunting down the latest gossip. He dug in his pocket and pulled out the yellow call slip.

"Well, let me get your package." Mary gently took the slip of paper.

"Hey, Mr. Marino, I think she likes you!" Tim had a broad grin on his face.

"What's not to like?" Joseph joshed.

"One package from Maine, coming up." Mary placed the package on the counter with a flourish. A package from Maine.

Joseph stared at the brown wrapping and then took it over to a corner table. Tim followed.

"So what other package are you waiting for?"

"Hmmm?"

"The lady at the counter made it sound like you were waiting for something."

"Oh that? Nothing..." Joseph said dismissively.

"Well, are you going to open this one?" Tim goaded.

"Give me a second," Joseph said, unsure why he felt such tension.

"It came from Maine." Tim pointed at the postmark.

"Just like my wife and I..." Joseph interrupted himself and looked back toward the post office counter. A scene appeared gradually in his mind.

It was many years before. Joseph had gone to the post office when Anne was visiting her mother back in

Maine. There was a package. It was full of cookies and dried fruit…cranberries, he remembered. There was a card and a couple of pictures. Annie.

"Did I say something wrong?" Tim was confused by Joseph's silence.

"Huh? Oh…no…it's just that I, years ago, got a package from Maine like this…"

"Then you know what it is?"

Joseph shook his head. "No, that one was from Anne." He pulled at the wrapping paper to reveal a nice white box with a logo from a store in Maine. He recognized the name instantly.

"Yeah! We used to shop there when we lived in Maine. It's been so long…" Joseph was about to push the paper out of his lap when he noticed an envelope between the paper and the box. He quickly spared it from the drop to the floor.

Dear Mrs. Marino:

Please excuse the tardiness of this shipment. When you ordered it last March, the shipping date was beyond our usual advance time frame for parcels. Usually we allow only a three-month advance order. I hope that you understand. It is difficult to schedule and keep track of the thousands of advance sales orders we receive each month.

In reviewing our records we noticed that we

failed to ship this for delivery on or slightly before the eleventh of October, as you requested.

Enclosed please find a coupon for twenty percent off of your next order; this is our way of apologizing.

Sincerely,
Hank Solomon, Vice President, Sales

Joseph let out a small laugh. *Imagine*, he thought, *that one of her perfect plans hadn't worked out so perfectly*.

"What's inside?" Tim prompted.

Joseph opened the top packaging—but he already knew its contents. Chocolate chips were carefully placed inside a tin which displayed a creek scene landscape. Joseph lost himself in thought. He was interrupted by a large crunching.

"Tim!"

"Hey, they're great cookies!" Tim smiled.

"I hope they taste better than they sound." The old man smiled at the boy who busily chewed the old cookie. *What the heck*, Joseph thought. He picked up a cookie, closed his eyes, and shed all of those years. It was Maine again…

Chapter 35

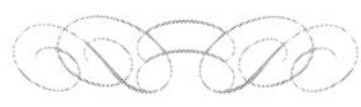

JOSEPH STOPPED TO CATCH HIS BREATH. IT always seemed to him that the stones weighed more when the weather was cold. Heck, nowadays, it seemed that everything was harder for him to do when the weather turned cold. He sat on the wall and looked up at Pine Mountain. The gray clouds were beginning to obscure the peak. Winter was about to descend to lower ground.

He pulled in a chest full of air, savoring the crispness, and watched his exhaled breath float away. The world was closing up for the winter. The plants had gone dormant. So many people had left the little valley; retirees moving on to warmer climates.

He looked back at his house, and it hit him. There would be no Anne to hold in the dark, cold night of winter. *God*, he thought, *it would be a lonely winter.*

Before his eyes a few white speckles drifted by. At first he continued to stare at the house, but after a short time these frosty visitors began to block his view.

"Snow?" he questioned.

"All right—snowboarding!" Tim had a wide grin on his face.

Joseph scanned what was unfinished on the wall. A couple days at most.

"This snow won't last. It's the 'pioneer snow.'"

"But the real stuff isn't far behind!" Tim obviously loved the winter. "We better climb soon," Tim said, looking up at the mountain. "If you keep putting it off, then winter will cancel the plan for you."

"We'll get there."

"You're not afraid, are you?"

Joseph ignored his question.

"We'd better keep going. We won't be able to get much done with the landscape covered in snow. Besides, I don't want to sit in my house staring at this unfinished thing all winter!" Joseph felt a new determination. Tim returned to the pile of stones and picked one up.

"The mountain, Mr. Marino—what is it?" Joseph was silent for a long moment.

"It will just be different, that's all," he mumbled.

"What will be different?" Tim asked.

"Having the wall done, the mountain climbed—it just seems so..."

"Final?" Tim offered.

Joseph nodded. How had all these things that seemed a zillion miles away come so close, he wondered. The wall would be done; the winter was settling; Anne was gone—he had thought about all this stuff so many times—but now it was all happening.

"I think we should do it," Tim encouraged.

"What—finish the wall?"

"That—and climb the mountain." Joseph looked at the mountain for a long moment, knowing he was right.

Tim interrupted his thoughts. "What are the stones behind the shed for?"

"They're the last capstones."

"What about the blue tarp next to them? What's under it?"

"You'll see—real soon. It's a surprise," said Joseph.

"I called Shannon yesterday and left a message with her sister," Tim sat down next to the woodburning stove in the kitchen.

"I hope she can make the hike with us," Joseph said.

"Well, I'll try again. Another message." Tim rose and went toward the living room. He picked up a piece of chocolate from the bowl in the middle of the table as he left.

Joseph shook his head and looked out the window. He admired the wall and wondered if Anne could see it. It was almost done. The gray clouds seemed to invade Joseph's kitchen. His mind drifted to times long before.

"It's beautiful, Joey! You made this for me?" Annie asked, blushing slightly.

"Only the best for someone like you!" Joseph had replied.

"I've always wanted a wooden cross with my initials carved into it!"

"It's the bestest one in the whole Sunday school!" Joseph proudly boasted.

"Because you made it," she finished.

She had shared her cookies with him those many decades ago…in that church long gone.

"Hey…isn't that Shannon?" Tim crashed into the old man's reverie.

Joseph followed Tim's gaze to see the young gal walking toward the house. Tim leapt for the door, wrestling slightly to get it open.

"Shannon! You got my messages!" Tim opened the screen door.

"Yeah, and the yelling started right after!" she rolled her eyes. "But I wouldn't miss this for the world. Besides, I'm eighteen now. I'm going to live my own life. The way I want to."

"How is the baby?" Tim asked hesitantly. Shannon pulled up her shirt, over her navel. Her hand rubbed her stomach in gentle circle as a motherly smile spread across her face.

"So," Shannon asked, changing the subject. "When are we doing the hike?"

"Tomorrow! We want to leave as soon as the sun is on the path on the east wall." Tim answered quickly. He took a big bite of ice cream.

"Isaiah is coming, too," Shannon said simply.

"What?" the two men said in unison. Neither of them had heard from the boy since the argument.

"Isaiah. He'll be there for the hike. I told him that if he doesn't, I'll tell the sheriff all that I know about him. And that's a lot."

"What do you mean?" Joseph asked.

"Your flag, he has it. And some other stuff. I heard him bragging about it at the café."

"Really?" Joseph sat up.

"Really," she affirmed. "Besides—I figured we all started this—might as well finish it—together."

Joseph nodded at Shannon's courage. As much as he loved the thought of finally completing this goal, something left him terribly uneasy. "Shoot," Joseph said aloud.

"What's wrong?" Tim queried.

"The Dannebrog flag—I left it out last night. I've just offended the government and people of Denmark—leaving their flag up without a light." Joseph grabbed his jacket. "My poor Dannebrog…" Joseph said as he hurried to the door. The door slammed, and Joseph faded into the darkness. Tim leaned over across the table.

"Hey…Shannon…don't let Mr. Marino know…"

"Know what?"

"I told Edie about tomorrow."

"Really? Is she going to be there?"

"She's going to meet us at the top."

"With the flag?" Shannon asked excitedly.

Tim nodded and smiled.

Tomorrow they'd reach the peak!

Chapter 36

Lovingly the old man pulled his favorite coffee mug down from the upper shelf. It was ceramic white with many of the flags of the world embossed on it. Anne had given it to him as a birthday gift one long-ago March. He saved this mug for very special days, like this one.

As he poured the steaming hot chocolate mix into the mug, he stared out the kitchen window. It wasn't quite dawn, but the lightening in the sky foretold it. Pine Mountain was a dark specter, outlined by the deep azure of the pre-morning sky.

"Well, Old One, today is the day. It's either you or me. For forty years I've run from you, but no longer."

Joseph rubbed his lower back. Too many stones had strained his almost-eight-decades-old muscular system. But there were still stones to place. Not many, but it seemed as if the work would never end. He stroked his left arm as he allowed his fingers to slide along the rim of his mug. He believed that his upper arms were much larger now. Exercise had made him much healthier. Joseph chuckled when he thought of the stone wall.

"You should see it, Anne. It's only a few stones short now." Joseph sipped on the hot chocolate and stared for a long time at the pattern on the tablecloth, mesmerized in his thoughts.

"You don't know how much those notes you left behind mean to me, Annie. God, I wish I could tell you how much. There isn't a day that I don't think of you." Joseph rubbed his eyes. His hand moved up to his forehead, and he stared down into his mug. The wisps of steam from his hot chocolate played against the tablecloth's design.

"You know, Annie, I don't know what to do anymore. I can see the wall being finished, and I'm scared of what happens after that." Joseph sniffed. He started drawing shapes on the tablecloth.

"There is a lot to do, I guess. The back garden is really overgrown, and I still need to repaint the side of the shed. And then there's that old squeaky front door!" Joseph looked across the table.

"I could fix that noisy..." he stopped in mid-sentence. The words wouldn't come. God how he wished she was there to hear his words.

Joseph rose quickly and went to the sink. He carefully and slowly poured the remainder of his hot chocolate into the drain. It became much lighter outside. He scanned the side yard, and his gaze stopped on the stone walkway. That walkway had changed his life so many months ago.

He could still see her face from that day…

"You still show off! Only now I can see through your 'muscles.' You are still trying to impress me!" Anne laughed.

"Hah! You should see them now, Annie! I'm a regular circus strong man!"

He remembered how he had regained his balance after wrestling with the wheelbarrow. Strange, he thought. He never wanted to remember those days last spring. He thought he couldn't. But here it was, a half year later, and the door to those days was slowly unlocking.

"Joey…Joey…" Anne had called out.

Strange. Once again he felt the cold, clammy sensation of panic welling up inside of his chest. He could feel, as if no time had passed, his labored breathing as he stumbled up the rocky path toward her. He remembered how he prayed.

"Oh, my God! No! Jesus…NO!" Joseph shouted. In the darkness of his closed eyes he could see her. He saw it again. She fell first to her knees, then slumped over on her left side.

Everything was clear again. Her right arm was holding her blouse, over her heart. Her left arm was extended away from her body. Her head was back, and she appeared to be staring at the sky. He remembered how he felt as if was running at half speed.

And there it was. The moment of horror. The terror of death was upon him.

"ANNIE! ANNIE! Talk to me! ANNIE! You can't die..."

"Grandpa! Wake up! Grandpa!" a voice called from behind.

"Huh? You're alive? It's..." Joseph lifted his head.

He was in the kitchen.

"But...?" Joseph looked around. A young girl stood next to him, rubbing his shoulder.

"Shannon?"

"You were dreaming. Are you okay, Grandpa?" Shannon moved closer and hugged him.

"I guess so. As okay as a lonely old man can be." Joseph pulled her hand to his cheek, relishing the youthfulness of her touch.

"You were dreaming about Grandma, weren't you?" Shannon whispered.

"Sorry...I'm just a sentimental old fool."

"No...you are just someone who's lonely. I understand."

Joseph looked out the window. The sun had been up for some time. He stood and moved toward the back door.

"Tim should be over here soon. It's almost ten."

"I'd better get my gear together."

"Well, are we ready to go?" Joseph stared up at the trail ahead. It was full of worn gravel; worn with the footsteps of untold numbers of people who had gone before.

"Let's do it!" Tim eagerly replied.

"I'm ready," Shannon added. "It looks like Isaiah is doing his usual 'no show' thing."

"Who needs him anyway," Tim mumbled.

"Move 'em out," Joseph said loudly, in his best movie star imitation.

"Who is that supposed to be?" Shannon laughed.

"What do you mean? Don't you watch any of the classic movies?" Joseph smiled.

"No. Why should I?"

"Because they're classics!"

"Who said?" Shannon squinted in the midday sunlight.

"Uh…oh, I don't know. I was imitating John Wayne." Joseph waved as if swatting a fly.

"Never heard of him. Was the imitation any good?"

"Never heard of him? I must be getting old…"

The trail started out easily enough, and the sunlight brought each rock, plant, and old log into easy view. Joseph felt blessed in the day they had chosen for the venture.

"Well, Tim…I…see…where…our…rocks came from…" Joseph's breath was labored as they climbed bit by bit up the side of old Pine Mountain.

"I'm glad we didn't have to come all the way up here!" Tim replied as he worked his way over a boulder.

"Come on, you two," Shannon called from a few lengths ahead.

"Hey…I'm old. This…takes time!" Joseph responded.

"What's your excuse, Tim?"

"Somebody has to help the old man."

"There's a good excuse!" she laughed.

"I…need…to…rest…" Joseph huffed as he struggled toward the boulder on the side of the trail. Shannon and Tim were ahead. They stopped and turned back.

"Are you going to make it? We're only about halfway up, Mr. Marino."

"I am going to make it! I don't care what it takes. I am going to make it!" Joseph strained to catch his breath.

"Let's sit for a while, Shannon…" Tim tilted his head toward the large boulder.

"Yeah…it has been a long road up here." She sat next to Joseph.

"Look…there's my house." Joseph pointed to a building that seemed like a dollhouse from this distance.

"Which one? How can you tell?"

"The one with the red and white Danish flag flying next to it! See…" Joseph squinted and also spotted the wall.

How beautiful, he thought. He felt the old familiar emotions again. He wished Anne could see her wall from the mountain.

"I see the flag! I think I see the wall, too!" Shannon exclaimed.

"Yep! It's there!" Joseph smiled broadly. He turned his gaze up the slopes of the mountain.

"You know… it doesn't seem as horribly huge from up here. It seems like a lot of little rocks piled up."

"We're near the last hump!" Shannon smiled.

"Last hump?" Joseph asked, pausing to catch his breath.

"Yeah. The last big climb before the walk to the top," Tim replied.

"When…do…we…stop?" the old man asked. His breath was not coming easily and sweat poured off his matted and disheveled hair.

"We usually stop at the little bench by the rock up ahead," Tim pointed.

"A…popular…spot…huh?" Joseph replied.

"Yeah. It's sort of a tradition… we eat a candy bar there!" Tim smiled.

"That's Tim's favorite part!" Shannon added.

"Here…Mr. Marino…only a little bit more…" Tim pointed.

"I'll…stop…here…for just a minute…then meet you…there…"

"Are you sure? Are you all right?"

"I'm fine," Joseph lied. "I just need a minute alone."

"Okay. We'll be up there." Tim pointed.

Joseph reached for the large rock to the right and lowered himself slowly. Everything hurt. His legs hurt. His arms and back hurt. Breathing hurt. He closed his eyes for a long moment.

"I'm up here, Annie…I'm doing it!" Joseph whispered as he turned his head and looked up into the pale blue sky. "Do you remember how you thought I'd never do it?"

The wind caressed the old man's hair, pushing it back into place. The breeze smelled sweet. He closed his eyes.

"Jooooeeeyyy…" the wind called. He opened his eyes.

"Annie?" He looked around. A cloud crossed in front of the mountain, casting a long shadow across the slope. Complete silence followed the brief gust of wind. It was cold, and Joseph pulled his coat close to his neck.

"Get your hands off of her!" a voice crackled down from above. Joseph turned and looked up the trail, but he saw no one.

"Shut up! I've taken enough crap from you! You heard what I said!"

Joseph stood up quickly and found the strength to climb a bit further. The voices were coming from around the next ledge. Within a few steps Joseph found Tim and Shannon. And Isaiah. He shuddered. Isaiah, with his back turned toward the old man, had his arm around Shannon's neck. Joseph saw a glint of silver beneath the sun's rays. He squinted and recognized it was a gun. Joseph crouched down, to conceal himself from view.

"Are you going to give them back or what?" Isaiah growled.

"Leave her alone…just leave her alone!" There was no mistaking the panic in Tim's voice.

"Hand them over…*now*!" shouted Isaiah.

"They belonged to Joseph's wife!" Tim's body curled with anger.

"She's dead…and they're mine!" Isaiah yelled. Shannon whimpered softly beneath Isaiah's grip.

Joseph knew what he had to do. He had quietly crept close enough. He knew he could get the gun. All he had to do was make it over the sticks strewn in the path and between the two rocks before him. He just needed one more step…he looked once more at Tim. And then he saw them. Clasped tightly in Tim's grip were Annie's pearls. Joseph gasped as he put his foot down.

Crraacckk! A twig broke from Joseph's weight.

Isaiah wheeled around quickly and the old man seized the moment to lunge for the gun.

The thick sound of gunfire broke through nature's silence and a bullet pierced Joseph's chest.

Joseph screamed, grabbing at the massive electric shock piercing his body. All he could feel was the ripping inside. More pain hit him when his shoulder impacted with the side of the ridge. A final shot of pain stung him when his body came to rest against a dead tree.

"Uhh..." Joseph tried to call out, but his voice was too soft, too quiet. Every breath brought more pain. The sky began to whirl as blue blurred into black and back to blue again.

"Oh my God!" Joseph heard a distant scream and then footsteps.

"Oh, no! No...oh, no...no...no!" Tim cried as he tumbled down the slope toward Joseph's lifeless form. Joseph tried to raise his arm, but wasn't able to get it very high. The scream of the pain forced him to lower it.

"Tim! Tim!" Shannon was screaming from above.

"He's breathing! Oh, God! Mr. Marino!" Tim was crying.

"Ugghhh...Ti-Ti..."

"Don't talk," Tim urged. "We are going to get help. We are going to get you up to the top, there are people up there who can help."

"Shan..." Joseph attempted to make out a sentence, to no avail.

"Shannon's okay," Tim assured him, resting his palm on his cheek. "Please Mr. Marino—you can't die."

"It's okay now." Joseph forced out what words he could. His eyes were so heavy, he had to close them. The light hurt. He felt the warm sun on his cheek.

"Grandpa?"

Joseph slowly opened his eyes at the familiar girl's voice.

"The...pearls..." he quietly whispered.

"Here, he didn't get them. Tim wouldn't let him." Shannon gently handed the pearls to the old man. Joseph raised his hand to touch the pearls and was shocked to see blood covering his hand.

Shannon gently placed the pearls in his palm and wrapped his fingers around them. Joseph pulled them close, his lips softly brushing the necklace.

"Annie..."

"You have them back now, Grandpa!" Shannon smiled. She looked down at the old man's chest, and her smile changed to a twisted look of horror. Joseph knew it was bad. It was getting harder to focus.

Everything seemed to twist from dark to light and back again.

"Mr. Marino? Can you hear me?" A voice from far away called.

"Mmm," Joseph whispered.

"You're at the top! We're going to get you down!" Joseph recognized the voice, but couldn't place it.

"The flag! Here! Take it!" the voice continued. Joseph tried to raise his head. A woman was handing him a piece of blue and yellow cloth. A flag.

"Swe…den…" Joseph smiled. Shannon came up behind the car and looked down.

"You're on top, Grandpa! You made it!"

"Made it…" Joseph weakly mimicked the voice.

"Grandpa! Grandpa!" Shannon was crying.

"Annie?" Images blurred. Memories became visions. Visions became the past. The past became the present.

"I love you, Grandpa!" Shannon called out.

"Shannon?" Joseph was barely able to speak.

"I'm here Grandpa…"

"Remember the stone…"

"Stone? What? Which one?" Shannon asked, urgency thick in her voice.

"Oh…God…Annie…" Blue turned to gray, and gray became black and breath became a part of the past.

Part Three

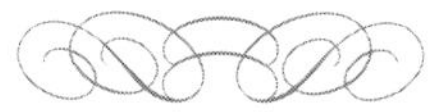

The Stones

Epilogue

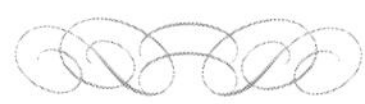

"Do you see? I know he meant something by 'remember the stone!'" Shannon was still sitting on the edge of the couch. Paul was staring out the window, with his fist below his chin.

"Hey…we're sorry, Paul. We didn't mean to drag you through the emotional swamp of the past." Tim was rubbing his pants legs nervously.

"No. No. You've answered a lot of questions. Oh, God, I've been in so much pain for so long about my father." Paul grew quiet again.

"He talked about you all the time, Paul…" Tim comforted.

"The last time I heard from him, he talked to my wife. Meredith said he called. I yelled about how I was angry that he forgot my birthday. How damned selfish can you get?"

"He loved you. He'd want you to move on," Shannon whispered.

"I think about him all the time." Paul looked out of the window again.

"I think of him often, too. I still look at this old album. I have a few pictures of him. A few things your mother gave me," Shannon offered.

"He meant a lot to both of us. The way we raise our kids. How we treat each other. Heck…look at what we named our kids!" Tim smiled and turned toward Shannon.

"What do you call them?" Paul asked.

"Joey and Anne."

A fleeting smile spread across Paul's face.

"Do you have any idea what he could have meant with the 'remember the stone' comment?" Tim asked Paul again. "Maybe if we go out and look at the wall?" Tim threw up his hands.

"Well, why not? Can't hurt." Paul slapped his leg. He rose slowly from his father's chair, much like Joseph used to do.

They walked through the house and Shannon noticed how so little had changed. The stove and refrigerator were still the same. Inside the small cabin, it seemed that time had stood still.

Together they walked outside. The air was crisp with fall's embrace. Leaves from past fall seasons circled through the yard, caught in the wind.

Shannon knelt down and inspected the wall, running her hands around the curves of the old stones.

"Anything?" Paul asked.

Shannon turned toward them both and shrugged.

"Joey! Get down from there! Do you want to break

your neck?" Tim shouted. Joey was doing daredevil tricks on the stone ledge.

"He's all right, Tim." Shannon touched her husband's arm.

"Hey…look. The last load of stones we dropped off is still there. Oh my God! The cart is still there…or at least what's left of it!" Tim slowly made his way toward the stones. "It's as if eleven years have disappeared."

"This was the last load?" Paul asked. Tim turned to face the older man.

"Yeah. We were going to finish the wall when we came down from the mountain. I can't believe we didn't." Tim's mouth dropped open. A yellow slash on the shed next to the house seemed to point at an aging blue tarp beneath a decade's debris.

"The stone!" Tim whispered. He covered his mouth with his hand.

"What? What is it?" Shannon pleaded as she looked around.

"There!" Tim pointed. Paul and Shannon turned and followed Tim as he ran to the side of the shed. He worked feverishly to sweep the garbage off of the tarp. Paul and Shannon joined the effort.

"More stones…" Shannon was crushed and shook her head.

"No…there is one…a special one. I know it's here somewhere…it has to be." Tim furiously pulled at the tarp to reveal a stone unlike the others.

"There!"

Together, Paul and Tim dug out the stone and carried it away from the pile. Using the back of his shirt, Paul brushed away the dirt.

Shannon smiled and wrapped her arms around her husband. "Look…there is an engraving."

In letters lovingly and deeply scratched into the stone the final writing of an old man spoke across the years.

Remember these things…
Every generation is the foundation of the next…
Love is our desperate need…
Joey loves Annie…

"Look…a pink envelope!" Paul exclaimed as he pointed at the ground between the stone and the tarp. A stained envelope was lying in the dirt. "It must have fallen when you pulled the stone out."

The envelope was moist in Shannon's hands and she carefully removed the cracked and faded paper.

The words had faded with time and were slightly blurred from the moisture. The three huddled around the note, squinting to read its message.

"Looks like your mother got the last word, Paul!" Tim laughed.

About the Author

Edward Mooney, Jr., was born in Massachusetts and raised in Tustin, California. After receiving degrees from Montana State University and the University of California at Riverside, he worked as a computer analyst until becoming a high school teacher in 1988. Edward currently lives in Southern California with his wife Carrie and their five children. His interests vary widely and include collecting flags and maps, travel, reading, writing, computers, web page development, and camping.

Reading Group Guide

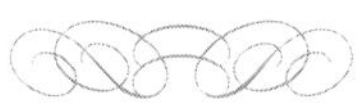

1. The locals in town refer to Joseph as the "Stone Man." Where does the nickname come from? Are there other interpretations of this name that the locals don't fully recognize? Does Joseph?

2. Why would the book be titled *The Pearls of the Stone Man* when the actual pearls in the story belong to Anne?

3. What is it that makes some of us procrastinators, like Joseph, and others more determined to get things done, like Anne?

4. It appears that Tim and Shannon have been together since their teenage years. What lessons did they learn in the course of their time with Joseph and Anne that could have contributed to the longevity of their relationship? Do you think Tim and Shannon's relationship would have been as successful without their experiences with Joseph and Anne?

5. Even before the car crash, Paul and Joseph struggle to get along and often butt heads. What are some of Joseph's and Paul's personality traits that may have contributed to their strained relationship?

6. Joseph is often surprised by how accurate Anne's notes are when he discovers and reads them—almost as if she knew ahead of time how he would be feeling. Did Anne really know how Joseph would be feeling or was it simply just having been married to each other for a long time?

7. Why did Joseph begin talking to Pine Mountain? What function does this non-speaking character have for Joseph? Is there any place in nature that you feel especially attached to?

8. While he works on the wall with the teens, Joseph describes how to place stones together so they fit snugly and form a solid wall and how one occasionally must knock a piece off of a stone to make it fit into another stone. How do these lessons work as a metaphor for human relationships?

9. Joseph observes several stark differences between his generation and the younger parents and children he sees in town. Clearly much has changed in recent years, and growing up in the world is not the same as it was when Joseph was a boy. What issues do families face in contemporary society that can make raising a child difficult?

10. How do our experiences as children affect our parenting methods? Do you think people are more inclined to mimic their parents' techniques or deliberately take an opposite path?

11. Did Joseph's suggestion at the trial surprise you? Which punishment do you think was more appropriate—the judge's original sentence or Joseph's alternative? Would justice be better served by allowing the victims to have some say in the punishment?

12. In Chapter 4, Joseph finds himself the emotional support for a weepy Anne returning from the hospital. Do you believe this is the way their relationship normally worked, or is this a reversal of their traditional roles? How and why does Joseph choose to be strong at this point?

13. The original set of pearls Joseph buys for Anne are relatively cheap, but as years go by, with additional purchases, the jewelry becomes more highly valued. How does the history of the necklace make it different from a set of pearls that is expensive in the first place? What things do you own that did not cost much to purchase but now are very valuable to you?

14. Joseph occasionally has vivid recollections of memories, seemingly out of the blue, of Anne that are years and even decades old. What sort of triggers, after half a century of marriage, would

spur such memories? Have you ever experienced this kind of sudden involuntary memory? How does it compare to memories that you consciously try to remember?